I0788779

TO SWAY A PRINCE

TEMPTING THIEVES

JESSICA M. BUTLER

CONTENTS

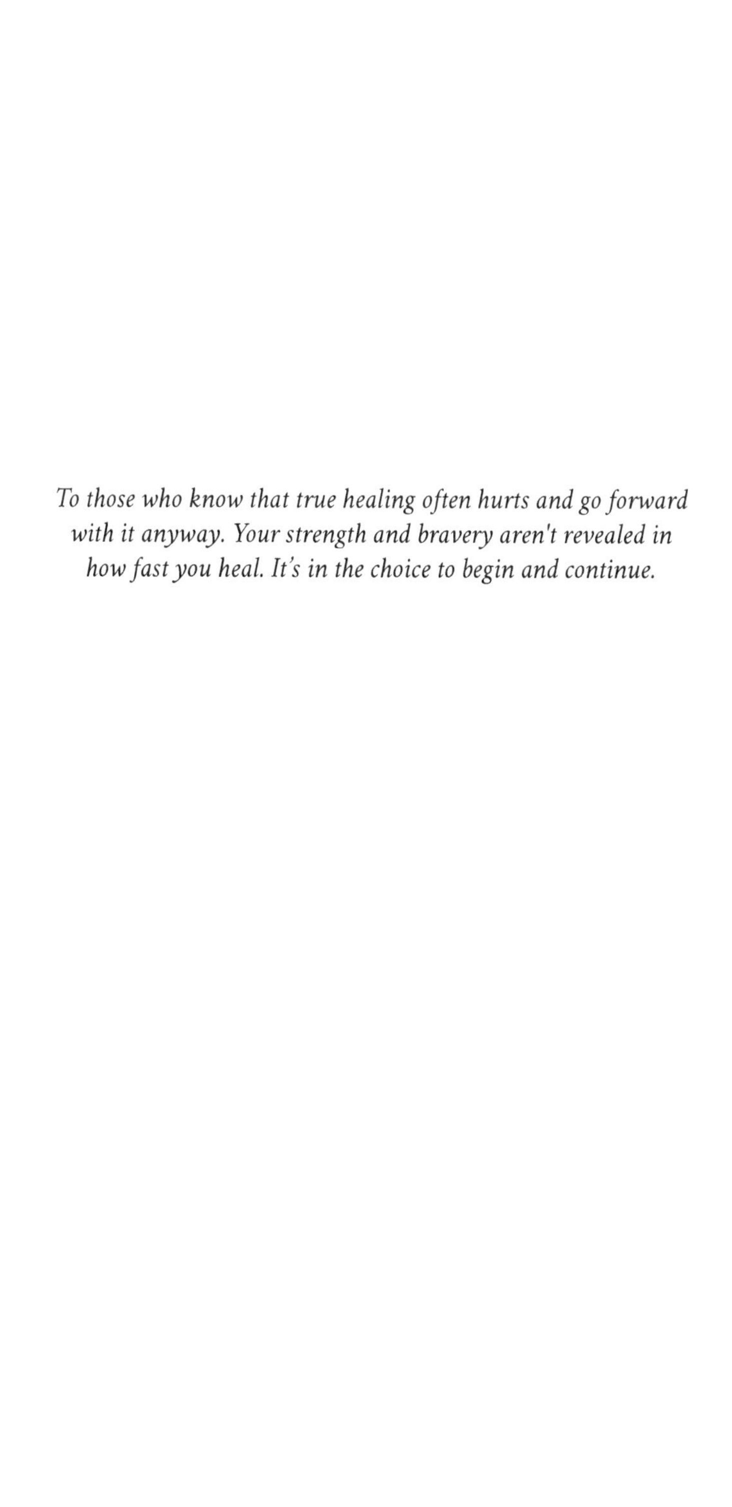

To those who know that true healing often hurts and go forward with it anyway. Your strength and bravery aren't revealed in how fast you heal. It's in the choice to begin and continue.

1

RESCUING A DRAGON

Wasn't breaking into the Sentinel's tower supposed to be hard?

I shoved my hand into a crevice in the dark stone and hauled myself higher. The crisp night air caressed my face and tugged at my dark hood and cloak.

Rumors abounded that the Sentinels were weakening in power, the Chasm nearing implosion. But then some said that the sorcerer prince who lived in this tower was a cursed fiend with the heart of an ice spirit, a spoiled child who thought being the prince of the Sentinels was enough to allow him to get whatever he wanted. I mean, in fairness, that last part was me and the people in the village of Irca agreeing with me after I learned who took my dragon. Really, they hadn't said much at all. Mostly just listened aside from offering the idea that it was Ramiel. But they didn't disagree with my assessment. And he certainly didn't seem to be loved. Most barely knew anything about him and his Sentinels, except that they were to be avoided and protecting the Chasm, though exceptionally dangerous, was crucial.

I pressed my body tighter against the cool stone. The winds picked up, fragrant with the sweet pleasant scents of lavender and moon fruit. The tower itself smelled of damp stone and runic magic, a cold scent like an oncoming storm. Ancient wards protected the perimeter, and this tower hummed and pulsed softly, vibrating deep into my marrow.

For anyone who didn't know magic, these glimmering wards might be enough to make them draw back. A pale-blue one spiderwebbed across the stone above me. Clear, well-constructed, and…easy to dismantle. Almost insultingly so. I'd always been a good knotweaver, especially when it came to undoing the central threads and spiraling away the strength of a well-formed ward or sigil. Few things other than Zephyrus brought me as much joy as seeing a vibrant bond slip out of that first knot, then the second, then the third all the way to the end.

But these—these were insultingly easy, and that didn't sit right with me. Ramiel or his minions had slipped into camp while I slept and stolen Zephyrus without waking me. I'd recognized the tang of magic on my tongue when I woke, a sweet but dark flavor like persimmons and plums. Whoever had done it had been sophisticated and skilled enough not to trip any of the guards I set up. Not even my aura had stirred as I slept. And that meant tremendous power.

So why these fluffy little nothing wards?

This one pulsed above my head like a ripe moon fruit, its natural light mirroring that of the moon above. Tendrils of mist curled around my boots as I reached higher. Hmmm, interesting. This ward was newer, the energy fresher. I didn't even need my blade to direct my focus. The tendrils came through, and those central threads came undone as easily as if they wanted to come apart.

Was it possible that because the Sentinels were neutrals they were prohibited from having certain kinds of guarding magic?

That didn't add up.

Shaking my head, I adjusted my grip and continued upward.

Even if this was a trap, I'd figure it out. If I got in too much of a jam, I'd pulseport back to the willow by the river where I'd left my few belongings, regroup, and return. But if all went well, I'd be riding Zephyrus out of here. He'd been my faithful companion and dearest friend since I was a girl. So many years together, and that giant scaly beast had never abandoned me once. I wasn't going to leave him in this forsaken tower on the edge of the Chasm.

I moved a little higher and tackled the next one. This too fell apart as easily as it if were simple string, the strands of energy vanishing as soon as that central thread pulled free.

My fingers twitched as I adjusted my grip on the stone. Just a bit higher.

The broad stone ledge of the open window jutted out above me less than fifteen feet away. I made my way up. My fingers ached, and my calves cramped, my boots gripping and pressing against the stone in an awkward position. An easy enough climb, all things considered, and my unease grew with each moment.

Up, up, up I climbed. Two more wards suggested I depart, and I insisted they vanish, their knots giving way to my focus within seconds.

At last I reached the broad ledge of the windowsill. Another thicker ward hummed over the window space, angry and alive. It pulsed with its own life. I clicked my tongue at it and channeled my focus through my eyes and index finger, tracing the strands. My energy hiccupped at the knot point, curling around and struggling with three of the strands. I pressed harder against the stone with my left hand and reached for the pale gold blade fastened on my right.

Finally, a ward that was more of a challenge.

I scrunched my nose as I lifted the blade as if it were a wand. It might as well have been. It accomplished the same thing and was even halfway decent at stabbing people. For now though, I simply summoned my energy up and focused it at the point. It hummed through my veins and then shot out, almost invisible. The air wavered around its path, and the ward flickered. Two of the three strands came undone. Then the third. The caster's essence flared through it, sharp and cold with an undercurrent like white moonstone, frosted silver, and glacial petrichor.

My lips curved. Ramiel, probably. Whoever it was, he liked his spells with bite. It had a depth about it, similar to the dark sweet aftertaste of magic left in my mouth after the abduction. With skills like that, he could obviously have done something far worse. So…why make it so light?

My energy rippled along the blade. Though the central thread resisted at first, my aura pressed against it and forced it to reveal itself. A darker purple and blue against gold light. Runes flared against the stone behind the ward, but instead of activating something more sinister, the threads came undone. For a moment, the intricate pattern hung in the air like frost, then it vanished.

Knots take me, what was I missing?

I seized the stone ledge and swung myself up. The dark-blue wooden shutters had been pressed back quite some time ago if the faded paint and the cobwebs and bits of leaves clinging to them were any indication.

A stronger gust of wind surged around me as if to shove me inside. My golden hair snagged on the faded paint. Hissing, I caught hold of the errant strands. How annoying. Carefully, I tucked my hair back beneath my dark-blue hood and surveyed my surroundings.

I could see most of the chamber fairly well from this crouched position. The stone ledge opened into a room large enough for a dragon to fly out of. It was rather bare, just a simple wooden plank floor and dressed stone walls. Functional like a barracks. A single table occupied the space to my left. An ebony inkpot and a glass case with a quill as well as a simple paper box suggested this was an observation point of sorts. Upon closer investigation, I noted that talon marks scourged the wood at multiple points and some of the stone had been chipped a little. Probably just from landing or easing inside. If there had been an actual fight here, it would have been far worse.

Oddly enough though, there were no traps up here. Not even any wards. The only sigils present were a few that merged with runes in the walls, and those were all focused on health, strength, and rhythm. Ancient, yes. Like prayer stones that remind you to pray and give thanks.

I eased myself down and took it all in. The moon through the window cast eerie shadows across the tower floor. Though my ears strained, all I caught was the distant call of a dark blade owl, plaintive and lonesome. A floorboard started to shift under my boot, but I drew back at once. All the rest were far more secure, allowing me to remain silent. No wards here at all. Curious. Not even a sign of this prince.

Maybe he lived somewhere else. People said that the Chasm was a rift that led to places between the worlds. Maybe he had another home somewhere else.

A chill pulsed through me. What if he had taken Zephyrus with him?

Swallowing hard, I shook my head. No, no, Zephyrus was here. I knew it. And I'd never been wrong about where Zephyrus was.

I slipped up to the wall and continued forward, gold blade tight in my right hand as I pressed my aura out in search of any kind of threat.

There. Not a threat. A staircase. It was behind a thick hickory door. The stairs curved down into darkness. My eyes adjusted swiftly, moving between the moonlit night to the close darkness of the stairwell. Steps silent, I made my way down deeper and deeper, counting each step as I went, nerves tense and aware. Thirty-nine, forty—there!

I lifted my head, breathing in deeper. Yes, there! I caught that familiar earthy, fiery scent: Zephyrus!

Willing myself to remain cautious, I continued down, ever downward. The air thickened. The Sentinel's magic bit into my senses as well, proof that he had been here as well and recently. It wasn't as ancient as some of the wards, but the undercurrent was the same. He was blood to whoever had cast the originals. He was also colder, angrier, and bitter if I read the remnants of his magic properly. I hoped he was somewhere in the Chasm.

The warmth intensified as I went lower. Deep grunts and low growls as well as heavy thumps punctuated the silence. Something stirred down here, and while Zephyrus's scent grew stronger, other scents took over. This staircase was large enough for him to come down, and there wasn't evidence of a struggle. Perhaps Ramiel had used an enchantment to keep Zephyrus compliant.

Then I reached the bottom. A door halted my progress, but already I caught new smells. A charred scent with undertones of smoke, leather, and sweet hay filled my nostrils, and a sharp mineral-rich flavor stung my tongue. Several dragons were down here. Those low rumbles suggested snores.

Pressing my hand to the door, I eased it open and peaked inside. A massive chamber—perhaps a dungeon— spread out before me, lined with what looked like iron-barred cells. My heart clenched, my fingers curling into fists as I searched for any sign of danger. I'd found the dragons, all right. But…what was going on here?

The bars were spaced wide enough for a dragon's head to slip through. Thick cushions of straw and scraps of fur and fabric spilled across stone floors. No signs of waste or neglect either. Each cell contained a large feeding trough. A few had dragged out the bones of their most recent meal, leaving bloody carcasses. Nothing rotted either. All fresh and bloody as if they had just been fed hours ago.

A deep blue-green dragon's tail curled out between the bars of one cell, flicking in sleep like a cat's. Another cell held a pearly-blue scaled beast whose snores echoed off the stone especially loud and made the water in its trough vibrate. I counted at least six dragons, all more peaceful than any I'd seen elsewhere. And there was still more to the stable.

I couldn't quite place what magic had accomplished this. Dragons were wary creatures. Even in family packs, at least one always remained on guard. But all slept here. That either meant they had been enchanted or another protector watched over them. Someone they trusted as much as blood. The latter seemed far more likely.

Zephyrus wouldn't be sleeping, of course. Based on his size and the patterns of his scales, he was older than some of the nations we traveled through, and you didn't get to be as big and powerful as him without being constantly on guard. Each night when I tucked in beside him, he slept with one eye half open.

Pursing my lips, I whistled a couple low bars. It was a mimic of the throaty call he made when looking for me. But no answer came back. The dragons continued to snore. Stepping farther in, I whistled once more.

Only snores and grunts greeted me.

Hand still gripping my blade, I continued into the dungeon. Still no sign of guards or attendants or anyone. No wards here either. Only the same runes and sigils, providing encouragement for health, strength, and stability. If there was anything else here, the caster had been especially good at masking them.

I took a few paces farther in. My heart leaped. There he was!

Zephyrus lay curled in one of the larger cells near the back, his dark-blue scales catching the torchlight. His massive head rested on his forelegs, eyes closed. Steam rose from his slanted nostrils. Not a mark or scratch marred his hide. No chains bound him. No signs of struggle or resistance scarred the stones around him.

Relief flooded through me at seeing him unharmed, but alarm quickly followed. Why was he here, sleeping so contentedly? Why hadn't he tried to escape? The Zephyrus I knew would never willingly stay caged, no matter how comfortable. He had to be drugged or enchanted. Or both.

A low rumble vibrated through the chamber as one of the other dragons shifted in its sleep. I needed to wake Zephyrus and get him out of here before anyone realized I'd broken in. But first I had to figure out what kind of enchantment held him so docile. I couldn't catch anything specific about it. Even as I reached out with my aura, nothing changed. Would he even recognize me?

I whistled once more, a little louder this time.

Zephyrus grunted, a stronger blast of steam searing from his nostrils as his pointed ears twitched. His horned eyelids fluttering open. His amber eyes were calm. A low purr rumbled through his chest as he cocked his head. With a deeper, lower growl, he stretched out like a cat, his claws scraping over the stone.

"What's going on?" I whispered, moving closer to the bars. He had only been this relaxed once or twice in the past, and that was when we were in the abandoned dragon tower or with two other riders.

He stretched his neck forward, nudging his snout at the gap. If he wanted, he could put his whole head through. He purred louder.

Tentatively, I placed my palm against his jaw. No signs of injury or distress marked his hide. His eyes were clear and alert, showing no signs of enchantment. No commands had been bound into his scales either.

Knots take me, I didn't like this. I was missing something. Part of me half expected to see Ramiel staring at me from the darkness, eyes glowing, magical energy pulsing.

I scanned the chamber again, more thoroughly this time. The torches burned steadily, no flickering that might hide motion-triggered wards or proximity sigils. The floor showed no trace of spell circles or runes. Even the ceiling, often a favorite place for trap-makers to hide their work, held nothing but smooth stone and iron brackets for the braziers. Some sort of mechanism suggested that the ceiling could be opened at the center of the dungeon.

Zephyrus bumped my shoulder with his snout, nearly knocking me over. His tail swished back and forth across the straw-covered floor of his cell—a gesture I knew well. He was...happy? Content even?

"I don't understand." I ran my fingers along his thick neck and then over onto the bars. Still nothing. Only iron. "You could break these easily. Why are you still here? You wouldn't abandon me, would you, Zephyrus?"

He drew back slightly, tilting his head in that way he did when I was missing something obvious. Another dragon snorted in its sleep nearby, sending a puff of smoke curling toward the ceiling.

Nothing made sense. The minimal security, the well-fed dragons, the cleanliness of the cells, Zephyrus's calm demeanor - this wasn't a prison.

That didn't mean it was safe for me. My gut clenched. My nerves tightened. I needed to get us out of here and fast.

His cell was deep, the gaps between the bars wide enough for me to slide through with ease. A dark, empty doorway was situated in the back. No. I wasn't going back through there. We'd go up through the staircase to the observation room.

A heavy iron lock secured his door. It too seemed completely ordinary, no magical signature or sigil work. Strange.

I sheathed my blade, pressed my hands together, and summoned an intricate series of knotted threads to press out through my aura, a small veil that enhanced my aware-ness, similar in form to a knotted shield but focused more on analyzing the points of contact with each knot and whatever touched the threads. I draped the magical web over the lock. It passed through easily, highlighting the tumblers.

Straightforward. Unprotected.

That was…very unusual. I didn't like it.

I slipped my fingers into my pocket and removed my lock picks. With care, I inserted the tension wrench and worked the pins.

An odd scent struck me. Sharp, cold, bitter. Thread rot! How had he managed that? I tried to counter.

It was too late.

Cold metal snaked around my ankles. The world twisted upside down. My picks clattered to the floor as more chains wrapped around my arms and torso, suspending me from the ceiling.

Blood rushed to my head as I dangled there, my hood falling away and my hair tumbling free. "Polph!"

2
SUSPENDED

*H*ow had that wretched sorcerer prince hidden that trap so well? I hated him even more now. Thread rot, this wasn't going well.

I half expected a loud gong or a pressurized wail to go off and inform everyone within miles of my presence. But there was nothing except the clanking of chains and the blue flare of a sigil binding the chains together.

Zephyrus made a rumbling sound that sounded suspiciously like laughter.

"Why are you laughing?" I demanded. Though I twisted in the chains, they tightened. My left arm was completely pinned, leaving me with nothing more than the ability to twitch my fingers. Whatever magic I channeled that way would be weak. My right had snagged and twisted in an awkward pose. Not much room to work with. These chains bit into my ribs and ankles, metal links cold against my skin even through my riding leathers. "Do something helpful, you big oaf! This is serious. Don't you want to get out of here?"

He cocked his head as he watched me swing and twist in slow circles. Poking his head through the bars, he nuzzled me. His hot breath steamed my hair.

"That's not helpful," I grumbled.

A dark thought occurred to me: what if there was no alarm because anyone who broke in wound up fed to the dragons? It would have been no trouble for Zephyrus to bite me in half. As it was, he just seemed sleepily amused, not doing anything to help me.

"Zephyrus," I whispered sharply.

He huffed again and bumped me with his snout, making me spin faster. His tail smacked the bars with playful energy.

"Zephyrus, no. This isn't the time or the place. Why aren't you being helpful?" Wincing, I wriggled, struggling to loosen my right arm as the chains clanked around me.

My blade pressed against my hip, still in its sheath. If I could just—there. My fingers brushed the hilt. The chains shifted, my arm aching, but I managed to grip the blade with two of my fingers.

A low growl echoed through the chamber. Then another. The other dragons stirred in their cells, their eyes gleaming in the darkness. Some made chirping sounds, others rumbled deep in their throats.

The nearest one—a female with silver-blue undertones beneath her dark-purple scales—stuck her head out. Her long serpentine neck allowed her to get uncomfortably close, though I remained out of the range of her broad jaws.

Another dragon—a silvering dark-green beast who looked like he had centuries on Zephyrus—twisted his head on the other side and leaned in. Torchlight glinted on his teeth.

Best not to make myself swing any more than I had to or else either of those two might nab me. These dragons seemed more curious than hungry or hostile, but curious dragons often used their teeth to nibble and test.

Blade in hand, I twisted my wrist. It was easy to spot the central knot where the energy of the sigil was hosted. It pulsed with an angry purple-red light. Four central threads inside had been bound so tightly there were no gaps.

Hmm. This sorcerer had made these with far more strength, and he'd managed to hide them as well.

"Wretched magic," I muttered to myself, channeling my magic as best I could. Something in the sigil repelled my energy, making the blood in my head rush and pound. Thread rot! My blade focused the energy, but this time the strands did little more than whinge.

Zephyrus's tail swished back and forth as he chuffed again. Some friend he was. I glared at him, comforted that he didn't seem to be in distress but confused at his lackadaisical manner. None of this added up.

Straining, I fought to get a better angle. Hopefully his relaxed manner meant there wasn't anything too dangerous nearby.

As I focused on the sigil, it flared brighter. Still it resisted.

More dragons awakened. They chirred and coughed and grunted, calling back and forth between one another. Zephyrus offered a few chuffs and growls.

With a frustrated mmph, I channeled another burst of energy through the blade. My magic hummed and seared along my veins, singing its way up. But whatever was in the sigil combined with my awkward position and…only the edges of the threads frayed. Sweat beaded on my forehead, and a stitch formed in my side. My breaths tightened.

Then one single strand on the outside of the sigil frayed.

Really? That was all!?

Furious curses rose to my lips, but Zephyrus's head snapped up. His attention was no longer on me. It was on the heavy wooden door at the far end of the chamber. His nostrils flared. The other dragons also fell silent.

Thread rot.

No sound reached my ears, but a sharp frosted silver and cedar scent reached my nostrils.

There was no simple way to explain my presence here or like this, and I couldn't pulseport out with that horrid chain wrapped around me. So if I didn't figure a way out soon—

The door thudded open and struck the wall. Rich violet eyes glowed in the darkness for a moment. A tall figure strode forward, silent as if his feet did not touch the stone.

Zephyrus pressed his snout through the bars, huffing warm air against my face. His amber eyes flicked between me and the newcomer.

The other dragons remained motionless, watching in a silence so complete it chilled me.

"Well, well, dare I ask what you're doing in my tower?" His deep voice rumbled low, far more pleasant than I had expected.

I twisted around in the chains, my muscles protesting the awkward angle. They clanked, but at least I didn't spin. "I'd rather not have this conversation while in such a position." I kept my fingers wrapped around the gold blade.

"Hm, is it wise for someone in your position to make such demands?" He stepped closer. His dark boots now made the faintest of clicks. That frosted silver and cedar scent followed him. The torchlight shone in his long silver hair, making it seem to have undercurrents of purple. "Then again, I suspect you might be one who finds it exceptionally easy to outrun wisdom. So let's try this again. What brings you to my stable, woman?"

I flashed him the best cold smile I could manage. "Well, it's a funny thing. See, someone stole my dragon a couple nights ago, and I just so happened to be passing through and I saw him down here all caged up. What a coincidence. I'm sure you had nothing to do with it. So get me down, let Zephyrus and me out, and I promise no harm will come to you." My long golden hair brushed the flagstones.

Zephyrus snorted.

I shot him a sidelong glare. He wasn't being as helpful as he should have been.

The fae's well-formed eyebrow arched as he studied

me. "Do you intend to have a serious conversation with me, gnat?"

"I'm serious as a blade through your chest: if you do not let both Zephyrus and me go, I will make you rue the day you met me." The energy I focused on the sigil continued to pulse and cut slowly. A second thread had frayed free. At this rate, I'd be down in a few hours. If he had noticed my attempt to escape, he wasn't acknowledging it. Once I was free of the chains, I'd pulseport out if I couldn't get Zephyrus free, and then I'd launch a counterattack.

"Well, I already rue your existence. You're like an insect in the wine. Small, annoying, and pointless except for getting on my nerves and using up my time and a perfectly good glass of wine. Do you even know who I am?"

My upper lip curled, and my head pounded. "One of the Sentinels probably." I couldn't remember the names of the individuals, but I'd heard of them in passing. Guardians over the Chasm. Technically, this land was theirs and they ruled themselves because no king tied to a people could ever have ownership of a liminal rift that theoretically could reach other worlds. The Sentinels were loyal to their purpose, which was the Chasm and all it held.

"I am Ramiel, Prince of the Sentinels." He now stood directly in front of me. The torchlight made the lavender notes in his hair all the more apparent and highlighted the dark circles beneath his eyes as if he had not slept in a long while. Even so, he was quite striking in appearance, his features elegant and sharp but pleasant. He clasped his hands behind his back as he stood before me now. "And aside from being an intruder and a dragon thief, you are?"

"Astraia."

His eyebrow lifted. "Just Astraia?"

"Just Astraia." My throat tightened. I never told anyone about my family these days if I could help it. Part of me still felt as if I had betrayed them by not speaking of them, but it was for the best. No one needed to know. It always led to the same conversations anyway. "Now that the introductions are out of the way, release Zephyrus and me at once."

A humorless laugh escaped his lips. "Not even an attempt at an apology for trespassing and robbing me?"

"You stole Zephyrus!" I gritted my teeth.

"I brought him home." Ramiel's eyes narrowed. He stood directly in front of me now. "He belongs to no one in the Rune. Least of all a slip of a knotweaver."

Heat flared in my cheeks, rising with my indignation. "I never said he belonged to me. Zephyrus is my friend!"

Zephyrus grunted. He leaned against the bars of the cage and nudged me again, making me spin. "Zeph!" I scolded. The chains clinked as I swung like some damnable lamp in a slow circle.

The deep, throaty chuckle that followed was unmistakable. The large blue dragon nudged me again, his broad snout tapping my stomach in a teasing nuzzle. He snorted again.

The other dragons also chortled and grunted, their tails raking the floor and the bars. One especially high-pitched voice sounded almost like a bird.

Ramiel held up his hand. All fell silent, even Zephyrus. "Well, it is clear they do not see you as a threat." He made a loose gesture with two of his fingers at the chains. Silver-blue light flared. It crackled at the sigil that bound the chains at their heart, and that internal thread I hadn't been able to reach came undone.

The chains loosed, the knot at the center of the pulsing sigil unraveling from the inside out. The metal shifted then.

Oh, knots take me!

The tension gave way.

I flung my arms out to catch myself, bracing for impact and planning for the fight.

It never came.

Instead, my body halted, suspended in air like a feather caught in an updraft. An odd sensation crawled across my skin—a distinct but foreign magic, cold and precise. Not unpleasant, but definitely not mine. My hair floated around me as if I were underwater.

Ramiel's fingers moved in a small, controlled gesture. His eyes narrowed in concentration as he righted me, then lowered me to the floor. My scuffed boots kissed the stone before I settled flat on my feet. With a loud clatter, the chains fell away and pooled on the floor.

Well, that had gone far better than I'd hoped, but I squirmed inwardly. I couldn't feel any magic suppressing my ability to pulseport out or even run on foot. But he'd surprised me more than once already. My fingers curled tighter around the blade. While it was intended for focusing magic, I could certainly stab people with it. If it became necessary.

The way Ramiel studied me, I wasn't sure. He looked more like he wanted to give me a scathing lecture than stab me. But he was a sorcerer as well. One strong enough to not require a blade to focus, and he carried himself as if he could level the whole tower with a single command.

With quiet grace, he circled me. His violet eyes tracked over the entirety of my body, cataloguing every detail.

Resisting the urge to wrap my arms around myself, I glared at him and turned my head to ensure we didn't break eye contact for even a breath. I felt exposed under his gaze, like a specimen pinned for examination. "Looking for something?" I demanded.

"How is it that you continue to act as if you were the one who was wronged?" he asked, his tone still dry. He turned to face the purple dragon as she chuffed particularly loud, his back to me.

At once, I rolled my shoulders and rubbed my neck to ease the tension. I hated hanging upside down, even when flying with Zephyrus. When he started to turn, I dropped my arms at my sides. "I am the one who was wronged. You snuck into my camp, and you abducted my friend."

"No. I summoned him home. No one owns a dragon

without the dragon's consent." He halted in front of me. His gaze slid to the dragons, settling on Zephyrus. "How did you know his name?"

I shrugged.

Zephyrus snorted again from his cell, his tail swishing against the bars in that infuriatingly amused way. He rested his head as close to me as he could be. That low chortling laugh of his annoyed me now though. Traitor.

Ramiel's eyebrow arched higher. "Well?"

I shook my head. "I just was talking with him, and I knew it. I felt it."

Zephyrus nudged me again, his neck braced against the bars. I reached back to stroke his snout. Even if this was his home, he wouldn't have gone without me or communicated it in some way. No…something was off here. I could feel it.

Ramiel paced a few steps more and then traced his finger through the air, marking the shape of my shoulder. "Your magic…it's runic knotwork. Fascinating. No trace of thought weaving or mind binding skills. No. Nothing like that."

He was at least six feet away from me, but my skin prickled in response as if he had traced his hand over my shoulder directly. I wrinkled my nose at him. It was impressive he could recognize both forms of my magic based on sight or magic alone. Especially when I took such efforts to hide my runic skills. "And how is that relevant?"

He circled me once more and then began to examine Zephyrus. Placing his hands on the large dragon's throat, he ran his fingers along the dark-blue scales. He turned sideways and entered the cell, continuing his examination.

"What exactly are you looking for?" I crossed my arms over my turquoise and dark-brown bodice. My right bracer snagged on the laces. Did he really think I had charmed Zephyrus? If anyone here had charmed Zephyrus, it was him.

"Dragons do not easily take commands. Not even from those they cherish."

"I would never charm Zephyrus to force him to take a command from me," I snapped. "Unlike you."

He circled Zephyrus and met my gaze once more. "I command the dragons of the Chasm. Zephyrus is one of the twelve weavers. They often wander for periods, but they always return home. Rest assured, I would only enforce a command upon one of them in the most dire of circumstances."

He stepped out of the cell sideways, his long silver hair a curtain against his broad shoulders. He moved directly in front of me and folded his arms. "I believe you. And I will grant you this one boon, Astraia. You may leave my tower unharmed if you vow never to return. Consider it a mercy—one I rarely offer."

Behind me, Zephyrus let out a low, rumbling growl. His tail slapped against the bars with clear disapproval, making the metal ring.

"A boon?" I laughed, the sound sharp and brittle in the chamber. "How generous of you to offer me permission to walk away from my own friend." I planted my feet firmly, mirroring his stance. "I'm not going anywhere without Zephyrus."

"Your stubbornness does you no credit." Ramiel's mouth tightened into a thin line. "The dragon stays. That is not negotiable. He is necessary to ensure the Chasm's protection."

"You got along without him for at least fifteen years, possibly more," I said sharply.

"Things have changed, and he is finally ready to come home."

That dull unease spread further within me. What if he was even partially telling the truth? I lifted my chin. "He would *never* abandon me, and I won't abandon him."

He closed the distance between us in three sharp strides. The scent of frosted silver intensified, almost covering the cedar notes. "Do not mistake my patience for weakness, little gnat. It is unwise to underestimate me." His voice dropped to a dangerous whisper. "You've seen but a fraction of what I can do. I am the last Sentinel, guardian of the Chasm, and this tower has stood for centuries against threats far greater than one stubborn knotweaver. This matter is far bigger than either of us. Bigger than you can even begin to conceive."

I refused to step back, though my heart beat faster. "I don't care if you ruled the whole continent and all the islands beside. I will not turn my back on someone I love, Your Highness. I will get Zephyrus free, and I will find out what you did to him. You have my word on that. You may be powerful, but I have my own tricks up my sleeve. So do not underestimate me either."

Zephyrus huffed behind us, a sound somewhere between amusement and concern. His claws scraped against the stone floor of his cell.

Ramiel's eyes flashed.

Had I gone too far?

3
THE CELL

I kept my chin up. Yeah, I'd probably pushed him a little too far, and I wasn't in the best position for an outright fight.

"If you name a price for a ransom, I will pay it though." My throat tightened. Not that I had any resources available beyond my wits. I'd have to negotiate for time next. All I owned was on my back or in the pack I'd hidden beneath the old willow at the deep bend before the forest. Everything I owned could be sold for half a copper ingot. But I was clever. I'd always found a way. And if I had Zephyrus back, it would be manageable.

Ramiel studied me, his gaze moving over my face with unsettling intensity. Something shifted in his expression—a flicker of something—warmth, perhaps? But the silence deepened.

My skin prickled beneath his scrutiny. The dragons had gone still as well. Even Zephyrus stopped his huffing and chortling, his heavy-lidded eyes now open wide and studying both Ramiel and me.

I swallowed hard. "Please."

The faintest hint of a smile curled at his lips. He canted his head as he drew closer. "So that's it? You will not give Zephyrus up?"

"Never." Surges of emotion rose at the mere thought, but I choked them back. "I will never abandon him. He is family."

A slight smile curved his lips more. The edges of his eyes wrinkled as well. "Such conviction."

That didn't sound like he was about to agree with me though. My mind raced. Perhaps there was a way through this—a bargain, a trade. Most men of power wanted something. "You have all these other dragons who look as if they are all quite healthy and whole. Let me take Zephyrus, and we will find another to take his place. We'll go to the south. To Bone or the Ash Lands. Even the Umbral Kingdom has dragons that might be trained for these duties. Just name your price, and—"

"Enough." He cut me off with a sharp gesture. He pressed two fingers together as he did, silver-purple light blooming from his fingertips. Runes blossomed around us.

Knots take me! I snapped my hands up, weaving a shield with my fingers and blade. Golden threads of knot-work magic sprang up, forming an intricate lattice that pulsed with protective energy. The barrier materialized just as Ramiel's silver-purple magic shot toward me.

"I'll be back, Zephyrus!" I gathered my focus to pulse-port away and envisioned that point beneath the willow. The familiar sensation of magic coiled in my stomach, ready to whisk me away.

Nothing happened.

Zephyrus snarled, his head snapping up in the first true show of alarm since this started.

Cold dread spiked through me. No burst of heat or tightness of energy cut across my consciousness. The ground remained painfully firm beneath my feet. No! Bands of purple runic energy bound my feet to the floor. I hated undoing runic knot magic. They never had one central thread. And somehow these had slipped beneath my protection shield. Damn him, he was good.

"You thought it would be that easy to leave?" Ramiel

scoffed, his hand still lifted, his wrist straight but his manner so casual he was clearly not using all of his strength. "I warned you not to underestimate me." He dropped it then against the hilt of his blade, his wrist now limp though the power in the magic remained strong.

My breath hissed through my teeth. "How—" It didn't matter. I shook my head. No one had ever blocked my pulseporting and knotwork shield so effortlessly before. "Let me go!" Rage boiled through me. I thrashed against the bonds at my feet, my knotwork shield still flickering between us. Whatever he had done, I couldn't feel the heat within. It was as if he was blocking the entirety of my magic as well.

Zephyrus roared, throwing himself against the bars of his cell. The metal groaned but held firm. His massive claws reached through the gaps and gouged at the stone.

Ramiel was just beyond his reach, his expression impassive. "I warned you, and now you have upset Zephyrus. That is bad for all of them."

"Let us both go and it all gets better!" I snapped.

He sighed and shook his head. With a flick of his hand, runes appeared in the air before me—ancient symbols that twisted and coalesced into a shadowy creature with too many limbs to count. It lunged at me, passing through what remained of my shield as if it were mist.

Cold fingers wrapped around my arms, my throat, my waist—the creature's grip unyielding as ice. I struggled, my knotwork magic sliding out and falling away. Its fingers moved through the shield as I struggled to keep it up, even as each knot strained and buckled. My breath snagged.

Zephyrus bellowed louder. His tail slammed against the bars with enough force to make the entire chamber shudder, and the other dragons took up the call, roaring, snarling, and howling.

Ramiel just watched me, his shoulders squared and his expression hardened. An expression almost like regret flickered in his eyes, but he lifted his hand and said something.

I couldn't catch the words. The shadow creature wrapped over me at once, pulseporting me away.

Darkness swallowed me. There was nothing but me, that cold shadow, and my struggling knotwork shield. I couldn't move—couldn't even draw a breath! A voiceless scream locked in my throat.

Then the darkness vanished. Something hard and cold slammed into my shoulder and side. I gasped for air, choking and sputtering as the entity pulled back.

Dozens of questions poured through my mind. Where was I? Where was Zephyrus? My head pounded, the roars and bellows of the dragons now muted and far away. I rolled to my feet, fists clenched. My hair slid over my face. What—I was in a cell now. A heavy iron door glared down at me. Not even a scrap of light slipped beneath the ledges.

"No!" I slammed my hand against the door, the impact stinging through my palm. The bite of a sigil on the other side warned me of the kind of magic he'd used to seal me in. "Let me out!"

The shadow creature had vanished as well.

Falling back, I drew in a long, shaking breath and took in my surroundings. Only a single torch lit this cell, too far up for me to easily reach. A scowl creased my brow. Yet another surprise. Ramiel was full of them. This was no dank cell with mold or rats. The stone floor was smooth, clean stone, swept free of dust. The bed—an actual bed, not a pile of straw—looked softer than what I'd slept on in years, with thick blankets folded neatly at its foot and a soft white pillow stuffed with duck feathers from the looks of a few wisps poking out.

"What kind of prison is this?" I muttered, running my fingers along the wall. As I focused, I willed my energy into my aura. Slowly it expanded out. The fine lines of magic even through the door became more and more visible.

Yes. There!

More sigils and a ward etched into the doorframe.

I managed a bitter grin, pleased and annoyed all at once.

Complex patterns of runic magic interwoven with sigil work, their edges glowing faintly purple in the torchlight. This was more what I'd expected from the fabled Sentinel —powerful, ancient magic that practically hummed with energy. The knotted centers were five strands thick but likely held together by a single particularly strong thread. Once I spotted the weakest one within the five, I could draw it out, work it loose, then make my escape by pulse-porting through the gap.

I pressed my hands against the door all the harder, seeking the threads of magic that bound those sigils and wards. Golden light flickered from my fingertips and down my blade as I worked to unravel the knots, searching for weak points in the pattern and that central thread.

The magic resisted, slipping away from my grasp like water. Whatever that shadow creature was, it had drained some of my strength. An uncomfortable emptiness had settled within me. I tried again, digging deeper, my teeth gritted with effort. "It makes no sense," I grumbled. "Why leave the dragons with so little protection and focus so much down here? Wherever here is."

"You're not asking the right questions, little knotweaver," a voice chuckled, seeming to come from the air itself.

I spun around, searching for the source. The underlying shimmer and vibrato of the voice suggested some sort of magical entity. Possibly male. Definitely not Ramiel. "Who's there? Show yourself!"

"I am Caein," the strange voice responded. "And I assure you, this tower is well protected. But it was clear you were not a threat to the dragons."

I set my hands on my waist, my fingers tapping with anxious rhythm. "You mean he knew I was coming?"

"The wards and sigils are intelligent. The magic that

holds them together is wise enough to recognize certain elements of intruders."

I scowled even more. "What do you mean?"

A low laugh rippled through the cell.

My skin crawled. I didn't like this. And I didn't like this disembodied voice. It sounded like he was one of the Nolches. Souls who had chosen to become incorporated into a building of sorts. While I hadn't run into too many over the years, I still had strong opinions. What kind of person decided to incorporate their living consciousness into a building? It sounded like some sort of esoteric torment.

"I like you, Astraia," Caein continued. His voice hummed in my ears as if he had drawn closer. "And if you weren't someone I liked, you'd have been incinerated before you stepped across the ledge. There is little more precious to Ramiel than his dragons. They're all he has left. But he doesn't believe in killing the innocent. It would go against everything that being a Sentinel stands for."

I scoffed. "That's not what they stand for. The Sentinels guard the Chasm and keep the other kingdoms from leveraging it—"

"The Sentinels protect the rest of the world from the creatures within the Chasm and the creatures of the Chasm from the rest of the world," Caein said, his voice firm as if he were speaking to an unruly child. "The dragons assist in that. I assure you Zephyrus is as safe as any dragon here."

That hollow sensation agitated me even further. As I folded my arms, I brought my focus inward and tried to build my magic up again. It was difficult to do without food and rest. "I could have been an assassin though. Most assassins wouldn't be asked to target dragons."

Another chuckle followed as if that was a good joke. "Had you been an assassin, you would have encountered very different wards and sigils, little knotweaver."

I rolled my eyes at the ceiling, pretending to be unimpressed. "So the wards sensed my intentions? That's ridiculous." It wasn't. It was actually incredibly concerning. Very few magic practitioners could accomplish that.

"The wards sensed your connection," he corrected. "The bond between dragon and rider cannot be disguised any more than the bonds of family, friendship, loyalty, mates, and love."

My fingers curled against my collarbone. My energy was replenishing slowly. Keeping my breaths focused and steady, I channeled my magic throughout my blood and lungs. "Then you should be able to sense just how close I am with him. You know I can't leave without him." My magic surged a little stronger within me, pooling hotter in my solar plexus. The corded magic that bound the wards and sigils together became more clearly visible, the individual threads brightening on the other side of the door. Good. Now if I could just get this Nolche to leave.

"I realize this must be quite hard and exceptionally distressing," Caein said, his voice softening. "But there are forces at work here which you do not understand. Ramiel is not your enemy. Zephyrus belongs here."

I pressed my palm against the cold stone wall. "Why do you talk like he wants to be here? He's been with me since I was twelve. He chose that! He doesn't belong in a cage."

"This is his home. Ramiel did not steal him. He summoned him, and he was reunited with his family, and it was a joyous occasion. He has been missing for so long," Caein continued. His voice grew a little more distant as if he moved up higher toward the ceiling.

I steeled my expression. Zephyrus had left me? No. No! "If that was so, then why would Ramiel not speak to me? Why steal him in the dead of night like a thief? Someone used magic on me! I know the taste. I am not a fool."

"I suspect it is because he wished to avoid conversation and all its complications. You might ask him the next time you see him."

"If all goes well, I'll never see him again," I muttered.

"Given that you are here in the secured guest quarters of Ramiel's tower, I doubt you can forever avoid him."

That note of laughter and smugness annoyed me to no end. But let him laugh. I'd be out of here soon. Ramiel's magic might be unusually powerful and well masked, but I had my tricks. That thread I'd been worrying on the other side was pulsing brighter now, and the hollowness in my chest had faded.

Caein continued, that faint chuckle still in his voice. "I do not recommend that you continue to fight this. Either make peace with Zephyrus's presence here or don't. But perhaps if you make peace, Ramiel will permit you to remain." He stopped. The air chilled a little, then warmed. An odd contemplative hum vibrated above me. "We'll speak again soon, little knotweaver."

The shifting in the air above me confirmed Caein had left. Now was my chance to escape.

Returning to the door, I pressed my palms against the flat surface. The pulse of magic within me went at once to that weakened ward. There. Yes. I removed my blade and pressed the tip to the edge of the metal and focused. The metal warmed against my skin as I channeled my magic through it. Golden threads of energy spilled from my fingertips, weaving through the air as I searched for the ward's structure.

Yes! I'd found it—right in the center five threads I found a runic knot. It was complex, a rich purple, pulsing and living. Unlike the outer wards, this one shifted and writhed as if alive, sensing my intrusion. A smile pulled at the corners of my mouth. No matter how strong, every knot could be undone.

Breaths steady and focused, I hooked the energy from my blade into that thread and eased it toward me. "Got you now," I murmured softly. The thread resisted once more, then snapped free. The ward pulsed. Snatching at the next thread, I forced it out of its pattern as well. The ward sputtered.

That was all it took. I weakened the rest of it and swiped the threads away. Though the other wards and sigils pulsed in response, there was now a gap large enough to pulseport through. Closing my eyes, I envisioned Zephyrus's cage—the iron bars, the clean straw, his massive blue form waiting just beyond. I gathered my remaining energy and pushed.

My body folded and shot through that gap like Zephyrus diving into a canyon. Bile crept up the back of my throat and coated my tongue, my stomach twisting and rolling. Darkness engulfed me, then spat me out.

I struck the stone floor harder than intended, stumbling, then cracking down.

My head spun, and I knew I wasn't in the stable before I could even open my eyes. It smelled of old books, faded magic, and candle wax rather than smoke, hay, and leather. Eyelids fluttering, I struggled to focus.

What had gone wrong? And why was I even surprised? I'd slipped out of tighter and harder holds than that cell countless times before, but this was Ramiel's tower, so why not bungle it?

All remained heavy and quiet. I lay on the floor of a long stone corridor. Silver-framed paintings lined the wall on both sides with small memorial tables beneath each. Probably former Sentinels and the items that had represented them in life. They all had appearances rather similar to Ramiel: sharp features, purple or purple-blue eyes, contemplative expressions, hooded eyes. All wearing silver and blue.

I pushed myself up slowly, my head throbbing. It hurt worse now than it had with the runes on me or when I was hanging upside down. My aura screamed at me, exhausted and shaken. Whatever was hidden in this place, it had drained me more than expected here as well. Thank goodness there was no sign of that shadow creature.

I cradled my temple as I took this place in. So which direction was the stable from here? I swallowed hard, my mouth dry. It didn't feel like I had the strength to manage even a small pulseport now. Thread rot.

I swallowed hard. Well, at least I had my wits, my blade, and, soon, my friend. Limping along, I took care to remain as quiet as possible.

A few steps farther in whatever direction this was and I caught the first notes of sound other than the faint hissing of torches. Ramiel's voice, low and measured, drifted from a room farther down the hall. A warm glow spilled from an open doorway. "This is unsustainable," he said. "The seals are weakening faster than before, and if I do anything beyond what I have already done, the omenfang will return. We don't have much time."

4

ANOTHER RESCUE ATTEMPT

I stiffened, my ears straining to catch every trace of information I could. Who was Ramiel talking to? Caein? My gut said Caein. Something in the air felt similar to his presence now that I focused on it.

Keeping my boots from scuffing on the polished stone floor, I eased closer. No wards or sigils here, but that was obviously not proof enough to move with any sort of confidence. Another two steps forward, and I halted.

"This will not be enough," Ramiel continued.

"You have made great progress," Caein responded. "It's fully contained."

"For now. But how much longer before it breaks free? I spent far too much on gnat."

I cocked my head, almost amused at that nickname. I'd certainly been called worse. Peering around the corner, I spotted him leaning over a glass orb on a desk, both hands pressing on it. Silver frost stretched over the orb, hints of purple and blue sparking among the runes in the frost patterns.

"Yes, well, you should have done more to ensure Zephyrus hadn't gotten himself attached. That woman is quite determined to free him," Caein said. "Do you simply intend to keep her until it is finished?"

The muscles in Ramiel's hands flexed though he kept his fingers near motionless. "If she refuses to swear to leave Zephyrus, I have no other choice. I can't let her interfere. The ritual requires at least eight of the weavers. Even with all twelve..." He fell silent. "I doubt she was any more reasonable when you went to her."

"No. You may need to be frank with her about everything regarding this situation, Ramiel. This is an exceptionally serious matter."

"Be frank with her? Yes, that sounds wise," he responded, the dryness in his voice intensifying. "If she thinks Zephyrus might even be wounded, let alone die, she will never leave. And we both know that it may be unavoidable. All may perish."

Bastard! My fingers curled tight against my palms, fingernails cutting into my skin. Cold rushed over me. I set my jaw as I drew back to avoid being seen, but I listened intently.

"Perhaps so," Caein said. "But you know what this is. It's a true—"

"Yes, I know it's a true bond, Caein, but that doesn't matter," Ramiel snapped. He continued to trace patterns over the glass. "He disappears for all those years, goes out, and bonds with—" His jaw worked, surprising emotion cutting through his voice. "You have no idea how difficult this is."

"No, I don't. I'm certain Zephyrus never intended to, even though no one truly controls a dragon. Commands do not hold if they go against the dragon's will. If you just explain to her—"

"I don't want to spend these last days explaining anything. This is challenging enough as it is. It is taking every ounce of my will." His shoulders tightened, his eyes hardening. "We are down to the final weeks. Possibly even days. They should not be spent in useless conversation. And Zephyrus should be allowed to be with his kin."

A bit of guilt twisted inside me.

"The bond between a dragon and rider is one of the sacred bonds. She knows his name. He chose her."

"I am aware," Ramiel said, his voice growing more stern. "This isn't going well. The leviathan stirs already. He is getting worse, and we're running out of time. Especially if the omenfang can't be stopped—ithoks!"

That sharp burst of profanity made me go rigid. The air had taken on a stronger scent, more like burning metal. I peeked in again in time to see that the glass orb was cracking. A pitch-black storm cloud had formed within it, and lightning flared inside.

"Steady, Ramiel, don't be so swift to believe the worst. If you become more agitated—"

Ramiel made a hissing sound in response. He hunched over the cracking glass, arms braced. "Check the perimeter wards. Strengthen them. Cut them off from the aether of the Chasm. Make sure it doesn't enter, then return."

"If the omenfang—" Caein started.

"It won't make a difference if the wards are breached. The defenses will have to hold here. Go!" Ramiel shot an enraged glare up at the ceiling. The air pulsed for a moment.

I crouched down, still watching and unable to tear myself away. The magic in or around the orb carried a bitter, caustic scent now—like burned copper mixed with rotting seaweed. My stomach tightened, some instinctual part of me repulsed by the presence of that—that thing. What evil was that?

The glass shattered. Runic symbols flared around Ramiel's hands, bright purple lights that flared in all directions. Dark shadows coiled out like a wind funnel—a spectral kangaroo, towering over seven feet tall with eyes like burning coals. It reared back on its powerful legs and struck Ramiel viciously in the chest and against the wall— once, twice, three times.

Terror spiked through my veins.

Ramiel collapsed, gasping and clutching at his chest.

I barely caught myself before I rushed in to help. What was I thinking? Why would I help him when he was the reason Zephyrus was here and willing to sacrifice him?

Drawing back, I took stock of the hall and decided to continue straight ahead. Ramiel could sort out his own problem.

A low, pained groan confirmed he was at least alive in there. I stole a glance as I slipped past the doorway and padded down the hall. He lay on his back, gripping his chest. There were no signs of wounds, and he was breathing well enough. Whatever it was—the omenfang maybe?—had probably come close to knocking the wind out of him, but there wasn't any trace of blood on his silver brocaded tunic. His straight silver hair fanned out on the dark floor like a disheveled aura, and he had his hand pressed to his chest. Steady breaths at least. He'd be fine. Served him right for putting Zephyrus in harm's way.

My chest tightened, that thrum of guilt intensifying. Enough of that. I didn't have time, and I owed him nothing. If he'd been some stranger on the side of the path, I'd have helped. But he wasn't a stranger. He was a Sentinel prince who had summoned Zephyrus away and apparently intended to let him die.

I slunk along through the tower's twisting corridors, swift and silent. The walls seemed to breathe around me, ancient dark stone veined with faint blue. My fingers traced the cool surface as I moved and my aura reached out, searching for hidden mechanisms, secret pathways, traps—anything. The sigils and wards did not come near me. They did not even seem to notice me.

The hall branched again, and I chose the left. A few steps later and I caught that familiar scent. Zephyrus! Relief pounded in my chest.

A few steps more and I found another door like the one I'd found in the observation tower. The silence in this tower cut deeper and deeper. I half expected Ramiel to pop up at any moment or Caein to speak above me. But only silence surrounded me.

A few moments later, and I had picked my way back down into the stable. As soon as I was through the door, I set up a knotwork net that would mask my presence and muffle any sound. It stretched out with golden shimmering threads that vibrated ever so slightly with a light all their own.

Most of the dragons were sleeping again. Except Zephyrus. He lay with his head on his crossed forelegs like a cat before a fire, his tail flicking back and forth and overlapping with the purple dragon's. The larger deep blue-green dragon was curled up at the side of his cell, leg outstretched toward Zephyrus and tail reaching into another dragon's cell.

Zephyrus lifted his head as soon as I drew near, blinking those large amber eyes. His tail flicked.

My heart clenched. Though my plan was for us to run, I knew I had to handle this with care. There was no chance of moving a dragon who didn't want to be moved. And panicking might send him into a rage that resulted in either or both of us getting injured.

Besides, now I saw how many similarities there were between him and the other dragons. While each had different colored scales, there was something in the eyes and the shape of the head that had the look of family. Could I really take him away from his family when all I longed for was to be reunited with mine?

With the heavy clicks of his large talons, he rose to his feet, his leather wings rustling as he tucked them against his back. He chuffed, softer than before.

I approached, my brow furrowing. "Is this where you want to be?"

He tilted his head and blinked slowly. Then he stuck his head out through the bars and nudged me.

I hugged him, tears pricking in my eyes as I wrapped my arms as far as I could around his thick neck. "If this is your family, I'm not trying to take you away. I'd never do that, I swear. But I heard Ramiel. If you stay, you'll die. I'm not going to abandon you."

He growled low, then nuzzled me again. A blast of steam from his slanted nostrils followed, along with a croaking churr. One of his contemplative tones. Another rumble followed, similar to his laugh.

"This is serious," I said, moving back a step. "I heard him." Thrusting my fingers in my long wavy hair, I pushed the locks back. "I'm sorry. It's all so complicated right now. Maybe we can come back for the others." How much time did we really have? Was Zephyrus the only one at risk? I didn't even know what weavers and dragons did.

He chuffed again. His voice rumbled and vibrated, a soothing sound that I enjoyed most of the time. The way his ears pricked forward though, it was as if he was simply telling me that there was something I was missing. I glanced around. As I turned, he shoved me with his head and chortled with that low, growly voice of his.

I struck the flagstone hard, landing on my butt. "Hey!" I huffed back at him and scrambled up.

He snorted again, giving me that chiding look.

I struggled to my feet and scrubbed my hands on my trousers. "Come on. Let's get out of here. We'll sort out the rest later." To whom could I even go to learn the purpose of the dragons? My fairy friends at Thistledeep or maybe Star Petal might have some knowledge, but on foot, it would take me days to get there. And more importantly, I didn't want to leave Zephyrus here.

The other dragons slept on, and Zephyrus regarded me with that same quiet amusement he usually did after a brutal training session when he knew I was on the verge of remembering a technique.

"I wish you could talk," I said under my breath. But even if he could, we didn't really have time for this. I pressed my forehead against the cool bars of his cage, thinking it through. No, this was the right call. Ramiel had said

Zephyrus could die, and Zephyrus did not belong in a cage. "We'll get out, and then we'll figure out what to do about the rest of your family." I wasn't sure that I could promise we would be able to save them, but it felt wrong not to at least try.

He nudged me again, and I stroked his neck while he purred. The first trap had been hidden inside the lock itself. My gut still warned against entering Zephyrus's cell even though there might be a door farther in. No. Not unless I had no other choice.

And…there were choices. I spread my hands and reached out with my aura to uncover any additional wards, mechanisms, sigils, or spells. The warm hum and tickle of the healing sigils as my consciousness neared them comforted me. And—yes! Yes, there on the far side of the dark-grey dragon's cell two down from Zephyrus were several levers. Hidden deeper within the wall was a series of mechanisms.

My magic made them light up briefly, and these mechanisms pulsed in response. Not quite what I expected. An ordinary mechanism, like the ones in old barns used to roll down special walls. And that mechanism also ran up into the ceiling but with stronger braces, suggesting that the entire ceiling truly could be rolled back, likely to allow the dragons to fly out.

All I had to do was select the right lever to release the proper counterweight, and Zephyrus's cell would open. Then it'd be a simple matter of going up the stairway. Probably best not to risk opening the entire tower unless I had no other choice.

Zephyrus nudged me again with his nose and gave a low rumble of approval.

I smiled at him wryly and pressed my cheek to his jaw. "Yeah, was that what you wanted me to see?"

A gentle chuff was his only answer, his head tilted.

That wasn't quite the response I wanted. It sounded more like he expected something else, but it wasn't a warning. The only ward or sigil specifically connected to those levers was intended to make it hard to see by outsiders and those unfriendly to the Sentinels and dragons. Still I moved cautiously, examining the air, floor, ceilings, and walls for any hint of a hidden trap. Ramiel had fooled me more than enough for one lifetime, and—

The air crackled. Runes surged around me in a blinding spiral of light as a deafening hum filled my ears. A great force slammed into my aura like a battering ram, and a translucent barrier encased me. I fell back, striking curved walls and suddenly suspended once more in the air in what looked to be a glass prison shaped like a tapered bud.

5

BLOOD BOUND

"Damn it!" I shouted as I struck the inside. The sound bounced back at me, vibrating along the deceptively strong, clear walls. Another trap! How did he mask these so well?! I had literally broken into the Library of the Celestial Spire. I'd eluded dozens, maybe hundreds, of bounty hunters and mercenaries over the years. I'd unshackled the Beast of the Low Fiend's Pass with just my magic even though he'd killed more than a dozen others. And I'd done that in the air with Zephyrus threatening to do barrel rolls. Yet somehow—once again—Ramiel had snared me…like a gnat in a web.

Thread rot, I hated this!

Zephyrus huffed at me again. That blast of steam followed by the arching of his horned eyebrows annoyed me. He didn't seem bothered by this. Another steamy breath made the glass fog up on the one side. I narrowed my eyes. "You think this is funny? Use your tail and break this thing open." His low rumble was his only answer, and I set my jaw. Utterly useless.

I wove a series of knots, rubbing them between my fingers until they hummed with power. Then I bound them together and released them in a burst. They struck hard but slid off, unraveling into thin threads before they fell away entirely.

Thread rot!

Options. I had options. Even if the knots weren't enough, I still had my runes.

Breathe, Astraia.

I tried again.

Nothing.

I traced runes with my fingertip and with my pale-gold blade. Despite all the power I poured into them, they simply flared and vanished. My aura remained contained in this as well. But no matter how much I coaxed the runes or knots into their full strength, they simply crackled or sparked. Twice the bulb wobbled, but the walls always held. Pulseporting was entirely pointless. I tried three times, sapping my strength more. But whatever this bulb was, it kept all my magic inside even when I just envisioned standing on the flagstones just a few feet away.

Ridiculous. Utterly ridiculous. I screamed and struck it with my fist. It hurt as if I had just punched a stone wall rather than magical glass. I tried again and again until my magic was exhausted. Then I slid down to the bottom of my prison, drawing my knees to my chest.

My pulse pounded in my ears as I focused. Exhaustion tugged at me, my head throbbing from overextending. "Zephyrus, break this bulb open." I gestured toward him and then to my prison.

He huffed another column of steam at me and shook his head. Then he cocked it like he wanted to play.

I glared at him. "This isn't a game—"

"No, it is not. Games are actually fun," a familiar deep voice said.

Thread rot...I resisted the urge to drop my chin against my chest. Well, this shouldn't be surprising.

Ramiel strode closer. He had combed his hair out so that it was no longer mussed as it had been when he lay on the floor. He'd changed his clothing as well, now wearing a deep-blue surcoat over silver trousers. Those dark circles under his eyes were more pronounced though, and he favored his right side. The way he looked at me made my skin prickle.

I lifted my chin in defiance, despite not having a single clue what I could do next.

"Why do I feel as if this is simply a look into what is to come?" he demanded.

"Because I will never stop." I squared my shoulders.

"You need to be reasonable," he said, his voice tight. He strode up to the glass bulb, his gaze fixed on me intently. "You should not be here. Zephyrus should."

"I won't abandon him!" I struck the glass with my fist. "Zephyrus is my family. He's all I have left. I won't let you kill him."

"Kill him?" he repeated, his eyebrow arching. He looked at me as if I had suddenly sprouted scales and insisted I was a dragon.

"Kill him or let him die or whatever it is. I heard you talking with Caein!"

His mouth pinched in a tight line. "I see…and how much did you hear?"

"Enough to know that Zephyrus isn't safe with you."

He pinched the bridge of his nose and then swept his hand through the air. Runes formed on the outside of the glass prison, and the walls evaporated as it lowered me back to the ground. The transformation was smooth enough that I easily unfolded my legs and slid out.

He still stared at me hard as I straightened my embossed bodice. My fingernails snagged on a loose turquoise thread. "Glare all you like," I said. "I don't abandon those I love. Especially when they're abducted by strange sorcerer princes in strange towers." Zephyrus huffed over me and rested his jaw lightly on the top of my head.

"I did not steal him or abduct him. There was nothing malevolent about any of this," Ramiel growled.

"If it was all so innocent, then why not come and explain it to me?" I snapped. "I know you were there."

"How could you possibly know that?" he demanded. "You speak confidently but without evidence."

"Except I have evidence. I know well the taste of magic and what it means even if I don't know exactly what you did. You did something to make me fall asleep. A spell. An incantation. How do you think I managed to track you here?"

His mouth pinched even tighter, his lips almost disappearing. "You have proven yourself quite resourceful. I would have assumed it was the bond that guided you here."

"It helped, but I also knew roughly where to start because of that magic. Sentinel magic is well known even to the farthest reaches of Taldao." That was perhaps a bit of an exaggeration, but I'd first heard of it back when I was much farther south. "You were in my camp. You came while I slept and made my sleep deeper, and you stole Zephyrus." I still didn't know how he had convinced Zephyrus to leave me. Part of me quailed just to remember that.

Even worse was that the dreams right before I awoke were among the best I had ever had. So soft and soothing, gentle. A welcome reprieve after the usual nightmares I suffered. It had felt as if someone had wrapped me in warmth, comfort, love, and peace. But then the cold, harsh reality had crashed over me, leaving only that taste and a longing for so much more. It was almost enough to bring me to tears, but I swallowed them and straightened my shoulders.

A sharp scoff escaped his lips before he at last lifted both hands. "I mean you no harm, Astraia. And I would never do anything to harm any of these dragons. But the Chasm is dangerous, and there are risks in defending it. That is why I cannot guarantee their safety."

There was one gamble I could try. "You can kill me, or you can let me leave with Zephyrus."

Zephyrus huffed again, his head cocking over mine.

I reached up to stroke his jaw as I kept my gaze fixed on Ramiel.

"I'm not going to kill you." His nostrils flared as he studied me. Annoyance flashed in his eyes with something else. "That would go against everything I stand for." He tapped his hands in the air as he drew in a deep breath. "There are things I cannot explain to you. Please. I am asking you to leave."

"Never. I will never stop."

He met my gaze, unblinking. I could tell that he was calculating the possibilities and how likely it was that I meant what I said. I did, of course. My entire life revolved around Zephyrus. We'd been inseparable since the day he found me on the outside of ruin and fire. He'd been part of the Resistance. And when I chose to leave, he stayed at my side.

"If you continue to speak that way, I will have no choice but to blood bind you from reaching him."

Zephyrus's head snapped up, and a low growl rumbled in his chest.

"Zephyrus." His gaze snapped up to the dragon.

My eyes widened at the sudden aggression in his voice. Zephyrus drew back in response to the raised tone, his ears lying flat against his skull as he withdrew back into his cell.

"You bastard," I growled. "Don't you dare speak to him like that!"

"He understands more than you, and he knows why this is unacceptable and dangerous." His gaze returned to me. "Give me your word and bind yourself, making it clear that you will not make him to leave this place in any fashion."

"By make, do you mean ask?" I demanded.

"By any means."

"I make no such promise." If he hadn't required that I bind myself, I might have tried to lie. But even agreeing to something with that term might bind me. I couldn't risk it with how well Ramiel had hidden his other spellwork. He was a rune fae, and unless a rune fae formed a binding spell rooted in love, it always had a weakness. But just because there was a weakness didn't mean I could find it. "And I ask that you please look into your heart and take pity on Zephyrus. Don't condemn him to death."

His jaw worked. "I am not condemning him to death. This is his calling as it is mine. None of us are safe in this place," he said sharply. "Do you even understand what the Chasm is? What it does, woman?" He dragged his hand across the back of his neck, shoving aside his long, sleek hair. "Astraia—"

My core tightened when he said my name. I folded my arms tighter, pushing that feeling down. Not the time or the place.

He released a heavy sigh. "I am not sacrificing them. But they are our last line of defense in protecting the Chasm from this world and itself. Without the dragons, I cannot shut the rifts that are tearing open within it. Without the dragons, I cannot defend our world. Without them, the Eye of the Needle falls, and once it falls, all of Rune may fall as well or at least be deeply and grievously wounded. I'm sorry." He then lifted his hand. "Do not make this harder than it must be."

My gut clenched. I tried to rush him, but he moved too fast, silver magic spilling from his fingertips. Runes spun around me in a silver column, a cyclone of letters and light, and then—something cleaved within my spirit.

The stable pulsed and hummed with energy, jagged streaks of lightning arcing across the air. Zephyrus's ears pinned back against his broad skull as he snarled. The other dragons roused as well, their hoarse bellows and rasping roars filling my ears. My hands flew to my chest, clawing at the runes that swept over me.

"Zephyrus!" I screamed.

Everything went dark.

6

FINDING THE LIMIT

Something had changed. The binding wrapped around my spirit like a girdle, tight, uncomfortable, but not precisely painful. More emotional than physical. Its weight held fast as I struggled to comprehend what had happened and how Ramiel had accomplished it so swiftly.

The darkness faded, and I found myself in what appeared to be another section of the tower. Fat globed oil lamps hung on the walls, casting flickering shadows all around me. Though cracks and crevices lined the aged walls, it was well kept and clean, smelling like stone and magic. My nose tickled, the musky scent of stagnant as well as biting fresh magics mingling. Hints of old parchment reached me as well, coating my tongue along with the acrid taste of the binding.

Swearing, I struck my fist against the wall. Bright pain flared through my wrist, and I screamed, just as much from frustration as pain. How had he managed to do it so fast? Binding rituals were supposed to take whole minutes, and he'd just shorthanded the whole thing. Somehow. Somehow!

Maybe he'd messed it up going that fast. Straightening my bodice and adjusting my cloak, I started down the hall.

Wretched silver-haired bastard! If he thought I was bested, he had another thing coming.

I didn't even try to stay quiet this time. I just hurried forward. My aura flared out, aware of the sigils and wards. None were hostile. None even slowed me. They weren't even trying. He hadn't sent me back to the cell either. A strange choice, and one I'd ensure he regretted.

A staircase spiraled ahead, and as I neared it, warmth spilled over me in strange and intense waves. My heart skipped at the unexpected sensation—tenderness, heat, affection—almost like a caress that lingered on my skin. It was just like those dreams. So soft. So warm. A distinct mark on the inside of that wall made it easy to remember: a shield with three swords.

I couldn't afford any delays or surprises. So I pushed the sensation away and hurried down the hall. The binding within me tightened with each step, twisting but not painful. It pinched my breaths a little and then settled in. I paused, pressing my hand to it for another breath as I studied it. This was…different. Ramiel could have made the binding curse painful, but he didn't. Even though it tightened, it never reached a point of pain. Essentially just an awareness.

I carried on, scowling at this. Why would he do that? I certainly wouldn't show that courtesy to a trespasser who was trying to free a dragon I'd imprisoned for some purpose. Was it a mistake or perhaps intentional?

Within minutes, I found the staircase that led back down to the stable. The runes and sigils and wards did not react to my presence beyond pulsing a little with light. Nothing new so far. My muscles tightened. He could have easily added a couple unpleasant surprises here.

Nothing in the stairwell either.

As soon as I reached the bottom step and peered into the stable, I slowed. All the dragons so far were fast asleep. I crept farther in, steady and silent. Their breathing filled the stable like a rumbling, rhythmic hum, punctuated by occasional snorts and huffs. Even as they slept as peacefully as if they had never been interrupted.

Zephyrus was still in his cell in the back. He cocked his head when he saw me, not greeting me with his usual enthusiasm. His tail struck the flagstones. I held up my hands to reassure him I was all right as I glanced around. "We're going to sort this out, Zeph." Where was Ramiel?

That miserable, frost-hearted bastard wasn't even down in the stable. He was so confident in his spell, he didn't even deign to be here to ensure it worked? I despised that man more with every passing moment. The sheer arrogance! Well, I'd make sure to be his undoing. He had underestimated me, and he'd regret that.

Zephyrus grunted and folded his wings back tight. He did not sound impressed.

"I'm going to figure this out," I said.

The chiding chuff that followed confirmed he did not believe me. But he didn't sound worried either.

Shaking my head, I drew closer slowly. The first thing was to determine the limits of the binding spell. The lack of pain and discomfort meant that there had been safety measures woven into it, so the pulseporting wouldn't take me somewhere like the middle of a wall.

I got within arm's reach of Zephyrus, and it pulseported me away.

Polph!

The world briefly spun as darkness swept over me. Then I landed in a dark sitting room. No torches or lamps brightened the dark, but my eyes adjusted swiftly.

White sheets draped over the furniture, dust motes swirling lazily from my disturbance. The musky scent of old velvet, ancient silk, and dry wood mingled with faint traces of arcane energy. A large stone fireplace dominated one wall, its hearth cold and empty. I swallowed a snarl of frustration. It was all right. This was just part of the process. I was going to find a way through.

The carved double doors swung open easily, the old

hinges silent despite their age and the dust. I charged through and ran down the hall, my boots striking the stones in rapid succession. If he thought he could stop me, he was wrong. This was only a setback. This time I'd get closer before it snapped me away again. And eventually I'd find the weakness and break it apart, rescue Zephyrus, and be on my way. He wanted to underestimate me? Fine! Let him.

I took the stairs two at a time, sprinting past the tapestries that hung along the wall like the Sentinels they commemorated. My instincts guided me back to the stable within minutes.

Zephyrus lifted his head again and rested it on the bars. That grunt of his told me precisely what he thought, his eyelids half shading his eyes.

"I'm not giving up," I said, striding forward. This time I came in from the right, angling for a point that just felt a little different.

He gave a short blast of a steamy huff, the grumble of a laugh confirming he wasn't hurt and found this more amusing than concerning. My aura stretched out, searching for any signs of the binding's limits. I hadn't felt anything change really once I got close to Zephyrus, which meant that it wasn't as weak as I would have preferred.

This time it pulseported me when I was barely four feet away from him and coming along the right side of the cell. It dropped me down in a storage hall on the same floor near wooden bins marked with runes to keep the food preserved. Thread rot! Fine, fine. I made note of the direction. The right side was even stronger. I drew in a deep breath.

Again and again, I charged back down to the stable, attempting another avenue. Each time the binding spell sent me to some other part of the tower. I was getting intimately familiar with this tower. Caein appeared and tried to convince me to calm myself and just enjoy the tower's hospitality, but I ignored him. Like most Nolches, he had some abilities to maneuver items within the tower, but he made no effort to stop me.

It was infuriating. And the angle I chose made no difference. Coming in from the left and coming in at a diagonal got me closest, but neither one allowed me to so much as touch Zephyrus. Worse still, Ramiel had made the binding extend to more than just Zephyrus. It reached the levers, the locks, everything that had to do with freeing Zephyrus.

I couldn't even get near the levers to open it and set him free. No, the bastard had bound that too! I hated him so much. He hadn't even added new wards to hurt me or push me back. The sheer arrogance of it. As if he could just cast a binding spell on me and go on about his business!

And…most infuriatingly of all, apparently he could.

By the sixth time, I was panting, my hair loose around my shoulders and sweat rolling down the back of my neck and along my temples. Once again, it had dropped me down in another hallway with paintings, incense, and rugs.

"Perhaps the lady would like to rest?" Caein proposed, his voice seeming to come more from the nearest doorway rather than just the entirety of the ceiling above.

I shoved my tangled hair back and bound it up. "No."

"You understand that binding spells are not easily broken."

"All binding spells have weaknesses," I said sharply. Before he could say anything further, I raced forward. Back to the curving staircase, back to the stable. On the way, I came up with new names and insults for Ramiel as I made mental checklists of other angles I could try. There was a weakness in this binding spell. There had to be!

As I charged ahead, my shoulder clipped the door frame. I yelped. I'd caught my cloak on a hook. It scraped across my shoulder and tugged at my sleeve as well, pulling it down just enough to reveal a trace of the scourge I'd inflicted on myself years ago.

Caein hummed. "You seared off your mate bond?"

Nolches were hard to fool. A knot formed in my throat. Searing off the mate bond wasn't precisely right, but it was right enough I had no desire to go into the details or correct him further. The burn was deep. It wasn't likely to ever heal enough to allow another to form or the original to continue. "Hired a witch." It took me a moment to free myself, and I rubbed my arm. "Enough people died because of me. Didn't need to doom my mate too." It was one of the many things I regretted. It had seemed so selfless and smart at the time, but grieving youths should not be permitted to make such choices. Now I had to live with it.

"The arrogance of you fae never ceases to amaze me," he said. His tone had softened, seeming more gentle than judgmental. "Why?"

"I don't feel like discussing my motivations with a stranger." I pressed my hand over the old scar on my shoulder. Sometimes it still ached and throbbed as if it were a fresh wound.

A low, contemplative sound followed. "Would you take it back if you could?"

"It doesn't matter. I don't deal in what can never be," I said. Squeezing my shoulder for one moment more, I drew in a deep breath and started back into the hall, slower this time.

I would take it back if I could. I'd practically been a child when I made that choice. A child who thought she knew her mind. I certainly wouldn't have been grateful to the witch for refusing me. But the older version of myself peered back on that child and wished someone had been there to shake sense into her or refuse to let her cross that line. Someone to tell her that as real as the pain and the fear were, it should not have dictated something so important. The worst thing about being alone was that your mistakes truly were all your own.

"Fate is a difficult thing to deny," Caein said in response. His voice swirled softly above me. "The bond of the beloved is one of the sacred bonds. Sometimes it all comes together in a way altogether separate from what we expected. In fact, I'd say that that is what happens more often than not."

"We all make our choices." And those we love suffer them as well. Even if they did nothing wrong. I quickened my pace and returned to the stable, grateful Caein did not seem to follow.

This time I tried to climb the bars of the deep blue-green dragon's cell and navigate my way over. Even though I was eight feet in the air, the pulseport snatched me up and dragged me away. I landed with a thud on a dark-blue rug in front of a massive bookshelf that spanned most of a wall.

"Having fun?"

Every muscle in my body tightened. "So you finally decided to crawl out of your hole?" I growled, struggling to my feet. The first time we'd met I'd been hanging upside down, but landing on my backside with my hair tangled and my face red with sweat and exertion was a close second for humiliating appearances. Not that I'd let him know how embarrassed I was. My anger and frustration were now high enough that even the passive enchantments I'd put on my hair were coming undone.

I was now in the same library I had seen him get attacked by that spectral kangaroo—the omenfang—that's what he had called it. Almost every inch of the walls was covered in shelves of some kind. The wooden floorboards were well oiled and well kept, not creaking even a little as I shifted my weight. He stood behind a massive desk, palms braced against the polished surface amid a massive array of books, bleached bones, a carved wooden bowl with rune stones, cracked gemstones scattered about, incense, dried herbs, and all manner of other odds and sundries. An inkwell sat on top of one leatherbound manuscript, the quill secured with a sparking bit of energy. A spindle with silver thread sat on the top of five books, almost at my eye level.

My gut clenched at that. I hated those things. Knotweavers typically used them to control the larger lengths of magic that they unwound, but I refused.

Ramiel did not act as if he noticed my reaction. His long silver hair was a sleek curtain pushed over one side as if he combed his fingers from right to left while thinking. "This is my home, and I have many serious tasks which require my attention. I couldn't waste more time babysitting you."

I lifted my chin. In the past hours, I had exhausted every angle of reaching Zephyrus except going under. Absent digging a tunnel beneath the cell and finding a way to create a line of sight, that wasn't going to happen. So...I was going to learn more and uncover the weaknesses in another way. "I get the impression I'm annoying you."

"Whatever gave you that idea?" He asked it in such a flat tone that a younger me might have thought he was genuinely asking.

"There's a very simple way to fix all of this. Let Zephyrus go and let both of us leave." I spread my hands wide as if making some grand new point.

"Your bargaining position is poor," he said.

"I have offered to pay a ransom for him if that is what you require. I'm sure we can come up with something. And just know that if you refuse, I will find a way to break this spell. So save us all some time and let us go."

"You can't break the binding spell," he said as evenly as if he told me the sun rose in the east.

"No spell is impervious," I responded. Not entirely true, but I didn't really want to go into those exceptions. The suggestion that he might love me even a little was preposterous, and just saying that reminded me that most likely no one except Zephyrus would ever care about me. Who would want the reason for the successful razing of Theodas City? I had to steel myself so that the tears did not rise to the backs of my eyes.

Except for Zephyrus, everyone who loved me died that day, and all because of me.

"No. I just know how to seal it so you can't break it," he said. His lips pressed in a cold, faint smile. "You are not as clever as you think you are, little gnat."

"Go ahead and think that." I strode closer, staying on the opposite side of the spindle. "You will have to kill me if you want to stop me from rescuing Zephyrus. And a Sentinel like you should have no trouble with that." Rage flashed sharper in me, and I spread my arms wide. "Is that what you want? Do you want to kill me now? Just go ahead and get it over with, rune fiend!"

He slammed his hand down on the desktop, and a great force slammed into me. I lurched backwards, striking the shelf. I barely drew a breath before he was on me, his arms caging me in.

7

NOT WHAT I THOUGHT

My mouth went dry as I found myself staring up into those fierce, unblinking violet eyes. For a moment, I didn't know whether he wanted to kiss me or kill me.

My insides twisted.

What was wrong with me?

I glared right back at him though, my heart racing. His fingers flexed against the wooden shelf, the board creaking beneath his grip. "That is more than enough," he growled. "I vowed I would not harm you."

"A strange statement from the man pinning me to the shelf," I said. I hated the little tremor in my voice as much as I despised the way my skin prickled at the nearness of his touch.

He drew back and squared his shoulders, though he kept one hand against the shelf. His jaw worked. That scent of frosted silver and warm cedar filled my lungs. "If I was going to hurt or kill you, I would have done so already. You are a terror. And I cannot keep wasting time on you."

"Then throw me out." I lifted my chin. "Those are your options. Kill me or throw me out."

"Or imprison you."

"I'll get out. I'll find a way around your binding spell."

He shook his head, fury flashing in his eyes. "Why are you so stubborn? This matter is settled!" Drawing back, he flung one arm up in the air. He turned and paced to the far side of the library.

"You bound me to keep me from reaching my dragon. My best friend! Even knowing he may be injured and die! I will not abandon him."

"I am doing this for the good of all this realm and for you. He belongs here. You do not, Astraia."

Again my stomach tightened. Something about the way he said my name…I shook my head, trying to dislodge the thought. "You have a dozen dragons down there. You yourself said that it might not take all of them."

His jaw clenched. Emotion flashed in those violet eyes of his. Pain? "It is dangerous work," he said quietly. "It is *our* calling."

Part of me wanted to now set all the dragons free. Commonsense warned me that that was a fool's quest. I didn't know these dragons. And they were at their core deadly predators who apparently played a role here. I had heard of the Sentinels and their work in the Chasm, but it was such a different matter when it was involving someone I cared about. Maybe it was selfish to want to spare Zephyrus that. Asking the others to be more at risk because he was not there? And yet the thought of sacrificing him broke my heart. It all confused me so much. "Will you at least remove the bond then and let him choose?"

He stared at me in somber silence for a moment so heavy I could not breathe. Then he shook his head. "I know what you are, and I cannot. He has bonded with you. He knows you, and he will want to make you happy. And at least keep you safe. He knows you should not be here, and he knows you are in no danger from me. So he is likely just to leave with you if he believes that's what you want."

"This is unacceptable—" I started, balling my fists.

"If you find my tower so odious, you are more than

welcome to leave," he said, his voice once more that gruff calm from before.

My temper rose again. Something about this man made me feel on edge and sharp. "Just leave, huh? I bet that's what you want."

His eyebrow crooked upward, and he cut his eyes at me as he reached the doorway. "I believe I have made it clear that that is precisely what I want. Now, if you'll excuse me, I have matters of great importance that require my immediate attention. As you are a guest here, you may avail yourself of the food. Guest quarters are on the fifth floor. You'll recognize it by the marking of a shield with three swords. I would tell you what areas to stay out of, but you strike me as the sort who would make that an invitation."

And just like that, he left me again.

I set my hands on my waist, my mind spinning. Why was he acting this way? I'd just disrespected him in his own home, and he was still allowing me to remain here as a guest? I dragged my hand through my hair, but my fingers snagged on some of my curls. Wincing, I freed myself.

"I'm missing something," I murmured. Nothing about this situation settled well within me. He was definitely a rune fae, so I could assume certain things. The laws of hospitality required that I not do harm directly to his person or to any of his beasts. Not that I would be inclined to do so anyway. But...that also meant that since he had allowed me to be a guest, he could not harm me either.

I crossed over to his books. Runic magic had to be written down. That was part of its power. It wasn't an oral tradition. And while he probably didn't have some sort of guidebook that contained absolutely everything I needed, perhaps I might find something.

Time faded as I pored over those texts. His library was well stocked, which was not particularly surprising. I pulled out book after book, scanning runes and translations. A few were so old I feared they'd crumble beneath my touch, but someone had taken care to enchant the pages and keep them whole. A lot of love had gone into the upkeep of this place. Hours passed, one flowing into the next, until my eyes burned. A headache cut across the back of my head and up along my temples.

I always carried emergency rations and supplies on me, so I ate those. Dried moon fruit served well to satisfy both thirst and hunger, but it did not do much for resisting sleep. Nothing really prevented that.

Rubbing the sides of my head, I sighed. This plan wasn't working well, but I hadn't come up with something better. Knotweaving magic wasn't particularly useful when it came to shifting through all this knowledge and all these possibilities. My own runic magic was built around supporting the knotweaving. More or less. I did have a few spells for life and Zephyrus. I rested my chin on my fist.

Maybe I needed to stop approaching this so logically. Ramiel was cold, calm, and clear. And I couldn't best him on that. But…I could be chaotic.

Yes…that was one of my skills.

Picking up the books I had been scanning, I crossed the room and shelved them elsewhere. Then I moved one of the small tables over just a few inches. On his desk, I rearranged the items, ensuring I avoided anything that looked especially important.

Part of me had expected him to return. His absence relieved and concerned me. But I'd make the most of it.

As I scanned for anything that might reveal his weaknesses, I rearranged the books. It was petty and annoying. Moving the furniture steadily over a few inches here or there was far more likely to attract his attention. Moving his wineskin and its small redwood stand to the opposite side of his desk would annoy him as well.

A small part of me twinged, almost regretting this invasion of his hospitality. Then I reminded myself that he was the reason Zephyrus was here. And I wouldn't do anything too horrid. Nothing that would threaten the safety of the tower or the Chasm. Just enough to really aggravate him.

The sort of thing I had once done to my brothers and cousins when they annoyed me or I needed to get them to be reasonable by wearing them down.

It really wasn't that hard. And in this, I could use some of my knotweaving. Magical trip wires that made you stagger or drop things. Someone as graceful as Ramiel probably wasn't used to that. Whatever he was up to, he'd discover this soon enough, and yes, it would annoy him.

As I finished, I surveyed what I'd done. Nothing obstructed the primary exits, so if some catastrophe with the Chasm did develop, I wouldn't be making it worse.

But I hadn't found anything to help break the binding. Cathartic as it was to sow some chaos into Ramiel's life, it didn't actually resolve my actual problem. I was behaving like a child.

I made my way back down to the stable. Fresh food had been set out. Droplets of blood stained the flagstones near each feeding trough. A few of the dragons were now in other cells, piled up on one another in a puddle. They'd all moved deeper back into the stable where it was warmer. Zephyrus remained alone in his cell, and his eyes fell on me immediately. He lifted his head as his talons scraped on the flagstone, an eager grunt rising from his chest.

I crossed closer, taking care not to trigger the binding spell. "I don't know what to do, Zephyrus. Is this where you want to be? You don't look happy in there."

Zephyrus huffed at me, his tone more chiding than usual. He sat up, peering down at me over his long blue snout. Cocking his head, he chirred.

I sat on the floor as close to him as I could manage without being close enough to pulseport. More than anything, I wanted to curl up against him and bury my face in his shoulder. To tell him it was going to be all right. To hear him confirm in his own draconic way that it would all come together.

He snorted again, steam rising from his nostrils. He looked lonely. Anger burned within me to see all the other dragons now curled up, and he was still here. Being alone was horrid. And I couldn't manipulate the levers to get him inside with his kin if that was what he wanted. "I'm sorry."

He tilted his head slowly. The low grumbling churr that followed sounded like a reassurance that everything was all right. A little deeper than his usual comforting rumble.

"Are these all your family?" I asked softly. "Do you want to be in there with them?"

He jerked his chin in my direction, and his amber eyes narrowed as he chirred again.

"I can't come any closer, Zeph. I'm sorry." A knot formed in my throat.

He grunted and growled, his eyes blazing brighter.

"I-I'm fine." I hugged myself. "I just haven't figured out how to fix the binding spell yet." An odd thought occurred to me. Ramiel had said Zephyrus wouldn't want to stay with his family because of his bond to me. What if he'd been waiting for me?

Swallowing the knot of emotion in my throat, I stood. "It's all right. I really am fine. If—if you want to be with them, it's all right. I want you to be where you want to be."

He glanced between me and then the nearest of the dragon snuggle piles four cells in. The low growl that rumbled in his chest sounded like a question.

I nodded, hugging myself tighter. "Yeah. I'm sure. Go on."

I wasn't even sure how I knew it was possible for him to reach them, but the thought crystalized in my mind. He cut his amber eyes at me once more and then strode back deeper into his cell through that dark space. Within moments, he emerged in the cell farther down. The purple and dark-green dragons lifted their heads sleepily. The grey-blue one nuzzled his neck and nibbled at the scales as he flopped down. Zephyrus's gaze remained fixed on me as if to ensure I was telling him the truth.

I forced a smile and nodded. Ramiel was right. I felt it

in my gut. Thread rot. "I'm going to go get some rest in a safe place," I said softly. "It's a little too exposed here."

The grunt that followed made it clear he understood.

Slipping out of the stable, I made my way up the stairs. My thoughts drifted to all the possibilities and what I should do. I wanted Zephyrus safe. But if he was supposed to be here, how could I manage that?

I halted, realizing my hand was on the door handle and I had already pushed it open into a hall. In all the pulse-porting, I hadn't been here yet. The air thrummed, a distinct but intense magic pulsing through the air. I frowned as I listened.

This wasn't the floor with the guest rooms. Then again, I wasn't going to sleep in his guest room either. Something about that felt too—intimate. It'd been years since I'd slept in a bed anyway. No sense starting now. I pulled back a step and looked at the marking on the central panel of the door.

There was nothing really unusual about it. It bore a similar crest to all the rest on this floor: three swords emerging from the mist. Each sword had a runic inscription on it, charges for steadfastness, courage, and honor. Interestingly enough, each carried the statement "to death, through death, and beyond death."

Yes. Death walked these halls. I wouldn't let it claim my best friend, but now I had to figure out how to protect him and let him be with his family.

That tugging sensation intensified. In fact, I wanted to go to a specific room. Maybe there was an answer up here. The air vibrated softly, no other source of sound in the long, dark, gently curving hall. My eyes adjusted easily to the dim light, but there was something even softer in this place. It was…comforting.

The only wards and sigils I saw were the standard ones for restoration and protection. They appeared in combinations that suggested this was a beloved place. Perhaps a hall of memories or remembering? Our palace had had both, but I couldn't remember the distinction any more.

One door seemed to call to me. The fifth one in. A marking for sand centered on this one, the etching so delicate it could almost be missed. There were other symbols that I couldn't fully translate, but I knew enough of the base to see that there was no threat here. I pressed the door open and peered inside. My mouth fell open.

8

THE WALL

I had never seen a room like this in my life and yet some part of it felt familiar. Something in this place called to me like the distant memory of a comforting dream, just out of reach. The ceiling within arched up like a cathedral, the eight pillars that provided support along the walls connecting in an interconnected design that was impossible to carve without magic.

This was some sort of sanctuary. Two walls were nothing but shelves, one mostly filled with large elegant jars of sand. The other held the same vessels but a far smaller number, and these were all empty. A soft glow came from the ceiling though there was no particular source, and the air itself shimmered with energy and magic. I drew in a long breath, analyzing the layered scents. It was almost too much. Rich colognes, fragrant perfumes. When I focused, I could pick out some specifics: smoked myrrh, crushed starblooms, oiled leather, charred pine, jasmine nectar, and so much more.

My eyelids slid shut. Across my mind's eye played a whole ballroom of couples waltzing and mingling. A rune fae ball, so runes glimmered in the air, shimmering and changing colors with the music and the mood. Obsidian chimes hung at intervals, floating amid the runes. And the orchestra played all manner of traditional instruments including rune string harps, shatterdrums, and violins. All I could think for music though was a lullaby.

When I opened my eyes, I saw the sand-filled jars once more. Beautiful. Sacred. They were filled almost to the brim with swirls of two colors. Except for one near the bottom. It was just blue.

I picked it up to study it. It looked as if it had been made of something similar to sapphires and lapis lazuli. Despite the beauty of the shades of blue, it somehow felt plain and small next to the rest. Only half full.

The wall next to it held a crystal geode that reminded me of an amethyst cathedral, easily twice as tall as me. It hummed and vibrated softly, its voice soothing but easy to miss.

The other wall was filled with dozens of elegant glass vials, each one tall, flawless, and empty. One had been set apart. Something had been etched into the side of one glass jar set apart from the rest: Natoumai ahme vahre. I frowned a little, uncertain what that meant. It wasn't a language I recognized. That pang of curiosity twisted deeper. Thistledown was a day's flight from here, and they'd probably know what this said. But I didn't have time for that now.

My goal was to rescue Zephyrus. Of course, if I really wanted to agitate Ramiel, I could always mix the sands together.

Some part of me recoiled immediately at that thought. Unlike all the other things I had done, this could not be undone. And there was something…sacred about this place. Maybe I'd done that with my father's hourglass and the sandkeeper, but it wasn't appropriate here. I held the jar a little closer as I contemplated my situation. It really wasn't as simple as I had initially thought. It was almost nice to remember my family though. Something about Ramiel made me think of them. Maybe because he was rune fae too.

Family.

Polph. I couldn't do any of this anymore. Was I going to have to let him go?

Guilt and unease tightened my shoulders and gripped my heart. Maybe Ramiel was innocent in this. Or at least not the monstrous thief I'd thought him. I frowned. Some parts still didn't add up. But that didn't mean Ramiel was evil.

I couldn't even deny that protecting the Chasm was good. It had to be done, didn't it? In my years of travel, I'd never actually visited the Chasm, but I'd heard loosely of its dangers and the general belief in the Sentinels and the value of their work. Not that I'd expected it to be a single fae in a tower with a dozen dragons. It seemed…disproportionate. And this tower was clearly intended for many more. Prince of the Sentinels now seemed more like a mocking title than a real one.

Tilting the jar a little, I watched the sand slide along its side. The flecks were beautiful too. Those subtle changes in color. It smelled a little like Ramiel, the cedar stronger than the frosted silver. Warmth tightened in my chest and core. His scent was…far more pleasant than I wanted to admit. Sorcerer princes should smell like…brimstone and body odor and no sunshine. That had to be a rule somewhere.

My cheeks burning, I put my back to the wall, slid to the ground, and set the vial of blue sand next to me. There really was something soothing about it. Looking at it up close, I admired all the deep shades of blue, ranging from cobalt to the deepest shade of blue violet I'd ever seen. It reminded me of the sands in the hourglass my parents kept in the study. Dark green, made of little gemstone chips. Father said he'd made it after saving all the chips and dust from carving his first two thousand runestones. Mother always teased that he had chosen emeralds and malachite as his stones because they were considered the hardest for fashioning usable runestones. He loved the challenge. And whenever she said that, he flashed her a special smile that he saved just for her and said that's what made him fall for her.

Setting the jar down, I fixed my eyes on it, pretending that the gemstone sand was shifting like it did through my father's hourglass. A few tears slid down my cheeks. Something about this tower had me thinking so much about family.

I closed my eyes tight and drew in as deep a breath as I could manage. I missed them. My parents. My siblings. My cousins. Their faces flashed through my mind. Emotion built within me, longing and sorrow. Then Zephyrus appeared in my thought.

My heart clenched, breaths shallowing. What was I going to do? Even with all the unanswered questions, I knew that some part of Zephyrus wanted to be with these other dragons. He'd given me so many years. This binding spell…I pressed my hand over my chest. I'd figure out a solution. I had to. Even if that did mean letting him go.

Darkness surrounded me. I didn't know precisely when I fell asleep, only a vague awareness that I had. It started like always with a general sense of unease creeping up my spine. As I sat there with my back to the stone and my head to my knees, I reminded myself it was a dream. Just a dream. Nothing but a dream.

Still my heart raced faster.

Only a dream and yet it felt so real. A dream that could never be controlled or avoided.

That creeping, crawling dread crept through the darkness to swallow me whole or strangle me.

Dark clouds formed around me in rough shapes. Some human. Some dragon. Some creatures I couldn't even describe. Mockeries of the people I loved and connections long lost.

Yes. I was alone.

My heart ached as if it had been pierced.

It would pass. It always did.

This was only a dream.

A dream from which I'd eventually wake.

I would.

Please, let me wake.

Threads dark as drying blood shot out from the darkness and coiled around me. Oil and mud sucked at my feet as I sunk.

There was a thread in that darkness. A double-coiled thread with runes etched into it. The runes lit up, and I put out my hand.

I always did.

The thread shot around me, spinning over me as if I were a spindle. My soul wrenched, and I tried so hard to cry out. But it just tightened—tightened—tightened.

Closing my eyes, I pushed out my aura and my arms. Neither responded. There was nothing—nothing but thread and darkness. No consciousness. No will. Only silence. Silence and crushing pressure.

And I was…alone.

Something gripped my shoulders. I gasped, my eyes flying open as I found myself staring into a now familiar violet gaze.

"Astraia?"

Tears formed along the backs of my eyes, stinging. Awareness stabbed through me. A dozen thoughts tried to surface at once. My shoulder ached beneath the scar, throbbing as it usually did after these nightmares. I rubbed it, willing it to stop. Then I realized Ramiel was holding out his hand.

Tentatively, I accepted it. As I stood, I realized I was cradling the jar of blue sand. "I'm sorry." Though embarrassment wasn't usually something I suffered from, an unpleasant heat and shame stole over me.

"Are you all right?" He guided me up. His gaze drifted to the jar in the crook of my arm, but he did not seem angry or even troubled. Just…concerned. "Did the guest room not appeal to you?"

I wasn't sure how to respond. "Y-yes." I shook my head, my mouth dry. I moistened my lips. "No, I'm sure the guest room is fine. I'm all right. Just…fell asleep in here."

"I gave you my word I would not harm you," he said, the chiding in his voice far gentler than what I expected or even deserved. His hand lingered for a moment longer, his thumb half stroking or accidentally brushing against mine. Everything in me tightened, and I felt the cold all the more as soon as he released my hand. "Are you afraid of me, Astraia?"

"No." That I answered confidently, and my eyebrow lifted as if to underscore the point. I hadn't feared him from the start because I'd been so confident in my own abilities. But now…now I couldn't find even a scrap of fear within me when it came to him. I'd slipped so easily into treating him like an antagonistic family member. Somehow I did feel comfortable around him. "It was nothing against you. You have been nothing but courteous and welcoming. Far more than I expected."

"From a rune fae?"

"From the person who owns the tower I broke into. Especially if you didn't do anything to make Zephyrus go with you. I—I know you did something to me to make me sleep. And I am still not pleased with that. I would have rather you spoken with me and told me what was going on with Zephyrus and then showed me how he was willing to make this choice and that this was what he wanted." The words were bitter on my tongue, but I spoke them none-theless.

His expression softened ever so slightly, the lines around his eyes crinkling. "I chose the course I did because it seemed like the best one. But I was wrong."

"I'm willing to do what's best for Zephyrus," I said. "I know he isn't mine. But you didn't even give me a chance to say goodbye and make peace. Why?" A strange sensation fluttered within my chest. Probably just because he was the first person I had talked to so closely in a long, long time. I hugged the jar tighter.

His eyes darkened, his gaze drifting momentarily to my lips and then back up. He stepped away. "I thought it would be easier. I was wrong."

"You really thought I'd give up looking for him? I'm ridiculously tenacious and quite petty. I would have hunted you down to the ends of this world and the next to soak your socks in slug oil if it would've taught you not to mess with someone who mattered to me."

"Yes." His nose wrinkled, the lines in his brow deepening. "I found what you did to the runestones. And my books. You do realize I have magic that allows me to assist in sorting everything with very little energy from myself."

"I knew it would be an inconvenience." That sense of shame stole over me once more. "I suppose…we both have made mistakes." I couldn't hate him right now. Especially not with him so near and that soft annoyance shining in his gaze. Or was that something else? "All I want is for Zephyrus to be safe. I want him to have a happy life. He's all the family I have left."

He tilted his head as he studied me through those half-shaded eyes. Stepping forward, he took the jar from me, his movements surprisingly gentle. "He's dear to you. You want to protect him. I respect and understand that," he said. "He and his kin are the same to me. I give you my word that if there is any way that I can prevent their harm, I will. While I cannot guarantee their protection, I swear to you that I will in no way be reckless with their lives or well-being." He set the jar back on the shelf. "Why did you choose this place to rest if I may ask?"

I shook my head, then answered simply. "I…felt like I was safe here. It was…comforting."

"It's a soothing place." He straightened his garments and offered me his hand. "I've found this place comforting since I was a child." His brow tweaked as his gaze moved along the shelves of jars with sand. "There are many memories in this place."

"What is it for?"

His jaw tightened. His tongue darted at his lips before he at last returned his focus to me. "Recognition of the sacred bonds."

The soft blue light highlighted the elegance and sharpness of his features. Those dark marks beneath his eyes betrayed his lack of sleep, suggesting that maybe he too needed a haven. How long had it been for him since he'd slept well? Perhaps decades. As with most fae, it was hard to tell just how old he was. Once we hit our twentieth year, most slowed significantly in the aging process. "How long have you been alone here?"

"I have Caein and the dragons," he said. "I am not truly alone."

I heard what was not said though. The heaviness of the meaning beneath those words, and that part of me sobbed in understanding. But all I did was nod.

A deep rumbling roar shook the foundations of the tower. Ramiel's hands flew at once to steady the jars. "The leviathan," he said, his voice grim. "He's breaching again."

9

WEAVER DRAGONS

"Caein, can you see him? How bad is the wound?" Ramiel demanded, striding down the hall.

"Uncertain. He seems worse today. The pain must have worsened if it woke him this soon." Caein spoke with crisp efficiency. "He isn't fully attacking, but the Chasm is tearing further."

I followed him. A chill rolled over me, my insides tightening. "What needs to be done?"

Caein's voice sounded above me. "Four wraiths have made their way from the Chasm and are trying to find a weakness to get through. They're feeding off the energy. The dragons are preparing. Thalorion is already leading the charge. Two nightfangs are nearing the surface."

He reached back to seize his silver hair and bound it with a tie. "Are the nightfangs within striking distance?"

"They haven't breached the final layer," Caein responded. The heavy thundering of wings and the rumbling of dragon roars resounded through the tower. One deep resonant rumble cut straight to me. Zephyrus. My attention snapped to the inner wall that hid the passage out of the top of the tower. He was joining the fight.

"How can I help?" I asked, quickening my pace to keep up with Ramiel.

He spun to face me, his expression grim. "You can stay in the tower and avoid causing problems."

"I'm a dragon rider. I can—"

He held up his hands, his manner growing more stern. "I don't have time to teach you how to battle wraiths and handle the Chasm creatures when they are already hostile. Stay here. Don't try to follow me. The protective wards will keep you here."

Though I opened my mouth to protest, he whisked around the corner. By the time I rounded it, he was gone. Clenching my jaw, I considered my options.

"The creatures that come from the Chasm are exceptionally dangerous, Astraia," Caein said.

I cut my eyes up at the stone ceiling. "I'm certain they are. But I'm not some helpless innocent who cannot adapt. If there is a fight to be had and I can help, then I want to help."

"Quite noble. It seems that when it is your own well-being on the line, you are willing to set concerns aside. But when it is someone you care about, then their well-being is paramount. Even when it is something they love."

I narrowed my eyes in his general direction. "This isn't about Zephyrus. It sounds like this is a tough fight. I fought in the Resistance of Theodas alongside the new king and his forces. I've been in countless skirmishes beyond that. I came here because I thought Ramiel stole Zephyrus. Now you all are saying this is Zephyrus's calling. Fine. At least let me help defend him. I give you my word as a knotweaver that I will not in any way jeopardize their mission," I said, hands braced on my waist.

Caein hummed in contemplation, then sighed. "I will not assist you in finding your way to the bridge. But if you can find your way out, I will not stop you."

Typical Nolche response. Or fae for that matter.

Hissing out an annoyed breath, I started to run, then halted.

This was a rune fae tower. Like all fae, Ramiel had his secrets, and this tower belonged to the Sentinels. Everything was about protection. He'd mentioned the protective wards. And Caein had made it clear that these were adaptive. Ramiel had said that they would keep me from getting through.

All right. Frowning, I reached out my aura, seeking out all the wards and sigils I could sense. Some I hadn't noticed fluttered into my awareness. Other points pulsed with a light awareness that might have been a current one.

The world grew silent around me as I drew back into the darkness of my own mind. When I focused, this was a place of peace. My strength was better than I'd expected after all my running around and attempting to pulseport. The soothing and restorative wards must have been doing their work for me despite my being a trespasser. A soft buzzing pressure filled my ears as I spread my aura out through the halls.

There.

A thrum of energy pressed along my mind, sending a chill down my spine.

Clever sorcerer. When had he formed these?

Three of the sigils on the wall near a shuttered window were attached to pulseport triggers if I came in contact with them. Not just any person. Me.

How quickly had he set these up?

The door had the same.

I could undo them with focus. The knots pulsed deep at their center, bright and clear. Getting closer would make it all the easier. That would all take time though.

Another rumbling roar shook the inner walls of the tower.

Oh. I knew precisely where to go.

Turning, I ran back to one of the staircases nestled in the wall. My boots struck the wooden stairs hard, sending dust motes flying. As I reached the stable, I flung the door open. All the cells were open. The purple-scaled dragon stood beneath the hatch, her head tilted back and up as she peered up the stone shaft.

The remnants of a hearty breakfast indicated they'd already been fed. And the special hatch in the ceiling was fully open. Small sigils attached to each of the mechanisms were now apparent, easily hidden and seemingly of such a nature that the dragons could maneuver it themselves.

The purple dragon's gaze flicked toward me as if asking whether I was going to be trouble. Her emerald eyes gleamed beneath heavy-scaled lids.

I held my hands up, palms exposed, and shook my head. "I'm not here to cause trouble. I'm here to help."

She huffed at me. The smoke curled about her broad muzzle, but she returned her attention to the opening.

More gears shifted. It wasn't the mechanism holding the doors open. No. It was lower. I scanned the stable again. There! I spotted more sigils that had been invisible before. A launch platform. Very clever indeed.

Another low groan and a shudder from the flagstones.

The opening stretched high, layers upon layers of stone leading up to the bright blue sky outside. A straight shot, albeit an exceptionally steep and high one. It was dangerous, but I could manage it. Yes. I looked from the chute leading up out of the tower back to the purple dragon and the outline on the floor.

The gears wound down farther and farther, the clacking growing slower as it neared the end.

Hands still held up to show I meant no harm, I moved alongside the purple dragon's left flank just out of kicking range. That long tail with the fur tip at the end might be an issue. Zephyrus could use his like a whip. "Easy, easy," I said, my heart racing. "I'm just going up to help you all. I'm just going to use my magic to make a rope, but I won't touch you."

She jerked her head toward the shaft once more, then chirred. It sounded like a challenge.

Well, I was ready to meet it. I assumed what I hoped was a good stance, summoning a knotted golden rope and holding it between both hands in a large overlapping loop. It hummed and vibrated in my grip, warm and familiar. It barely took the full measure of energy to form.

The gears clicked and locked once more, and the platform shifted ever so slightly beneath my feet.

Knots take me, this was going to be intense.

THWACK!

I barely registered what had happened before the platform sprang upward, shooting us up with magically enhanced force. It felt like I left my stomach behind, and the force of the wind against my face tore at my hair and skin, ripping at my clothes. The entirety of the shaft blurred around me as I shot upward, ever upward, just behind the purple dragon. She didn't acknowledge me at all, wings tight to her body and her neck fully extended.

My vision tunneled. I willed myself to keep my eyes open as that patch of blue sky came closer and closer. The wind battered against my ears. If there was a pulseport trigger up there, this was really going to hurt.

The dragon glanced down at me as we sliced out of the tower's opening. Another smoky huff followed. I tensed, watching for her to spread her wings or lash her tail. Magic sang in my fingertips.

She remained perfectly straight and poised. Her lion-like tail coiled as we emerged, but she did not strike me. The air rushed over me, cool and crisp as we soared higher and higher.

As soon as we emerged, that blissful moment of hang time began. I twisted about to take in my surroundings, scanning and filing it away as I gripped the knotted rope tighter.

A vast deciduous forest spread like an emerald sea, its gold-touched edges flickering in the sunlight. Beyond it, foothills rolled into a jagged horizon, a deep indigo mist swathing their peaks. And there—oh, there it was.

The Chasm.

A gaping wound in the flesh of the world, shimmering with an ethereal pale-purple light. Mist flowed from it. Dark shapes pulsed at the edges, a massive claw grasping outside it. The dragons soared and spiraled above it. Zephyrus was on the outer flank, half covered in tendrils of mist. I remained silent, knowing better than to draw attention to myself. His attention was focused on the Chasm, where it should be. And the Chasm—it was—it was alive. Or something close to that.

I curled my right hand to my chest, drew up my energy, and then swept it into the air, forming a hooked rune for flotation and protection. It seared into the sky, brilliant gold like the knotted rope in my hand. Then, before I could fall from the sky, I flung my knotted lasso over the rune. It hooked into place as gravity took hold of me, but my magic held fast.

My stomach lurched in protest as my feet kicked. It took another rotation to swing my arm up over the golden hook of the rune. Then I clambered up. My cloak snagged on one of the gaps, a few of the threads tearing. I swept myself up higher.

The purple dragon peered down at me, far higher now. Her dark-green eyes narrowed in on me as if to ensure I was safe. Then she thrust down her wings. The great gust that followed was almost enough to knock me loose. Almost. I clung to the rune, the knotted rope in my hands and the cool fresh air filling my lungs.

Beautiful. I adored the heights and the wind in my hair. The only way this would be better was if I were with Zephyrus right now. I cast one more glance at the Chasm and the frothing mist that seeped from that wound. Something was in there. Multiple somethings. The dragons still circled. I needed to get to a safer point.

The tower was only about twenty feet below me. The

gears clacked and shuddered as the sliding hatch closed. And the tower surrounded that passage, all dark stones with broad parapets wide enough to march shoulder to shoulder with a dragon on each side. I could practically smell that frosted silver and musky earth scent, though the wind was to my back at the moment. More roars, challenging and defiant, filled the air.

Crouching on the widest point of the rune, I launched myself at the tower. It was a fair distance away, but I'd made tougher jumps onto a moving target and I could always pulseport if I failed. The wind pushed me along this time. With a skidding thud, I struck the stone in between the stone merlons and landed on the massive flat surface of the tower.

Spinning around, I ran back and leaned out through the crenels. The strong stench of blood and ozone struck my nostrils. I winced, my eyes squeezing half shut against the brightness of the sun reflecting off that mist and the onslaught upon my senses. For the first time I realized just how precarious the tower's position was.

The enormous structure was built directly alongside a cliff. The Chasm was not simply in the air above but stretched down into that cliff. Something about it made it hard to focus on or to know for certain what you were looking at. The cloying purple mist spread along like a sea, lapping at the jagged stones that lined it. A single section of a stone bridge jutted out from the tower's entrance at the base and continued all the way to one of the rifts in the Chasm among shattered ruins of buildings long gone. Dark forms bubbled in that place. A claw dripping with something like oil lifted from the mist and fell back, but for that moment, all the color faded from around it. Another deep wet roar gurgled from within the Chasm.

Ramiel strode out along that bridge, his gaze straight ahead and the wind on his face. His arms were at his sides, his hands encased in brocaded silver air carver gloves. Most likely intended to make it easier for him to craft solid and powerful runes. Even from this distance, I could tell that they were ancient. Powerful too, most likely smelling of frosted silver.

The dragons spun in the sky.

Zephyrus! I spotted him again, now in a triangular formation with a dark-green drake and a silverish purple dragon. He was right in the center, wings thrusting powerfully and in perfect sync with the others.

My heart swelled with pride. Look at him go!

It was impressive. He was impressive.

Ramiel reached the edge of the bridge. He pressed his hands out into the air, palms facing to the sides. The wind whipped faster around him, tugging at his silver hair and his robes. He barely flinched as silver light coiled around his hands and vibrated in the air.

Then, unlike in the stable, he started to move to summon his magic. He sliced his hands through the air in a complex pattern. Several feet before him, the runes formed, mirroring his movements with great connected strokes of shimmering light that burned with their own life.

Three dragons swooped down, circled four runes, and then carried them away, their talons somehow gripping them. They carried them out above one of the wounds in the rift. Three others including Zephyrus dove in and defended, driving back the wraith-like creatures that clawed through the mist. Three more soared up into the heights, spun around, and descended toward each of the runes once they were put in place. The lines of the runes burned bright silver in the sky. Some dropped over the mist while others began to come apart and coil together like enchanted ropes.

Sections of the rift came together with the dragon flight and disintegrating runes. Their wings drove the mist down, intensifying its color. When the rune energy came into contact, the rifts sealed into a deeper and thicker mass.

Claws slashed up, emerging briefly from the mist. The three defending dragons dove down. Roars followed, and those three including Zephyrus shot up once more. Dark blood stained the maw of the purple dragon, and she wheeled about at the head of the formation like a commander. Zephyrus shook his great head and wheeled about as a massive blunt head emerged from below.

All color drained from the mist.

Zephyrus and his flanking partners pounced. They drove the creature down. The claws grazed the paler blue dragon's shoulder. It bellowed with pain, and Zephyrus's jaws shot out to seize the attacking limb. His jaws snapped through and cast that limb aside as the beast roared below.

Two more dragons shot down into the mist.

Ramiel carved more runes into the air.

My stomach clenched and twisted as I watched, my skin tingling and prickling as my own magic hummed with excitement. It was like watching a spectacular aerial dance that was brutal and beautiful. Zephyrus might have been gone for fifteen years, but he kept pace with his kin, sliding through the sky with the elegance of a swan.

They shifted between groups of three and groups of four with ease. No dragon ever went down into the mist or carried a rope alone.

An enormous beast emerged, revealing only its head. Crocodilian. Enraged. Vicious deep-orange eyes blazed. Its jaws snapped at the mist and the barrier, thrashing and tearing it as it struggled to force its way through.

Ramiel summoned even more runes and coiling strands of silver thread. The light sputtered and pulsed at his fingertips and along his forearms. His jaw tightened.

A scowl creased my brow. I'd seen something like this before...in the resistance. Fae warriors who were blocked or cursed like that couldn't properly channel their magic. He wasn't using all his strength. Something about these particular runes was draining him.

I crouched down on the parapet, focusing in on him

now. He moved at the edge of the narrow bridge with what would have seemed like an easy command if not for the fact I had seen him do more with greater force. He was flagging. His coloration had gone paler as if someone was cutting off his blood flow. The light no longer flared as strongly in his runes.

If I didn't know better, I'd say he was being suffocated. What was happening?

His jaw tightened. His gaze moved along the wavering rift in the light. Then he coiled his hand. He bowed his head for a moment, his shoulders tensing. Then he adjusted his stance, braced himself, and snapped his hands out once more. Energy arced out with each movement of his hand, far stronger and crisper than before. It seared along that rift. The silver light in his runes shone brighter than before.

The deep, bellowing roar faded into a low gurgle. The massive jaws slid down from the largest point in the Chasm, disappearing into the pale-purple mist.

A spasm of fear cut through me.

It wasn't over.

The air grew heavy and tense as if a storm brewed.

Ramiel's hand clutched at his chest. He waved the dragons back.

A dark column of smoke erupted in the air to his left. He shouted some command, but the words were lost in the wind. The three dragons nearest him wheeled back. Up above, the others circled. They roared and bellowed. The purple dragon landed on a broken wall, flung her head back, and screeched.

"Don't engage with it!"

I could just make out Ramiel's words as the wind whipped faster around me. Dust rose around that dark, ominous column, and then…it emerged.

10

STRUCK DOWN

I stared down at that smoky column. A shape had solidified within it—a tall, long-limbed creature that crouched low, legs bent and ready to spring. But those molten red eyes were what I remembered.

The omenfang.

A chill spread through me.

No laughter rose in my chest this time. Only horror. Ramiel needed to move. Get out of there. Time slowed.

The spectral creature lunged forward.

Ramiel marked out a large silver rune to block it, but the omenfang whipped through it. Violet-black static radiated across its form. It burst through the silver.

Ramiel dropped, dodged, and started another rune—no two runes. He was carving them into the air with both hands.

The omenfang vanished mid-leap, reappearing at his left. Its claws swept down. The two partial runes exploded, showering silver sparks across the bridge. Ramiel brought his arm up to shield his face and started cutting into the air once more.

The omenfang bared blackened teeth. As the wind howled around it, smoke and static merged in a chaotic cloud. The dragons howled and roared. They weren't to help? Why?

I gripped the crenels tighter, fingers pressing hard against the stone. I'd never seen a creature like this. Experience had taught me with brutal clarity to never rush into attacking a cursed creature. Fear bit deep, but I wouldn't hide up here.

I scanned the bridge and the surroundings, making note of the safest points to pulseport in. My aura recoiled from the omenfang, warning me not to go near it. I stretched out again, searching and scanning. What was I missing? What could be done?

The omenfang pressed its advantage. It reared back on its tail and lashed with its powerful hind legs. Then it slashed with its claws and headbutted, sending Ramiel reeling. Something had made it far more vicious this time. The wind howled around them, all of Ramiel's runes exploding before fully forming. The wild sparks flashed against the smoke and static.

Ramiel sprang back up and narrowly avoided a savage slash across his neck. He caught his footing, his left hand now gripping his chest. His lips were going blue, his mouth open in gasping pants as if he could not catch enough air.

A tremor shook the bridge and the earth. It vibrated up through the tower. There. I found the right spot, clenched my eyes shut, envisioned the place just beneath the shattered elm, and—in a dark flash, I shot down from the tower.

My head spun, and the golden knotted rope in my hands burned, my body protesting the rapid use of my magic while near this omenfang. I stood in waist-high grass on the edge of the cliff itself, my skin crawling as if thousands of insects had crawled beneath it.

Up close, the horror of this creation struck me fully. How had I ever laughed at this *thing*?

It wasn't a creature. Wasn't sentient. It was just pure

malevolence. Cruel magic twisted into a particular form with one singular purpose.

Ramiel countered another attack, his movements sluggish. He sliced his hand through the air to form another rune, but the silver light faded.

The omenfang drew back and crouched, the shadows and smoke whirling around it faster. The static sparked amidst the darkness. Ramiel's shoulders sagged, favoring his right side, but he still fought. Silver light sparked along his gloves and forearms, the air smelling of burning metal, charring rope, and some cold, choking scent I could not place. It coated my tongue, and I nearly gagged.

Neither had noticed me yet. The omenfang's muscles coiled, its gaze fixed unblinking on Ramiel. Ramiel adjusted his stance again. His hand shook as he carved the start of another rune into the air. Even from this distance, I could hear the raggedness of his breaths.

Setting my jaw, I crouched down and looped the knotted rope in my hand, preparing to strike. My fingers shook as I carved three runes into the air, looped them in the knotted rope, and then whipped them straight at the omenfang.

The runes struck it dead in the side, just above its vital organs—if it had any. For a moment, they hung there, but then they faded, dissolving into the darkness. The creature didn't even look at me. It didn't even flinch. It bared blackened teeth at Ramiel instead, the cold scent thickening, choking and reeking.

"Astraia, get out of here," Ramiel said, his voice stern though it shook at the end. "Get out of here before it notices you." The light from his hand sputtered, the rune wavering before it was even half carved.

"I'm not leaving you behind," I snapped, gathering up my rope. "Tell me how I can help."

He barely hinged a glance back at me, but in that moment, I saw pure fear in his eyes. Several strands of hair had come loose from the tie. "You can't. It's here for me. It's tied to my magic. I have to endure until it has had enough. There's nothing you can do. Leave! I can't protect you if you stay."

The omenfang swayed back and forth in its crouched position. Those red eyes blazed, seeming to savor the moment before the strike.

It lunged once more at Ramiel. The runes fell apart before it even touched them, and this time it struck him with the full force of its strength and a double blow, first in the thigh, then in the chest. Bones snapped with a sickening crack. And just like that the creature vanished.

Ramiel skidded to the edge of the bridge with a pained grunt, one hand clutching at his chest and the other gouging at the stone as if trying to scratch out another rune. His breaths were unnaturally fast and shallow like a man fighting against ever-tightening bonds. His left thigh was broken. Bone protruded from the dark trousers, blood soaking the fabric and pooling on the stone.

I ran to his side, dropping to my knees beside him. His silver hair was matted with sweat and dirt, his normally stoic face contorted in agony. The dragons peered down from above, their scaled bodies casting shifting shadows across us—several still circling in the air with wings outstretched like guardians while the others perched on rocky outcroppings or the remnants of crumbling buildings, their burning eyes watching our every move.

"It's all right," I said, steeling my face in calm. "You'll be all right." I pressed my palms together and formed a smaller, knotted thread. This one I bound around his thigh with my magic, forming the best tourniquet I could manage. Painful memories flashed through my mind. Battlefield dressings. Screams of agony. My hands remained steady, but my breaths trembled. "You're going to be all right."

"Have to. Have to get back in—inside." He drew in a long breath, filling his lungs more. But even then it wasn't enough. The tips of his fingers were going blue as were his lips.

"Back into the tower?" I turned my gaze up at the tower. We were at the base of the hill right before it dropped into a cliff, a good two hundred feet from the tower itself with stairs in between us and a stone path. I was strong for my size, but there was no way to carry him without injuring him. I couldn't even get him onto one of the dragons without risking breaking his bones more. If the knots shifted, he could bleed out within minutes.

The massive dark-green dragon with silvering scales landed on the edge of the spear. His long whiskers nearly dragged on the stone bridge, and his scaled tail lashed back and forth like an angry cat's. A long, gurgling roar rose from his chest. His eyes narrowed to fiery slits.

That was a warning, clear and simple. Just one of his teeth was bigger than my hand.

I remained kneeling beside Ramiel, but I held one hand up, the other still pressed firmly over the worst of his wounds. "Peace, elder dragon. I'm not going to hurt him."

The ancient dragon bared his teeth and snarled louder this time. Zephyrus landed heavily several feet away. His own growl resonated. His scales bristled like hackles.

Thread rot! I shook my head and pressed my palms out. "Zephyrus, don't attack. Elder dragon, this—"

Ramiel waved his hand weakly. "It is fine, Thalorion." His head fell back against the packed earth. He swallowed hard, his throat bobbing with the effort.

Thalorion drew back, his upper lip curling, yellowed teeth still visible.

"I need to find a way to stabilize you, and then I will—"

Ramiel gripped my hand, his strength shocking. "Cannot." His violet eyes grew unfocused, their color dimming.

Panic rose within me, choking me as well. Then an idea struck. "Zephyrus!" I cried, holding onto Ramiel. "Zephyrus, come here." I trilled the whistling notes to summon him.

I had no idea where in the tower the pulseport would drop us. But it would be far closer to where he needed to be than this. And even if the tower did not provide full protection, Caein would surely know what to do.

Zephyrus grunted, his shoulders dropping. Then he strode forward. His heavy footsteps echoed on the stone, and his talons bit deep, scraping on the stone. He wasn't as confident as usual.

"Faster!" I cried.

He lunged forward.

The darkness snatched us up before Zephyrus's jaw brushed the back of my head. Ramiel came with me. I held him fast, feeling his body pulse and waver against whatever evil the omenfang had wrought against him.

We landed in a hall in the center of a long, plush rug. The fourth floor if I was right about the paintings and incense. "Caein!" I shouted. "Caein, Ramiel is hurt!"

The air shimmered and hummed. "Hold his head. Give him support. Don't let his head fall back." The usually calm Nolche's voice carried tremors of fear I felt within my core.

I adjusted my position, my arm sliding beneath Ramiel's shoulders and lifting him up. My breast pressed against his shoulder, and my hair swung over his face. His weight made him difficult to move, but his fingers knotted against my leg, digging in as if to anchor himself. "Shhh," I whispered. "Deep breaths."

He managed a weakened nod. Each breath was a struggle.

I held him as best I could, trying to offer comfort and yet feeling entirely out of my depth. My cheek pressed to his brow as I studied him. "You'll be all right," I said, my voice thick. "Just breathe. Breathe." At least one of his ribs was broken. Possibly more. Maybe his sternum. I adjusted him just a little to a better angle so that there wasn't so much pressure on his lungs.

The air within the tower hummed around me, heavy in

my ears. Something was working even now. Whatever it was, I prayed it helped him.

A door slammed farther in the tower. Something fell, rattling across the floor.

"'ll. Be. F-fine." He struggled to speak.

I shushed him again. "Save your breath. Unless you can tell me something that will help you."

He drew in another shaky breath.

I glanced once more down the hall. "Don't use words. Shake your head or nod. I know a little healing magic. Some runes of soothing. Will that help?"

"Maybe," he rasped.

I narrowed my eyes at him, pretending to be angrier than I was. "That's not shaking your head or nodding." I placed my hand over his chest and summoned my energy to my fingertips. With slow strokes, I traced the runes onto his chest. Slow was good, but it was also necessary because I had to remember what to do. I didn't usually do much healing magic. Lessons in the old solar and adjoining library about layering runic symbols and enclosing them in a circle and infusing with focused intent murmured in the back of my mind. Battlefield healing wasn't nearly so tidy. This felt like a fusion of the two.

His breaths eased a little as the gold light shimmered over his chest. Something wavered inside though. Energy pulsed back, bitter and hard. Not him. Something inside him. I moved my hand up higher and drew another series of runes just above his heart. The same sensation was there, though not as strong. Something was constricting his very heart. The energy made my skin crawl like the omenfang.

I tugged at the ties of his tunic, opening the front. My mouth fell open as I stared at him in horror. Thread rot. No wonder he hadn't been able to breathe!

11

A PARTICULAR BARGAIN

The healing runes illuminated what was within Ramiel's chest. His very heart was wrapped in tight knotted threads that had coiled around it like a constrictor. The golden light from my runes only highlighted the starkness of these poisonous threads. They were like the omenfang. Probably from one of his attacks or connected in some way.

Broken ribs and femur aside, this is what would kill him. My heart clenched in sympathetic pain. "I'm so sorry," I whispered.

He shook his head weakly. "'ll pass."

Until one day it wouldn't.

I didn't know precisely what this magic was, but I had seen similar curses more times than I wanted. This was a curse with a particular trigger. Each time it was triggered, it drew in tighter. Eventually his heart would cease beating altogether, and then his spirit would be severed from his body. Probably trapped in some liminal space until the end of time.

A door several feet away opened, then shut. A roughly human form appeared at the corner, little more than mist and shadow. It held a chest and a large volume. Its feet stuck to the floor, struggling to hold together any form of cohesion and rising and falling in height. "T-take," Caein said with great effort.

I gently shifted Ramiel, wadding the rug up to serve as a makeshift cushion for his head, and hurried over. The Nolche lurched, his rough approximation of hands shaking. Glasses rattled within the chest. They weighed more than I expected, but as soon as I had hold of them, Caein vanished with a gasp of relief. "Open to the black ribbon. Use the vials to trace the runes over his heart."

Hugging the book and chest close, I returned to Ramiel. Though his breaths were a little steadier, that blue tinge in his lips and fingertips remained, his eyes glassy. I swallowed hard as I opened the lid. "That thing was pure evil." Inside were about a dozen vials of thick but colorful liquid, somewhere between the consistency of ink and paint.

"Yes," Ramiel said weakly. His head dropped back against the rug again, a weak cough shaking his body.

I opened the book and set it on the ground beside me, flipping it open to the black ribbon. It had been opened here so many times that the musty pages went there of their own accord.

The page held a detailed painting of three runes to be painted on the afflicted person. Complicated but manageable. But my blood chilled when I saw what they were. They weren't healing runes. They weren't cures. All they did was push back the effects of the curse. The Wyrdcleft Seal. One of the thirteen Grave Bane Runic Spells.

"Hurry," Caein urged. "There isn't much time." The air shimmered roughly near his voice. "Get the runes on him, and his natural healing will take over. Don't worry about the bones or bleeding any more."

Steeling myself, I removed the corks from each of the vials, pulled back the fabric of Ramiel's tunic, and painted the marks on his chest. Each rune had particular cuts and bents, the small flourishes more detailed than what I usually worked with. And each one required at least three colors with the final one requiring five. As I worked, I prayed and filled my thoughts and gestures with petitions for healing. That the Creator of All would hear and have mercy.

And I meant it. I meant every word. Even though sometimes I wondered if I was heard. So many prayers had been answered in silence and death.

What nearly broke me was seeing how far along this curse was. The bonds and the knots were so tight around his heart that I did not see how he was even breathing at all. My paltry attempts to provide relief had eased them only a little.

He remained still, glassy eyes fixed on the ceiling.

Caein murmured words of encouragement and direction. I held my breath, my breaths cramped until Ramiel's lips returned to their natural color and his breaths loosed. Somehow. Even with those knots still bound around his heart. "Thank you," he gasped, his voice strained and rough.

"You're still in pain," I said. It wasn't a question. I knew what that kind of spellwork did to a person.

He cut his gaze to mine, his eyes half shaded. Even with the dark circles beneath his eyes, the sweat on his brow, and his overall disheveled appearance, he was painfully beautiful. "I am alive. And that is thanks to you. Even though I told you not to come. The omenfang could have turned on you."

The way he said that made me ache. I wasn't even sure why. He said it as if that would somehow make it worse. "I don't leave people to fight alone."

"Sometimes there's no other choice." He pressed his hands down against the rug and sat up slowly. Already he was mostly healed. At least from all appearances. A low groan escaped him. "Should have known you would use the dragon platform."

"Ramiel, you need to rest," Caein said, his voice concentrating over Ramiel's head. "I will see to the wards and sigils."

Ramiel lifted his hand. He swayed a little, then steadied himself against the wall. "You needn't fuss."

Before I even thought about it, I was at his side, my arm at his trim waist and his arm resting across the back of my shoulders as Caein continued to speak. The nearness and heat coming off him startled me. His pleasant cedar and silver scent had returned, evidence of his magic. Not even the scent of adrenaline or sweat remained. That crispness combined with the earthy woodiness into a soothing combination. Probably some spell of his. I certainly had my own. In my early months of dragon riding, I had used vanilla and jasmine. Then I'd realized people didn't take me seriously. Vanilla and jasmine were the scent of a peace-time princess or at least of a woman who was safe. After it exposed me to an attack, I'd settled for making my scent neutral. Or at least as neutral as possible. My magic some-times smelled like cashmere, and I loved when that lingered. There was even a faint trace of it now.

I froze then, realizing that I was pressed up against him and he was standing there with his hand hovering over my shoulder as if not sure whether to fully rest against me or push me away. "You were going to fall," I said. My cheeks burned. Caein had stopped speaking, and the air was heavier now.

"I suppose I was." His gaze drifted over my face, drop-ping briefly to my lips before returning to my eyes. His arm started to relax against my shoulders, his fingers brushing my skin. Everything within me tightened.

"You should probably rest like Caein said." My mouth had gone dry.

His throat bobbed. "Perhaps."

"Do you want me to help you to your room?"

"You want to come to my room?"

I hadn't meant it to sound so salacious. But the way he asked that with that low voice of his and half-shaded eyes suddenly made it sound so much worse. The tension rose, burning in my cheeks and core, humming in the air. "I just

—I know you need to rest. So…it doesn't have to be your room. Anywhere you'd be comfortable."

Caein cleared his throat. "I will go and tend to the dragons. They have been unusually quiet. I suspect they understand more than might be assumed." A soft rustle in the air sounded above us. I couldn't drag my gaze from Ramiel's though. He simply nodded, his fingers brushing tortuously over my shoulder again.

Heat rose to my cheeks, my heart quickening. As I focused, I heard his. It beat almost as fast as mine, even with the knots around it. "I just want you to be all right," I murmured.

His fingers curled along the curve of my shoulder, sending sparks through my body. The air hummed and drew me deeper into the moment. His purple eyes darkened, pupils expanding as they fixed on my lips. He leaned closer, the scent of frosted silver and cedar enveloping me and mingling with notes of cashmere from my magic.

"You shouldn't worry about me," he whispered, his voice low and rough. His free hand rose to brush a strand of hair from my face, fingertips lingering against my cheek.

A thunderous crash echoed through the tower, followed by a dragon's roar. Ramiel jerked away, the moment shattered. His expression shuttered closed, walls slamming back into place.

"I should check on that," he murmured, pulling away.

The sudden absence of his warmth left me cold and hollow. I wrapped my arms around myself, aching for what almost was. Breathing deep, I tried to still my racing heart. More than anything I wanted to burrow back under his arm and hold him close. That was ludicrous though. What was wrong with me? I'd seared out my own mate bond years ago. Not falling hard and fast was supposedly a benefit. "Sounded like a play challenge," I responded, swallowing hard and trying to compose myself.

"Yes." He paced into one of the rooms and then back,

dragging his hand through his silver hair. "Yes, probably." He cut his gaze toward me once more.

My eyes locked with his. That look in his eye was one of pure hunger and need. Almost as intense as the fear when we were at the bridge.

I—I wanted him to hold me.

My hand flew up to the heavy scarring around my shoulder and collarbone, swallowing hard. I couldn't take my eyes off him. Couldn't bury this…need that was rising within me. To be held close. Loved as a person…as a woman.

Where had these thoughts come from? They were so blazingly vivid within my mind. Practically a plea. All these years I'd been alone. I'd learned the hard way to not ask for much for myself. The world was kinder when you didn't have expectations. And yet—

Another roar sounded. This one even more clearly a play response but breaking the moment nonetheless.

Ramiel swiped his hand through his hair again. "There's much to be done. We weren't able to fully seal the final rift in the Chasm or heal the leviathan, so it will only be a matter of time before he goes mad and attempts to break through again. His thrashing and biting near the surface weakens it enough that the other creatures can sometimes escape, and the chasm wraiths feed off his agony. There's a tragic irony to it. The leviathans are guardians of the Chasm. They help keep it safe on the inside, but that wound…it's deep enough that he can't fulfill his duty. He's got to be healed or else…."

"He's not the only one. Those knots and bindings around your heart only have one outcome." I followed him, steeling my voice to ensure I sounded far more focused than I felt. "I know what it means when someone is using a grave bane spell."

He grunted in response. "Well…it is what it is." Drawing in a slow breath, he straightened his posture and strode toward the chest with the vials. Carefully, he checked each of the stoppers and then sealed the chest. "Not everything has a cure. And everything has its time."

A deep ache formed within my chest. I shivered, feeling the cold more acutely now that he was no longer beside me. "I'm a knotweaver. I might be able to help you."

"A generous offer." His surcoat hung loose and crooked, entirely unbuttoned now. He moved it back as he straightened his tunic and then began to fasten the buttons one by one. "And one that is unlikely to be effective. This curse is beyond both of us, little gnat."

Was there a note of affection in his voice when he said that? Even the nickname...I brushed the thought aside. My imagination was not helping me. This was just loneliness talking. "You might be surprised. We've both underestimated one another. What would it hurt to let me try?"

"You mean aside from you pulling the wrong thread and killing me on the spot?"

I shrugged, trying to seem casual about this. But I genuinely wanted to help. "You're a rune fae. Your death does not end your spells. If you die and the binding spell remains on me and keeps me from Zephyrus, I'll never be able to journey with him again."

"That still doesn't account for mistakes." A hint of a smile curled at the right side of his mouth.

"No. But I won't make any. Besides, what other choice do you have? Do you have some great plan in place?"

"I have other plans I am pursuing." He adjusted his surcoat, lining it up at the shoulders, and then fixing the lapels. "I have many plans, little gnat."

"None of which have worked." I folded my arms.

Though he was moving a little stiffly now, he seemed more himself. With firm strokes, he smoothed down his hair. It returned to its sleek finery with ease. "So your point is...what's the harm in trying a desperate chance?" He glanced at me sidelong. "And what will you want in return?"

Now it was my turn to smile. "Well, I can certainly be

reasonable, and we both agree, no one owns a dragon. So...
I help you, and you remove the binding spell and—"

"Let you leave with Zephyrus," he said. His expression
had masked once more, returning to its more typical
stoicness.

"Not if he doesn't want to. And after seeing him with
his kin..." I shook my head. "No. It's his choice. But as you
said, if he remains here, he is in danger." More than I had
ever guessed, and Ramiel was clearly on borrowed time.
"So...that means you let me stay here and help you make
the Chasm safer and protect the dragons."

"So..." He smoothed the lapels of his surcoat down,
making the embroidery shine a little more with the
gesture. "You're saying that you want to help me in return
for letting you help me more? You aren't especially good at
bargains, are you?"

"I never claimed to be, but it isn't about helping you," I
said, sharper than I intended. He must have noticed the
way I looked at him, and he was certainly keeping his
distance now. "It's about making sure Zephyrus is all right."

"So if Zephyrus wanted you to leave, you would go?" He
tilted his head, those eyes of his piercing me in place once
more.

"Yes." What an odd question? Something else lay
beneath it. I frowned.

He gave a slow nod of his head, then looked away.
Dragging his hand back through his silver hair, he seemed
to be weighing what I'd said. "I think this is a point at
which you and I are quite similar. We both want to ensure
that the dragon is cared for. You would put his well-being
above all else. Good. So you swear it then? On your life—
on your spirit?" He turned to face me again and held out
his hand. Silver light shone in his palm, the runes for the
oath flashing in his flesh.

"I already told you I would." I frowned even more at
this. What was I missing in this? "Why do you require a
vow? Do you think me a faithless dragon rider?"

"You are not formally a dragon rider nor are you a Sentinel. I do not know you." Though his voice was calm and cool, each word enunciated as crisply as if for a vow recitation, something else lurked beneath.

"My word is—"

"If I am to trust your word, then make the vow," he said firmly. He stepped closer, lowering his voice. "Make the vow. Choose the words yourself if you fear I am trying to fool you, but ensure that it is at its core that you will not abandon Zephyrus and if he feels that you should leave, then you will leave. Make this vow, or I will rescind my offer of hospitality and send you from this place."

STRANGE VOWS

Why was Ramiel insisting on this vow? It unsettled me, but I could not spot a trap. It was just…intrusive. "I will vow that if Zephyrus no longer wants me to remain here, then I will depart…unless his life is at stake and I believe that in remaining I can save him."

I half expected him to protest or snatch his hand away and reject the vow. After all, if he was going to try to trick me into leaving, that was what made the most sense. But instead a smile broke over his face, far more satisfied than I expected. He kept his palm turned upward. "I accept this vow. Now make it."

My instincts prickled at this, my aura stretching out. I couldn't spot any deception within him. No harm toward Zephyrus or me. Only that this vow was exceptionally important to him. Turning my hand over, I scrawled the runes over my palm. They glowed golden, tickling my palm. "I so vow it and bind this to my spirit, my flesh, my soul, and my mind." I pressed my hand to his then, palm to palm.

A pleasant warmth flooded me as our palms connected —not just the heat and energy of the runes, but something deeper. I'd made such vows before, of course, but never one that felt so... binding. So permanent. And over something so basic and small. I would have obeyed Zephyrus's wishes even without the vow.

Ramiel knew this too. So why ask for the vow?

I stared at our joined hands. His dwarfed mine, strong and surprisingly warm, especially for a sorcerer. His fingers flexed slightly over mine, curling ever so briefly over the tops of my fingers. Calluses lined his index and middle finger as well as a point at the base of his palm. Heat flared within me.

What was wrong with me? This had to be loneliness. Maybe just a need for something more permanent. I'd spent fifteen years with Zephyrus, never lingering anywhere long enough to call home. Always moving, always watching over my shoulder. The thought of remaining here, even temporarily, made something inside me twist.

"Is something wrong?" Ramiel asked.

His voice cut into my consciousness. I pulled my hand away, flexing my fingers as the last of the golden light faded. "Nothing. Just...sorcerers usually have cold hands." I shrugged, pushing away the odd sensation. Forcing a smile, I lifted my gaze to his.

"Do they?" He sounded amused, one eyebrow lifting. "I've never noticed."

The heat was still unpleasant in my cheeks and up my spine as I gestured toward his chest. "We should get to work on those knots before they tighten again. The grave bane is temporary. We need to find a place where you can lie down. And you'll need to remove your tunic and surcoat."

He scoffed at me, his eyebrow arching higher.

More heat blazed through me. "Not like that." I tried to think of something to say to ease the tension. "I'm not just trying to see you without your shirt." The words stumbled out, making me seem more flustered than I was. "If it makes you feel any better, you're not my type." A lie. Bold and stinging. And it had stumbled past my lips so quickly. Polph, that wasn't what I meant to say.

"Well," he said dryly. "That makes me feel wonderful."

I shook my head, not certain whether the lie or shame hurt more. More importantly, I couldn't bear the thought of him believing that. "No. I'm sorry. That was cruel." I released a tight breath. I really had lost my ability to deal with people. The truth seemed the wisest course now, and I hoped he would accept it and let us move on. Thread rot, this man was getting under my skin. "You are very handsome, Ramiel. It was a poor excuse of a joke. If I were one who believed in mates or love, I'd certainly be interested."

He chuckled at this. The lines in his brow deepened, and some formed around his eyes. "You don't believe in mates or love?" He motioned for me to follow him, then picked up the chest and the book, and strode toward the staircase.

I twitched my shoulders, realizing how poorly I had expressed myself. This was so tedious. Why did he bring out the dumbest parts of me? "It's…no, that's not the right way to put it. I just…I decided that based on the life I lead, I was never going to be with someone like that. I…" What was wrong with me? I stiffened, blinking in shock. Had I really been about to tell him that I had scourged my mate bond? That I had eliminated that male from my life to protect him? "Some people aren't good for love. At least not like that." If I weren't so good at picking up on spells, I'd have suspected he had enchanted me. But not even someone as powerful or skilled as him could do that without leaving behind some trace.

A soft laugh escaped his lips, more relaxed and calm than at any point before. Oddly so. He started up the staircase. "I can understand that. I made a similar choice. No woman deserves the fate that would await her here with me." The stairs creaked beneath his booted feet. At the next landing, he pressed his hand against the door and pressed it open. The door yielded on silent hinges, opening into a hall that smelled of magic, cedar, incense, and smoke. "Do you love it though?"

"Love what?" I almost added 'being alone?' but I held off.

As I stepped into the hall, I realized that this was the one floor that the pulseporting had never dropped me, but it was clearly where Ramiel lived most of the time. The shield with the three swords was marked on the wall, that comforting, peaceful sensation present even more than before. The air was warmer here, quiet and pleasant. Dark-blue velvet curtains hung at the windows, the one nearest us partially opened as if he had been checking outside. A textured leather book lay on one of the tables beneath an oil color painting of a peace treaty signing among elementals and rune fae. Probably something he had been reading before he got distracted. White beeswax candles, some half burnt, littered the tables and shelves as well as the oil lamps, and a series of hooks held several cloaks, some weather-stained, others mended, all dark in color.

Somehow this floor felt like him. And I didn't know how to explain how that made me feel.

"Flying through the world with a dragon and your will," he said.

"Oh…" I dipped my head forward. A heaviness stole over me, but I forced a smile. "It's beautiful. The freedom. The wind in my hair. The possibilities." The cold nights. The hard ground. The never knowing how much longer this could continue. "Is that something you wanted?"

"Thalorion and I did our fair share when I was a child. But my calling is here. Some things cannot be escaped." He stopped in front of another door and pressed it open.

"Would you? If…if you could and no one would get hurt?" I followed him in. As I crossed the threshold, I halted.

This room wasn't what I expected. It was lovely, yes. Tidy and pleasant as well. It was all comforting, calming shades—deep indigo curtains covered the windows, pale lavender walls, and a velvet throw folded neatly at the foot of the bed over a periwinkle duvet. To the right was a blue velvet couch that looked comfortable enough to sleep on. A glass lamp lit up in response to a gesture from him and cast a gentle glow over the dark wood furniture, and the air carried the faint scent of chamomile and cedar. "This isn't your room," I said.

He glanced back at me and smiled a little. "No. I thought I would show you the guest room since I found you sleeping in the Covenant Chamber. As you can see, it's safe. You can lock the door. The window can be opened, and given your ability to break into the tower, I know you could easily get out. If you're going to be staying here, I feel it would be better if you had a more comfortable place to rest."

"I apologize if my being there caused offense—" I started. Once more that damnable shame stole over me. Why was I so concerned about what he thought of me? I didn't usually care so long as no one got hurt.

He crossed over to the small polished table before the couch. He curled his fingers and traced a design rapidly in the air. A silver tea service appeared, steam rising from the ornate pot's spout. "The chamber is a peaceful place. One I have enjoyed many times. It causes no offense to sleep there. But it is not good for restorative rest. All those commemorations of the sacred bonds can be disruptive, especially if one is sensitive. You were having a nightmare when I found you."

That didn't have anything to do with the location. Nightmares always plagued me. And almost always the same one or some variation of it. "It—it's all right. The room had nothing to do with that."

"Is there something that could be done to make the guest room more to your liking then?" he asked, his manner calm but curious as if we were not about to tug on the cursed knots that engulfed his heart.

"No—no, it's nice. Thank you. I'm just not used to it. That's all." His being kind to me and so hospitable made me feel worse and more on edge. Maybe he was feeling lonely as well. Perhaps that was all this was. I shook my head. "Listen. It's all very lovely, but why don't we just get to work on that curse?"

He glanced up at me, his expression almost coy. "Oh?" Picking up the teapot, he poured two cups of tea into the delicate porcelain cups. Each one had a series of runes worked into a floral design. "You want me to strip off half my clothes now? You're in quite the rush."

I folded my arms, refusing to back down and show just how embarrassed that comment made me. The worst part was that if I didn't find him attractive, this wouldn't be embarrassing at all. "Fine. It's your life that's on the line. I'd have assumed you'd want to do something important with what little time we have, but if you'd rather talk, we can talk. Why not answer my question? Would you travel more if you could do so and no one get hurt?"

"This is important." He handed me the cup and saucer, then sat on one end of the blue velvet couch.

After taking a long draught of the tea, he leaned back. "I would have traveled more, but in the end, I would always return here. It's not an easy life, but it is mine. And there is something to knowing that you are giving back to the world while also being able to live near such wonder and terror."

I breathed in the fragrant tea, chamomile and lavender filling my lungs. It had been ages since I'd had a hot cup of anything. I cut my gaze to him once more, then bowed my head slightly. "Thank you. It's delicious. But…you don't have long, Ramiel. Shouldn't we be focusing on eliminating this curse? You had your own solutions you were pursuing."

He took a long slow sip, then lowered the cup. "The

leviathan is what disturbs the Chasm currently. We sealed it. He has returned to sleep. He usually sleeps for at least a week in between attempts, sometimes longer. He'll rest and then hunt a bit. Over the coming days, the pain will likely worsen. We gave him some relief. When it becomes too much for him, then we are at risk for the others breaking through as well. It's become much trickier because I couldn't go into the Chasm to heal him after he was injured this time. So now we wait while he rests and try to heal him when he attacks. But the advantage of this is that we do have a little time."

"How can you be certain he will stay asleep that long and nothing else will try to escape? Things go wrong."

"The leviathans are the only creatures on their side powerful enough to break through the elements that keep that which is in the Chasm within the Chasm. And you're right. Unless there's a miracle, I don't have long. So..." A contemplative look stole over his face, his head slightly bowed. "Why not enjoy a few quiet moments with another rune fae?"

"I'm not completely rune fae," I said. "Only my father was rune."

"You must have been trained well. You cast with strong precision," he said.

"The ones I know well, yes. I'm better with knots." I took a sip of the tea. It stirred an old memory nearly forgotten. One of my instructors had loved a similar tea, though I remembered it was a touch more floral. "If I had to come up with something on the spot, it would be trickier."

A silence spread between us. To my surprise, it was... comfortable. There was a macabre undertone to it, knowing that he was savoring his last moments if we weren't successful. But we would be. Still...my curiosity pricked at my patience. More than halfway finished with my tea, I tilted my head. "So what exactly is attacking you? An omen—"

"An omenfang." He set his jaw. "Years ago when I was a younger man, I was with Thalorion. We were traveling and stopped at a river. I wasn't paying attention, and I crushed a spirit house. One of the tiny ones. Nothing lived in it at that time, but the witch who guarded those lands was understandably furious. And…she cursed me."

"With an omenfang?" I cradled the cup in both hands, its warmth seeping into my palms.

He nodded, his gaze fixed on the window past me. A little light streamed along the edges. "It was an overreaction. I offered to rebuild the house, to repair the damage. It wasn't enough. She was insulted and angry. I was barely an adult when it happened. My family tried to help me undo it. But the omenfang was bound to me with unusual ferocity. Each time I used my abilities, it drew it in closer until I reached a certain point. And each time that reservoir is smaller, constricting my powers and draining my life. Tending to the Chasm and the beings within is a task that requires a great deal. What has made it more difficult is that after a certain point, the curse itself began to…disturb the Chasm itself. It changed it, making it impossible for me to enter."

"Disturb it?" This curse he was under was certainly disproportionate, but that was also true to so many fae. We weren't really a measured people. Some did better than others, but some…well, they gave us all a dreadful reputation. "Did the witch who did this intend it to be that way?"

He shook his head. "No. At least not nearly so bad as it was. At that point, there were only a few Sentinels left. We returned to her and beseeched her for mercy. We had failed time and again to remove the strands, and it was becoming increasingly difficult."

I frowned. "And still, even knowing what you were doing and the risk to the Chasm, she refused?"

"No. She relented." His finger tapped the side of the porcelain cup. "She even agreed to come and remove it, but the curse refused to respond. She cast it when she was in a rageful and distraught state. As a result, it was not fully what she expected. She vowed to make things right, even if it cost her her life."

A heaviness pressed upon me, cold dread building within my core.

He let the moment linger, then sighed. "Sadly, she paid that price and it was not enough. One of the chasm wraiths destroyed her as we battled the omenfang and sought to calm the Chasm. It ripped her spirit out of her body, and by the time we found her, it was too late."

The dark poetry of dying in part because of something that had been done to harm another was not lost on me. "It sounds like a dangerous curse."

"It is." He cut his gaze back to me. "And beyond that, you should be cautious. Whenever someone tampers with a curse, there is the risk that it will have unintended side effects on the one who interferes."

"I know that well," I responded. My heart tightened. "Anyone who interferes with a curse risks that the curse comes upon them or fulfills in a new way. It's the risk of being a knotweaver." And I had seen just how devastating it could be. "But sometimes it is simply too dangerous to allow it to remain."

"Mine has been a part of me for so long I can scarcely remember life without it." He stared at me now unblinking. "I will not fault you if you don't want to continue with this. I don't want to harm you. Sometimes all we can do is our best and then we must let it be. I am at peace if this is where I end. It is not necessary for you to risk yourself."

"If I undo the knots, then the power evaporates," I said. "I just have to be right about what I undo. And I will be. If there's a central thread, which I'm sure there is, then removing that will be enough to unravel it. I can also loosen these knots in an emergency and give you more breath. Was the witch who put this on you truly unable to remove any aspect of it?"

"She said the magic twisted because my father and

mother and uncle attempted to remove it, but later she also admitted that in her rage, it had warped beyond her capabilities. She did apologize though."

I scoffed, placing the now empty cup on the table. "As if that did any good."

The small nod he gave suggested he had been through this many times before. His manner was of a man who had accepted what had happened and now worked to make the most of what remained. "I appreciated the sentiment nonetheless." Setting the teacup down, he sighed. "Are you ready to begin?"

I nodded.

He removed his surcoat and tunic, folding each one and setting it on the table. Then he removed his boots and stretched out on the couch, his head resting on the velvet armrest. It was a serious moment, and I tried not to let my thoughts drift, but thread rot, the man was exceptionally handsome. His muscles were as perfect as if they had been sculpted from marble. A few scars etched across his chest and back. Knowing the kind of fae he was, he had chosen to keep their appearance. That small bit of vanity made me smile. And they certainly drew attention to the broad planes of his torso and the sharp v's at his waist.

Kneeling beside him, I stretched out my hand and reached out with my aura as well. The gold light lit up his chest, highlighting the dark bonds and vicious knots. My stomach twisted. I would not wish this on my worst enemy. It was even worse than it had seemed at the start. The knots themselves were small, bound and twisted in such a way that they surely hurt him constantly even if all he did was breathe.

He closed his eyes for a moment as if steadying himself when I placed my hand above his heart.

"You're in pain."

"The discomfort is not because of you," he said firmly, despite the faint strain in his voice at the end.

I shook my head and leaned in closer, my fingers

pressing lightly against his flesh. A frown creased my brow. These didn't simply surround his heart, some pierced it. And some of the strands were layered and then knotted together. I swallowed hard, then flexed my fingers. "This will not be pleasant."

"But you're here. That makes it better." That small smile of his made my stomach flip, but I gave him a sharp look.

"Just stay steady." I swallowed hard and then drew in another deep breath. Carefully I searched over his heart with my aura, flexing my fingers and directing my energy over him. Not piercing. Not cutting. Nothing except examining.

"Thread rot," I breathed, unable to keep the shock from my voice. Never had I seen such a brutal weaving, a complex lattice of suffering and cruelty. It constricted the flow of his own magic far more than I'd ever thought possible.

"Your confidence inspires me."

I cut my gaze back up to his. And when our eyes met, I knew that this was already clear to him. He did not have real hope that I could help him. He was simply allowing me to see this part of his life...the very short breadth of what remained for him. So many questions rose within me. "I will help you," I vowed. Then I flexed my fingers over the bonds.

For almost an hour, I searched in near silence. He did not protest at my proddings, though his jaw sometimes twitched. A curse like this had a central thread, but it was guarded. There were a couple ways to potentially handle this, but first...I focused on the smallest knot at the end. Removing my pale gold blade, I held it above his heart and directed my own magic in. The knot pulsed, its light a sickly shade. Carefully I separated his energy from the knot itself, ensuring that only the witch's magic remained in that knot. Then I cut.

The knot snapped free, taking four small strands with it. Two rejoined, forming a straight line while the other two did not. I gave a small gasp of delight as I held the severed knot aloft.

"Astraia!" He sat up, gesturing toward my hand.

The four strands snapped around my wrist, trying to burrow into my flesh.

13

KNOTS

I winced, biting back a pained cry as the threads thrashed at my wrist and tightened, the ends poking hard.

Ramiel grasped my arm and placed the base of his palm just below the threads. Light flared from his hand. At the same time, I channeled my own energy back up into the threads, severing them. They tightened around my wrist again, then died.

Wincing, I cut them free with my blade. Though it was dull to cutting flesh, it excelled at slicing through these magical fibers. They vanished after a moment though the sting remained.

"That is concerning," Ramiel said, his voice grimmer than I'd heard it before now.

I raised an eyebrow. "More concerning than the fact that they are killing you?" I rubbed my wrist. "As far as I'm concerned, this is just wretched magic trying not to die. It's easy enough to manage." My skin prickled and stung from the patch, and a sharp sensation cut through me, fear piercing my heart. "It's not the first time I've seen something like this."

"Are you all right?" he asked. His brow was still

furrowed, and his hand curled over my arm, just below the point where the threads had tried to burrow in.

"Yes. I'm fine." The heat flared stronger within me, and I thought about tugging away. Yet I didn't move. "It's fine."

He gave a noncommittal hum, his gaze fastened on my wrist still. "Did it hurt you?"

"No." I planted my hand firmly against his shoulder and pressed him back. "But it will kill you if we don't deal with it."

His eyebrow twitched. "Look at you taking control."

I clicked my tongue, but that pleasant heat flared through me again. Thread rot, I was lonely. This was not the time to be getting all moony about this man. Though I had to focus a little more, I pressed my aura out again and highlighted the cursed strands. "Even with what you did, one of the strands did not grow back. Two grew back immediately. One grew back after you helped me. But one did not. That means we have an advantage."

That dark chuckle of his made me burn all the more. "Assuming nothing changes."

"Stop being so dour and let me work." I pretended not to notice just how handsome he was as my fingers stroked lines along his chest and sought out the next weakest knot. My preference would have been to go straight to the central knot and central thread, but I couldn't even spot it. Instead I continued working and succeeded in removing another smaller knot. It glowed, resisted, and then cut against me. This time I removed it even faster and dissolved the energy that remained.

The threads still coiled around my wrist and tried to bite and cut, the strands surprisingly sharp even though I tried to cut them as bluntly as possible. Ramiel tensed more at those moments, watching every movement of the threads and sometimes putting his hand over mine to destroy the threads. "You don't have to do this," he said after the fourth one.

The heat between us intensified. My mouth was going

dry. I moistened my lips with my tongue as I leaned closer, steadying myself with one hand splayed across his chest and the other directing my energy toward the knots. "No. But I want to."

"Are you in pain?"

My eyebrow arched like his as I tilted my head, the blade loose between my fingers. "Ramiel, you are the one whose heart is bound in cursed knots that defy standard magic. If we should be worried about anyone—"

He scoffed at this, cutting me off. Concern still shone in his eyes. "I am aware of what my fate is likely to be. I never wanted to drag anyone else into it with me."

As he crooked his arm back behind his head, I noted the charm on his pendant. Small. Likely disguised. A suppression charm. His magic was wavering at the moment. I found a faint but sad smile tugging at my mouth.

As I removed another four strands, they snapped along my wrist and tried to cut. One scraped especially deep. I winced and destroyed it. Damn it. That one did hurt more.

"You know, you really should consider working with a spindle for this," he said. "Give the magic something else to latch onto."

"I don't work with spindles," I said firmly.

He propped himself more on his side, angling toward me. His brow scrunched. "A knotweaver who doesn't use spindles at all? How do you manage the longer cursed threads?"

"I destroy them." There were a few techniques I had mastered over the years, but generally speaking I simply avoided working with such curses. My blade helped a lot.

His frown deepened as he contemplated this. "There's little sense in—"

"I don't work with spindles." I didn't care if the threads left me bloodied. So long as I lived, I never wanted to see a spindle or a spinning wheel. My stomach twisted, my throat knotting with emotion. I tried to swallow it, but a mist of tears blurred my eyes. "Just leave it be, Ramiel. We both know I'm not in danger from this. It's just uncomfortable. If it turns out I need a spindle, we'll figure something else out."

Though his eyes narrowed, he gave a small nod. Concern. That was what was in his eyes. And I hated it. Because I wanted to explain. And now wasn't the time.

I leaned in, putting my face closer to the cursed threads and trying desperately to focus on that.

It was a slow process, and the tediousness of it all made it hard to not let my thoughts drift. I needed to talk about something else—something that didn't involve me. "Did you start wearing suppression charms after you realized you couldn't escape the curse?"

His eyebrows lifted at this question. Then he gave a slow nod. "Yes. And usually I keep it hidden. You have a good eye if you saw through that enchantment."

"Your skills are a little sapped at the moment," I said, offering a small smile. "Who was she? Did you meet her and then decide this? Or is it just a precautionary measure?" An odd bit of jealousy curled within me. Foolish, I knew. It wasn't as if he would ever choose someone like me. So why be jealous at all?

"No," he said softly, eyes shaded as he drifted in thought. "No. I knew from the time I was a youth that I had a mate. I was the only one in my family to have one foretold by destiny, though others in my family of course found happiness and love. But I...I had someone intended for me. Only one person intended for me. Then I learned that if I wed and had children of my own, the curse would pass to them as well. And when I learned how swiftly the bonds were tightening and the dangers that it brought with it, I knew I could not sentence anyone to such a fate. Especially not the one person I was supposed to protect and love above all others."

I tugged at the knots, my heart clenching. The subjects of mates and love and happiness were complicated and nuanced among the fae. To have a mate carried with it expectations and sacred duties. "You sound like you love her." And a small part of me whimpered to admit that. It was a beautiful thing. A respectable thing. And all I could think of was how I wanted someone to feel that for me. It would not be hard for me to feel that for someone... someone like...

He nodded his head. "I do," he said, his voice quiet. "I love her even though I can never have her. She is far too beautiful and wondrous to be shackled to death."

I swallowed hard, the taste of regret bitter on my tongue. "Do you regret it? Cutting yourself off from her?"

"No." He said it so firmly it bordered on harsh.

I tried to swallow that knot of emotion in my throat. When I severed another knot, the threads coiled at my wrist and stung more. A few tears rolled down my cheeks, and I dashed them away. "You're better than me," I said, my voice thick.

"I doubt that." He put his hand over my wrist to soothe the sting.

I kept my eyes down, not meeting his gaze and trying not to think about the warmth and strength of his hand around mine. The urge to fling myself into his arms or curl up beside him thrust itself into my mind, and I had to shove it away. "You were trying to keep the omenfang trapped. Or you were trying to trap something else, and then the glass broke. Was that one of the other solutions you were testing?"

"Yes." He measured his breaths, keeping them slow and steady. The warm cedar scent intensified. "I still have a few more possibilities. You are buying me time and breath. For that I am grateful. Already I feel better than I have in days."

We talked about all manner of things, mercifully avoiding the topic of mates, love, and family. It had been foolish of me to even bring it up. Some of the knots were more resistant than others. It took minutes to dispatch a single one, and a few reformed entirely and had to be removed a second and third time before they only returned with fewer threads and eventually vanished entirely.

At last my hands cramped. They ached, and the well of my magic felt dry. I sank back and rubbed my hands. "It's a start," I said, though already I was calculating how many hours it would likely take to remove them all. We had a very long, long journey ahead of us if I was to undo them this way.

He eased the rest of his way onto his side. His expression was weary but relieved. "One for which I am exceedingly grateful." He nodded toward my hands. "Are you in pain?"

"It's nothing serious." I cracked my fingers and then flexed them, feeling the ache in my knuckles and wrists.

"You should eat. The larder is fully stocked." He stood and picked up his tunic and surcoat. Carefully he pulled them on and adjusted the shoulders. "I apologize that I cannot join you. There are matters in the tower that require attention."

"Do you need help?"

He took my hand in his. His thumb brushed over my palm, kneading gently to ease the tension. "You can help me best by recovering. By restoring your magic."

I tried to pull away, feeling self-conscious, but he held my hand firm. "You're sure?"

His gaze held mine. "Yes. Please. Sleep in the guest room tonight. Eat. If there is more you can do, I promise I will tell you. But you have already done more than enough."

"Given that I broke into your tower, I feel like I should make myself useful. Seems the best way to make up for it."

"Even accounting for that, you have done more than enough."

He helped me to my feet and then released my hand slowly, his touch lingering. "You need to eat too," I said firmly.

He gave another small, scoffing laugh. "I eat."

"I may need you to prove that." I folded my arms.

"Very well. We will share a meal together at some point soon. But for now, I must see to my other responsibilities." He took my hand in his once more and pressed a kiss to my aching knuckles. "Please make use of this room. All that you need will be in here. Including garments if you need them."

A teasing response leaped to my lips. Asking him whether he thought I smelled or if he simply preferred the thought of seeing me in something other than my riding leathers were both possibilities, but I found myself simply smiling and thanking him instead.

The air grew thicker and smelled more of dragons, hay, and blood as I descended the staircase back to the stable. It was warm, almost humid in the hollow core of the tower. Upon reaching the door, I peered inside.

Zephyrus was in the cell nearest the door this time. He lifted his head, a low growl rumbling up his throat that soon turned into a chuff. That deep, happy trill made my heart lighten even more.

The other dragons stirred and shifted, a few rustling their wings. They were likely exhausted from the day's endeavors. Thalorion was in one of the cells now, head resting on his forelegs like a large cat as two of the others curled up beside him. He watched me with half-lidded eyes.

I crossed as close to Zephyrus as I could. "You did good out there. You and the rest of your kin. I never knew you could fly in formation like that. It sounds like that isn't close to half of what you're capable of."

Zephyrus lifted his chin, his gaze still fixed on me. Steam curled from his nostrils. A series of low chirrs and the way he puffed his chest confirmed he was proud. As he should be.

I picked up a stick from the corner of the room and used it to scratch his jaw through the bars. He rubbed against it, curling his upper lip and pressing his teeth on the edge.

Soon I'd be able to hug him, and perhaps soon we could fly together again. I spent a few more moments giving him the best scratches I could, spoke to the other dragons, and then left. I really didn't want to sleep, but sleep was necessary to restore my magic.

As I neared the door to the guest room, I heard voices. Caein and Ramiel. My heart tightened, and my stomach somersaulted. I should just go back to my room and prepare for rest. But maybe I should say good night.

I slipped down the hall, drawing closer to the voices, then paused when I heard Ramiel say, "I don't understand why you are suddenly so antagonistic. You said you liked her, didn't you? You won't be here in a few days anyway. Why wouldn't you want Astraia here?"

AN INVITATION

I held my breath as I heard the two speaking about me. Pressing my hand to the wall, I listened closely.

Caein sighed. "It isn't that. I am fond of her. I'm simply surprised to learn that you invited her to remain. Especially given what she is."

Their voices were soft enough that I had to focus to hear all of the words. Ramiel said something I couldn't quite catch.

"This will only make it harder," Caein responded. "Remember what you told me: you don't want to burden anyone with the grief. She won't be able to remove the knots in time."

"I have other methods I am using to resolve the issue. But more than that, perhaps…" Papers rustled. Something scraped over the desk. A sigh followed as if Ramiel did not want to say it aloud.

"You know so long as the curse remains it cannot be so, your Highness. The omenfang is—"

"You don't have to remind me." His voice sharpened. "I am well aware of what it does and of the limitations. If I take some small measure of comfort in her presence, what harm is there in that? I am strong enough to endure."

"You're the one who told me—"

"She doesn't want to leave. If I cast her out, she will return."

"Yes, I was there when she launched herself up with Giselle. She's lucky Giselle is so patient with foundlings."

"They all like her. Even Thalorion."

"Of course they do now. They know she saved you. But given what you have said and what you claim to value, I do not see that this is wise."

Ramiel spoke again, his voice more contemplative yet still clear. "Perhaps it is not perfect, but there are advantages to this. Perhaps she will care for the dragons when I am gone. Perhaps she will help you find some new host structure."

So that was his game. He wanted me here to help take over his duties so to speak, even if I wasn't a Sentinel. Somewhat manipulative, yes. But part of me respected him for it. Knowing what he wanted made me feel more confident as well. I could work with that. I…I did care about him. Odd as it was.

"I do not require her assistance. I have three other structures which I can use. Just because the process did not go entirely as planned does not mean I am helpless," Caein responded tightly. "And I would rather you focus your efforts on surviving the curse, my friend. Survival matters little when everyone you care about is gone. I do not deny that it pleases me to know someone will be here with you when I must go to the other hosts. It weighs heavily on me when I do. But what happens when she learns—"

"Enough. Give me peace this night," Ramiel said, his voice rougher.

Caein scoffed. "There won't be much peace for you if she comes to comfort you in your dreams."

"Go on then, shade." It almost sounded as if Ramiel was smiling. "Other tasks are far more important than us prattling. And I doubt she'll visit me as I dream. If everyone sleeps peacefully and restfully tonight, then that's more than enough good to have come from this. I won't be greedy."

My heart warmed to hear him say that. In truth, to see him within my dreams would be welcome indeed. Especially compared to what I usually dreamed about.

I returned to the guest bedroom. Once inside, I found everything I could possibly need. And I used it.

It was strange to bathe with water and soap rather than relying only on my magic for personal hygiene. The simple night shift left me feeling vulnerable and exposed but more like a person than I had in ages. It was even stranger to lie down in a bed again. To draw silken sheets up over myself. This one smelled of lavender and cedar, comforting and warm. The softness made my body ache a little, and the sheets were cool against my skin. When I reached out with my aura, I noted several wards woven into the walls along with sigils intended for protection, peace, and rest.

I'd have felt safer with Zephyrus with me. It brought a faint smile to my lips to imagine him in here at my side. He'd insist on being on the bed, even though it would barely fit his chest. Most likely he'd smash the bed to kindling, then roll around on it and crush the wood into splinters before tucking in around me. He was back with his kin in a giant cuddle puddle of dragons, able to thrash and turn and grunt as much as he wanted without risking crushing anyone.

Those images made me smile. I closed my eyes, holding onto the good images, the warm feelings, telling myself there was a way through. Within minutes, sleep took me. Dreams found me swiftly.

This time Ramiel was there. Not the stern, guarded version but the gentler, warmer one. The one who soothed the sting of the threads on my wrist, who watched with shaded eyes. We stood together on a balcony overlooking the Chasm, its swirling mist ethereal and beautiful from this distance.

"It is beautiful even if it is dangerous," he said, his voice carrying on the wind. "It's all been worth it here. I'm only sad that it has to end so soon. I wish I could have visited it again without the curse. It was a wondrous place."

I turned to face him, surprised by how close he stood and yet longing to be closer. "It's not going to end."

"Everything ends, Astraia. All things have their time." His eyes were clearer than I'd ever seen them, the violet rich and bright. They warmed as he smiled, small wrinkles forming at the edges of his eyes and temples. He reached out, his fingers brushing against my cheek. "It's sad that ours is so short."

"It isn't over though," I said. The tears stung, and my body ached. It felt like I had a fever, and my shoulder throbbed, the pain beneath the scars almost as strong as it had been when I seared my flesh. "Why would you give up?"

"I'm not giving up." He cupped one hand along my cheek. "I chose the wisest course to protect what I love. Sometimes, Astraia, all we can do is our best and then we must let go and allow what is to be what is."

He said it so gently, and yet I wanted to sob.

His hand closed around mine, warm and solid as he brought it once more to his lips. I leaned closer, drawn to his warmth as his other arm moved around my waist.

"If there was no curse, I would ask you to stay," he whispered, his breath tickling my ear. "Not for the dragons, not for duty. Stay because—"

The balcony crumbled beneath my feet. Ramiel's hand slipped from mine, and I fell, screaming into darkness.

Then came the familiar nightmare—the one that haunted me since childhood.

No. No!

All right. The darkness engulfed me. I knew what to do.

Just a dream.

Just a dream.

I held myself tight, shaking as the air became thick and stale. Threads spun in the darkness and curled around me.

I was alone in a pitch-black space. Invisible cords wrapped around my chest, my throat, my limbs. With each breath, they tightened.

I tried to scream, but even my voice abandoned me.

It didn't matter.

This was just a dream.

A dream where I was alone.

No answer came. No one ever answered, but it would end. I could endure until it ended.

The cords constricted further. I couldn't move, couldn't breathe. But I couldn't stop fighting.

I strained and gasped. Knots appeared before my eyes.

I woke, flailing, my hands seizing the covers. Blankets and sheets covered my face. Where was I? Wait— the Eye of the Needle—the Sentinel tower. Zephyrus. Ramiel.

My shoulder throbbed and ached even more. I pressed my hand to it, wincing. Why was it getting worse? I'd scourged myself years ago. Couldn't it ever be done hurting? It was like one final indignity, an even more present reminder of my mistake.

My breaths ragged, I lay there. Was it the bed that had made it worse? I swallowed hard, my mouth dry. Maybe. Or maybe it was because I was still separated from Zephyrus. The binding spell didn't hurt, but its pressure remained steady.

Still, I needed to get this day started. The sooner I finished restoring my magic and eliminated the knotted curses around Ramiel's heart, the sooner the binding spell would be removed and I could ensure Zephyrus and the others were safe.

Time to get dressed.

As Ramiel had promised, the wardrobe did in fact hold numerous garments. As soon as I reached inside, a shimmer of silver light passed over my hand and into the garment I touched. The mossy-green fabric shimmered a moment as well, transforming before my eyes. When I removed it, I found it to be a soft woven gown with an embroidered neckline and sleeves that depicted dragons weaving through clouds and mountains. The silver sash hung low on my hips, and it smelled of lavender and cedar with just a hint of green tea and chamomile. It made me think of the tea we had shared yesterday.

That memory comforted me somehow, almost as much as being with Zephyrus. Funny. It had only been a couple days, and Ramiel was now the closest friendship I had with someone other than a dragon. Caein too, though certainly different.

I made my way out, smelling melting butter, warm cinnamon, and yeasty dough. The scent guided me to a kitchen several doors down. When I pressed my hand to the door, it gave way easily.

Inside I found a charming kitchen with stone walls and a wood floor. The large fireplace dominated the back wall with a massive cast-iron stove positioned to the left. Herbs hung from the hooks in orderly rows along with strings of onions and garlic. Slices of crystals hung in the window as wind chimes, singing and humming softly. The cupboards were all polished walnut with intricate runes etched into the panels. Blue porcelain bowls sat on the counter, a few eggs rolled up against one. The air shimmered and wavered over a lump of bread dough situated in the middle of an uneven circle of flour.

"Caein?" I hoped it was him. Usually there was only one Nolche in a single building.

"Ah, you're awake." All the utensils jolted and shuddered as Caein's voice rose in pitch. I had no idea what he had looked like in his fae form, but the image of an older man smiling flashed into my mind. "I wasn't able to offer you breakfast yesterday. And you did not eat dinner either. You and Ramiel can be so alike."

"He doesn't eat regularly either?"

"You both get caught up in your tasks." Caein sighed. The spoon rattled against a bowl of half-beaten eggs. "And I do not require food any longer so it is easy for me to forget. But good food is good for the soul, and that makes your magic stronger."

General health and well-being always provided positive results for one's magic so long as you weren't cursed in some way to prevent it. I stepped farther in, debating asking about what I'd overheard, then deciding against it. "Can I help?"

"I have it—" Caein swore in a language I didn't recognize as the spoon flipped out from the bowl and onto the wooden floor, spattering a sugary glaze. "Yes. If you would like to assist me, I would not object."

I stooped down to pick up the wooden spoon. Seeing a small blue and white check towel, I used it to clean up the floor. "Cinnamon bread?"

"Yes, an old, old recipe from my mother's side. Now…if you could add a pinch of crushed cloves and three pinches of nutmeg and mix it in, I would be most grateful."

It was a little surreal to be helping prepare cinnamon bread, but I enjoyed the hominess of it all. After I washed my hands in the basin, I measured out the cloves and stirred it together. "Where is Ramiel?"

"Trying to break the curses and tend the Chasm, heal the leviathan, all the usual tasks," he said. "The dragons were especially energetic this morning. They were up before the sun. He set them through their paces."

"Does that mean the leviathan will try to break through sooner than expected?" I hadn't removed enough of the cursed knots to give Ramiel much of a reprieve, and I didn't think he could take more than one or two more fights with the omenfang without the curse destroying him despite the ground we had gained.

"No, it means the leviathan has calmed. He'll likely rest, then hunt, and then sleep. It should mean we have more time." A long sigh followed. "Time. The one thing we need, and the one thing we're never certain we'll have." The bread dough squashed at an awkward angle.

"Would you like me to knead it?" I asked.

"If you wish." He sounded rather relieved. I couldn't blame him. If I were in his position, I'd hate it, and I guessed that what he was doing was an act of kindness specifically intended to bring comfort. There were other simpler cuisine you could prep and that would be easier to manage if you had to rely on your aura or telepathic abilities or will to maneuver objects.

I rolled the dough onto the flour and began to work it. It stuck to my palms and fingers, the yeasty scent growing stronger. My mouth watered. It smelled so much like the peace loaves my mother and sister and I made each year with all the other women.

"I'm glad you're helping him," Caein said, his voice vibrating around me. The whisk beat around in the bowl with the eggs, faster and smoother now. "I feared that when I returned from rest again, he would have perished… what happened on the bridge has been a grave fear of mine since the coming of this curse. When the omenfang attacks outside the tower, its power is always far greater."

"You're leaving? Or—I guess resting?" I glanced up at the ceiling. "Why?"

"I'm still adjusting to being a Nolche. It requires that I often…sleep might be the best term for it, but there are mercifully no dreams."

It was strange to watch the implements within the kitchen move themselves. The spoon in the bowl stirred in stuttering strokes, and the whisk moved in halting spins.

"No dreams, huh? That sounds nice. As long as you can get out of it."

"It is restful. The challenge comes in moving between the host structures. I am not the guardian of only this place."

"You're the guardian of the guardian tower?" I smiled at this. The rolling pin clattered toward me, wobbling as if someone had sent it rolling from the wrong end. Picking it up, I dusted it with flour and started to roll out the dough.

"A guardian of the Sentinels. I was a friend to the

Sentinels before my transformation. I am a friend to them now though Ramiel is all that remains. I divide my time between the families I loved in my corporeal life."

"What happened to the other Sentinels?" I rolled the dough. There was something comforting about his presence, despite his ghostly nature.

"That is not my story to tell," he responded. "But Ramiel may speak of it when he is ready."

Fair enough. We fell into an easy silence. As I kneaded the dough, I decided then not to mention the conversation I'd overheard last night. Caein was trying to protect Ramiel, just as I was trying to protect Zephyrus. And now we were all trying to protect the Chasm.

As I put the loaf in the oven, it startled me to realize how important that had become to me.

When Ramiel came to the kitchen, my stomach somersaulted again. He didn't remain, but he did smile a little.

I didn't know how, but…somehow we really found a beautiful synergy. Over the next three days, we did little more than work and prepare, but time passed swiftly.

Ramiel did not stop for meals, only pausing long enough to gather food from the kitchen and then returning to his desk or the rune tables. He barely stopped for sleep. And for a few hours out of each day, he stretched out on the couch and let me work at the knots.

I drew out the threads with great care. Each one when severed curled back on me and vanished into the air with a pulsing hum, cutting or biting at me. Though he sometimes winced, he often soothed or stroked my arm to remove that sting. Each touch from him made me grow warmer. Sometimes my hands shook a little.

Foolishness. Loneliness. Whatever it was, I had to be cautious. My fingers worked along his chest.

There was something undeniably intimate about this. Each time my thoughts drifted in that direction, I blushed but turned my head to hide that. If he noticed, he never mentioned it.

Still the energy thrummed stronger between us. Sometimes I just wanted to stretch out beside him, feel his arms twine around me, and rest my head on his shoulder.

I cursed myself for that desire. I cursed him for being so impossibly close.

Now wasn't the time or place.

Even if it would be easy.

So very, very easy.

Heat radiated through his parted tunic and into my hands and side. Part of me hated how much I longed to be close to him and how quickly I fell for him. As I spread my aura out over his chest, I thought I glimpsed the central thread. "It looks like it really is woven straight into your heart." If I could get a solid hold of it, it would undo all the rest. Magical knots were magnificent like that.

"Not surprising," he said, his arm draped over his forehead. He studied me from beneath his arm. "If that's the case, then that means you won't be able to reach it unless I fully engage my magic. But that will trigger the omenfang's arrival for certain. And…" His brow pinched.

I focused in on another of the knots. My magic shuddered as this one resisted. "And what? Don't tell me you're giving up?"

He shook his head. "Do you always have nightmares?"

The abrupt change of topic left me blinking. "Um…yes. I usually do."

"I'll see what I can do about it. True rest is essential for healing, and that is difficult to do when you have nightmares." A contemplative hum rumbled from his lips. "I should have asked sooner."

"Why?" That response confused me. "My nightmares aren't your trouble."

I focused my magic on the next knot, tracing the patterns with the blade. This one seemed more complex, with tighter coils and sharper edges. Six threads instead of four. As I worked to loosen it, I felt resistance—stronger than before.

"They're getting trickier," I murmured, pressing deeper with my magic.

The knot suddenly constricted, then snapped back at me like severed violin strings. The cursed threads lashed out, slicing across my palm and wrist deeper than any previous attempt. I yelped in pain, jerking my hand back. My blade fell to the floor, spinning until it struck the wall.

"Astraia!" He caught my wrist before I could pull away. His fingers were cool against my burning skin as he examined the wound. The cut was deep enough that beads of blood had begun to form.

"It's nothing," I insisted, though my voice betrayed me with a slight tremor.

Ramiel's brow furrowed as he traced his thumb gently across my wrist, his healing magic soothing the sting. His eyes met mine, concern evident in their purple depths.

"These threads are becoming more aggressive," he said softly. "They're fighting back harder each time. Did it try to enter your wrist?"

"I—I think it just coiled," I said, but I wasn't actually sure.

He continued studying it. "I don't like how it lashes at you." His fingers wrapped over mine. "Has it been hurting more, gnat? This is the first time it's drawn blood, but it seems to be getting harder."

I started to shake my head, but he chided me. "You don't have to pretend."

"Severing curses always stings a little," I said quietly. But it wasn't the sting that had absorbed my attention. His thumb pressed against my palm.

The cut sealed shut. He still held my hand, his expression contemplative. "I don't like seeing you hurt."

Witty words escaped me, my heart racing faster. So I just shook my head again. "I don't like seeing you hurt either."

That gentle smile of his spread. I loved how it reached his eyes and how his eyes crinkled. "I appreciate that you have been doing this for me, and I know that it takes great skill and focus," he said. "Let me prepare you a special dinner. Something restorative."

"Something we can scarf down as I restore my magic and sever the cursed threads and you pore over your texts and continue with your experiments?"

That smile pulled higher. His low laugh made my stomach somersault and tighten. "No…I mean a quiet meal at a proper table with good food and good conversation."

"You can spare that much time?" Though I said it in a teasing tone, I was also serious. My progress in removing the cursed knots from around his heart was not going as swiftly as I hoped.

He pressed a kiss over the point where I had been cut. "Yes. Some of the reagents need to rest anyway, and…I want to spend the time in this way. I will see you after sundown in the eighth door down from your room."

"Of—of course." I drew my hand back to my chest. My skin tingled from the memory of his lips and his breath wisping over mine. "Is there anything I can do to help?"

"Don't be late." He crossed to the door, cast one more look at me, and then left.

15

A QUIET DINNER FOR TWO

$\mathcal{M}$y stomach twisted and fluttered as if I had just dropped a thousand feet. I spent the rest of the time restoring my magic and strengthening my abilities. Then, shortly before sunset, I prepared.

I hadn't really fussed much about my appearance since I'd been here. It had been enough to have clean clothes, soap, and hot water. But now...now I wanted to do something special.

I stood before the wardrobe, hand hovering over the silver handle. A memory surfaced—my mother's smile as she held the pink fabric up to my shoulders, preparing me for my first ball where I was to be presented to the kingdom. Fifteen years old. Nearing the time when I would begin assuming royal duties.

"Pink is special to the crimson fae," she'd said, tucking a strand of hair behind my ear. "It reflects your soul, darling. Bright and warm, nurturing and soft."

Father just laughed, his eyes crinkling at the corners. "Blue suits her better—turquoise, like the rune fae. Strong and steady."

"It suits her, but pink is special," Mother said.

"I like the pink too," my older sister Sona said. "Especially the rich shade. It's like the roses in the desert."

"But blue is easier for the eyes when one is working with knotweaving," Father countered. "And it is easier to make stronger runes when using those shades in our family."

"I think green would be better," my eldest brother Loam said. "It still has the blue and works against the gold, but it's easier to hide. Especially dark green. Or black even."

"Princesses do not wear black at their presentment. This is our opportunity to tell the kingdom something particular about Astraia. Black must be reserved for the higher functions and for her demonstration of her powers when she is eighteen. These traditions matter." Mother tilted up my chin, then adjusted the fabric.

My brother Elim hooked his arm around my waist and flipped my hair out of the floral binding. He wove a quick enchantment that made my curls bounce and scrambled the colors of the flower petals together. "I think she should wear yellow so it matches her hair."

Sona rolled her eyes, scoffing at him. "We do not match our clothes to our hair. We contrast with our hair. If you must match something, match your eyes."

A knot of emotion formed in my throat. Little had I known then how soon I would wear all black and why.

Willing back the tears, I closed my eyes and focused my intention, picturing a gown of soft pink. When I opened the wardrobe, my breath caught. The dress that awaited me was exactly as I'd imagined—rose pink with flowing angel sleeves and the perfect flair and layering.

I ran my fingers along the fabric, turning it inside out to examine the seams. There, hidden from casual view, was an inner lining of turquoise and blue threads. My compromise, once upon a time, to honor both parents. The rune stitchings on the inside even formed the runic marks for family.

I hadn't worn pink since. It was far too happy a color. But now...now I wanted it. The gown fit perfectly, and even though I did not add perfume or alter my scent from anything but clean, I felt as if I was ready.

As soon as I opened the guest room door, I caught the mouthwatering scents. It was only a few doors down, and the carved door had been left ajar. The room beyond stole my breath.

A feast had been laid out on a table draped in midnight blue cloth scattered with silver stars. Platters held glistening roast duck with crisp, golden skin nestled among caramelized onions, carrots, sprouts, and potatoes. Beside it sat a steaming tureen of wild mushroom soup, its earthy aroma mingling with fresh-baked bread sliced neatly in a cloth-lined basket. Crystal goblets caught the light from floating white taper candles, and delicate pastries dusted with sugar formed a small mountain on a silver tray. Other smaller plates held honeyed figs stuffed with soft goat cheese and crushed walnuts, charred leeks drizzled with shadow truffle oil, and slivers of cold-smoked river trout wrapped in vine leaves with a moon fruit garnish. A shallow glass dish shimmered with starlight jelly with a tiny silver knife balanced over the top. The decadent scents made my mouth water and my stomach cramp with hunger.

Ramiel stood waiting at the head of the table, dressed in a tailored rich blue surcoat, embroidered with silver runes that shimmered when he moved. The formal attire surprised me—as if we'd both decided this evening warranted something special without ever discussing it. I hadn't even questioned the choice of dress, and that—that was remarkable.

I realized then we were both staring at one another, his mouth slightly open as if he had never seen anything like me.

"You look..." his voice trailed off as his gaze traveled over me. His throat bobbed.

"So do you." I kept my chin up even though heat spread

through my body and likely made my cheeks match my dress.

Straightening his shoulders, he stepped forward with that quiet grace of his, pulled out a high-backed chair, then held out his hand. "Please."

My hand slid easily in his. He guided me to the seat and slid it under me.

I settled into the chair, sinking into the cushion and painfully aware of his proximity. His hand grazed my shoulder as he stepped away, that wonderful scent of frosted silver and warm cedar wrapping around me like a sensual embrace.

He took his seat across from me, still within arm's reach. "I hope you're hungry. And that the food tastes good. It has been a while since I have prepared anything even remotely like this."

"Yes, if your habits over the past few days are any indication, I suspect you mostly eat whatever you can while working. But it smells wonderful." I curled my hands in my lap. Everything had been set up with such care.

He chuckled at this, picking up a bottle of mead and pouring us each a goblet full. "Especially lately." He raised his glass. "To unexpected but delightful company. Natoumai ahme vahre. Kahdahle."

I dipped my head forward, lifting my own goblet. I recognized the word "kahdahle." It was a rune fae toast that essentially meant blessings upon you and all yours and may all the good spoken come to pass. I didn't recognize the first phrase, though I remembered seeing it inscribed on the empty jar. "Kahdahle."

The first sip of the mead sent my senses reeling with delight. It was so delicious it was all I could do to not gulp it down. "That is amazing." Closing my eyes, I savored the complex sweetness. "I know what kahdahle means. But...I don't know the other. Natoumai ahme vahre."

"Oh..." He paused as if startled I asked. Then he tilted his head, his silken hair sliding over his shoulder like a waterfall. "It's a Sentinel's saying. An acknowledgment of the blessing that one's presence holds. Please. Enjoy the food. It has been ages since I have been able to share this with anyone."

The meal was delicious, reminding me of the cuisine in the palace. Especially on the rune fae holidays. For several moments, I simply ate with relish until I reached the duck. "You marinated the duck with wine and garlic and stone leaves," I exclaimed. The rich and savory flavors exploded over my tongue with the sharp bite of the acidic leaves. I held my hand up to my mouth as I chewed the bite thoroughly, delighting in every scrap of flavor.

"You know the seasonings of the rune fae well." That pleased smile of his sent a bolt of delight straight through me.

I took another sip of mead, another bite of duck, then shrugged. "My father was rune fae. Even though he was a king, he still loved to cook. He loved to cook so much that he had a special section in the private chambers so that he could." I paused, realizing what I had just said. I hadn't spoken about my family to anyone for so long, and now it was slipping out. As the princess assisting in the Resistance, most did not expect me to speak of my family specifically. My purpose was to be an inspiration. And eventually my purpose ended. I was part of the old ways. The old always gave way to the new. But I had gone back to something older still. Memories of my family before the massacre. It felt like lifetimes ago.

"Your father was a king? The king of Theodas?" His eyebrow arched. He set his fork down, the silver utensil clattering against the plate. "Forgive me, but…why would King Houtan allow his daughter to wander so freely? And why would he not have provided aid when she thought her dragon was stolen?"

My whole body tightened, and my gaze dropped to the goblet. "No…my father was Servas the IV."

His eyes widened slightly at this. Silence fell over the

table. "I'm sorry. I did not realize..." He shook his head. "Forgive my clumsiness..." A muscle jumped in his jaw. "I'm sorry. It was a grave tragedy, your Highness."

"Please...don't call me that," I said softly. "I'm not the princess any more. Most think I died in the resistance, but..."

He remained silent, allowing me the space I needed to choose my words.

I swallowed hard, staring at the mead in my goblet. The amber liquid caught the candlelight, shimmering like trapped sunlight. Part of me wanted to change the subject.

But something about Ramiel's quiet presence made me want to share this burden I'd carried alone.

"My parents offended a powerful fae," I finally said, my voice barely above a whisper. "No one knew where she came from. She appeared at my naming ceremony on my fifteenth birthday, uninvited and furious."

Ramiel leaned forward, elbow resting on the tabletop.

"She cursed me to a painful death," I continued, my fingers tightening around the goblet's stem. "Said I would die because of a spindle on my sixteenth birthday and be lost in the void until the end of time. My parents tried everything to prevent it—burning every spinning wheel in the kingdom, researching counter-curses, creating new spells, forming rune patterns..."

It was hard not to see their faces in my mind's eye. Though the tears burned, I held them back. It was the first time I had told anyone this. Before, others had told the story in their own manner and I had simply agreed to it. Yet now the words slipped from my lips. "They gathered up all the spinning wheels and spindles and set them ablaze with curse binding fire. It was...it seemed perfect. But...there was something in the wood. Some spell that we missed. Maybe a poison. As the wood burned, this green mist entered the air. Practically everyone fell asleep within moments."

He studied me, his violet eyes fixed intently upon my face. "You did not fall asleep."

"A handful of us remained awake. We were immune or something. And…that's when we realized that something far worse was coming. Our enemies—they were at the gates. And they knew. It was all part of a plan."

I closed my eyes, trying to block out those memories. The horrible squelching, the dull thuds as they cleaved through the bodies of the sleeping and helpless. "Some fought back. Others of us—we tried to rescue who we could. But…"

I couldn't bring myself to say those final words. To tell him how each member of my family died. I didn't want to see those moments again.

The silence grew between us, and he let it sit.

I took another long drink from the mead, not tasting it at all. "I was one of the few who survived. And barely. I fled into the forest that night, and I just…I ran until I couldn't run any more. I started crying. I don't know how I got there, but I found myself on a hill at dawn. I was cold and scared, and… Zephyrus found me."

I looked up at him as I reached this point. He gave a small nod, suggesting he understood. I swallowed hard. "I was so scared at first, but somehow…he got through all of that. And he taught me to be a rider. He was my whole family. I was so useless that I didn't even know how to hunt, but…he helped me. And he protected me. The attack on the nation continued, and I was so lost in grief, I didn't think there was anything I could do.

"But then Huntao came to get me. He was one of my father's generals. I don't even know how he found me. But he asked me to join him in the resistance. So I did. And in the end, we won. He offered to restore me to the throne, and I…I believe he would have. But in those years, I saw the kind of leader he was. And I knew what I was."

"What were you?"

"A scared girl who had no experience in politics or

diplomacy who turned out to be good at rescues and dragon riding but not really the finer points of ruling. I couldn't imagine marrying anyone, and serving as the icon of the resistance took its toll. Huntao proved himself wise and surprisingly kind for a general who was crowned king. And, of course, I had already scourged the bond mark. I couldn't be with anyone then."

Wait. Had I told him that before? The words had just slipped out. I halted.

He leaned back in his chair, one wrist draped over the wooden arm. "You scourged the bond mark?" He asked it quietly, not cruelly.

I nodded, staring down at the mead and the small ripples from tilting the goblet. Maybe it was for the best. The words tugged at my lips, eager to spill free. "My father was rune fae, but my mother was crimson fae. I found the crimson mate mark when I turned fourteen. It meant that somewhere—somewhere out in that grand world—my beloved existed and had also reached a critical point. If lore is true, then the bond would begin forming between us over the next decade until at last we met. And at first, I took great joy in that. Mate bonds are not common among crimson fae though apparently more common than among rune fae."

"If I may ask, why did you sever it when it had begun? You had already lost everything. Would you not desire the comfort and security of a mate?"

I pressed the tip of my tongue against my teeth, willing the tears back. "Because all I had left was Zephyrus and death and the resistance, and...I didn't think I would survive the fight. At that point, I thought the curse would find some other way to destroy me. And the lore masters said that if a bond was severed before it was fully formed, then my mate would have a chance to bond with someone else."

His brow furrowed, a soft yet knowing light in his eyes.

"Fate would be rewritten? Your beloved would find someone else?"

"And he would be safe." I bit down on my tongue. "He wouldn't know I'd rejected the bond. All he would know is that something changed."

"And you never pursued romance outside of that? Rejecting the mate bond does not mean you cannot love or be loved," Ramiel countered.

"What man would be interested in me? Especially once he knew that I had a mate…that the mate bond had started to form its mark on my flesh to draw me to my mate and I scourged it? I know that must sound dreadful and cruel—"

"No, I understand your choice." He tapped his finger against the pendant at his throat. His magic made the charm difficult to see but it was present nonetheless. "I did not cut my mate bond from my own flesh, but…I took other steps. I masked the bond and freed her. My reasons weren't so dissimilar from yours."

"Really?" I had never thought I would meet someone else who had followed such a similar path. Speaking of this so frankly and without judgment—I had never thought that would exist for me. It was as if an old burden was loosed from my shoulders.

His violet eyes softened. "Because I always knew I was coming to this point, Astraia. The curse hangs over me and keeps me from entering the Chasm and healing the leviathan. And that in turn means that the leviathan is going mad. Who knows what else has happened within those corridors?"

With a heavy sigh, he lifted the chalice to his lips. "I realize it may seem insane to you that the dragons and I remain here. I could live if I never used my runic Chasm magic again. But the Chasm must be protected. If it ruptures, then all the beasts of the Chasm starting with the leviathan will pour out into ours and the raw magic of the Chasm itself will undo the moorings of this realm."

"Then why are you here alone? Why not ask for aid?"

"Because I am all that is left. After the Battle of the Iron Fell, my great-great grandfather bound the duty and magic of the Sentinels to our bloodline rather than being something that could be passed to volunteers. Very few can stand to be so close to the Chasm." He set the goblet down, his gaze fixed on it. "I could have summoned my beloved to me, but I didn't want her to have this life. Especially not when I know where it must end. How it will always end. In darkness, pain, oblivion, and death."

"I haven't found it difficult." It hadn't been difficult at all. "Perhaps that curse has faded?" He did not respond, so I continued, more tentative. "At least I can help you."

He gave a small smile then. "I do not want to impose. You have your own life, and you have done so much."

"If Zephyrus is happy here, I would not want to separate him from his family. And…to be able to serve a particular purpose for a time…I feel like I could accept that." I took a long sip of the mead. The sweet flavors exploded over my tongue, but the nerves spasming through me made it difficult to enjoy. "Besides, you shouldn't underestimate me. I will get those knot curses off you, and then you will be able to use all of your magic and fix the Chasm. Simple."

"Elegantly simple."

"You don't believe I can."

His brow creased at this, and then his hands dropped to his lap. "I…I am not used to having hope, Astraia. And false hope is devastating. It is not that I don't trust you. I do. It is that I must be prepared to do what I must, no matter what I feel. That it very likely may require that I lay down my own life. The hope that you offer is one of the most beautiful things I have considered. But I have to be ready. And I do not want you to carry this burden or feel that it is your responsibility."

I bit the inside of my lip as I nodded. "I'm going to prove to you that it can be done. But you're right. You should do what you must to prepare yourself. But when this is over and you are healed and freed from this curse, I will tell you I told you so."

He smiled then, leaning forward on his elbow. "If you succeed, I will savor your victory as my own. I will admit freely that you were right and I was wrong."

"I'll hold you to that," I said, lifting my goblet in another toast.

He lifted his in acceptance of my toast, and we ate in silence at first. Then we spoke of little nothings as we ate, anecdotes about the small parts of life. The ordinary pieces that made life so precious.

After he refilled my chalice a third time, I set down my fork. A question had formed in my mind and refused to pass. "When I severed the bond and scourged myself, the witch told me she could try to see his face and describe him to me so that I could change my mind if I wanted. I—I didn't have the nerve to do that. Was it the same for you? Did you ever see her? Your mate, I mean. Before you masked the bond?"

His hand stilled halfway to his goblet. Something flickered in his eyes—pain, longing, or perhaps regret. "Not in person. But I saw her face a few times in a scrying mirror. She was—is the most beautiful woman to ever walk or fly. All pale embers and sunlight. And a smile that both wounds and delights me. The first time I saw her was in one of the sand mirrors that distorts time. I don't even know if she has lived the point that I saw, but...she was more than I could have ever hoped for. It was almost enough to make me reconsider until I really contemplated what a life here would mean for her. But there was comfort there too. Because after I saw her, I knew that in time, she would find happiness. Another would love her and do better by her than I ever could."

It was my turn to shake my head. The sentiment was sweet but seemed misguided. "And how can you know that for certain? Life can be so cruel."

"Because...she will. She's strong and clever and tenacious." His gaze drifted to the bottle of mead, and he added more to his goblet before taking another long pull. "I pray for her. I mark runes for her. I debated at times going to speak with her, but that is far too dangerous. Caein says..."

The silence intensified between us. I waited, fingers still wrapped around the stem.

The tip of his tongue moistened his lips, then he shook his head. "Regardless, it is done. Do you think of the beloved you cut off?"

His gaze held mine fast, and though it was not a subject I had ever really opened up about, I could not help but speak. "Yes. Not as much now because it hurts. But...I comfort myself to think that he is happy somewhere. I hope he is. Then I realize there's so little I know."

"That would mean a great deal to him if he knew," he said quietly. "To know that someone loved you so much they were willing to deny themselves their own happiness to protect you. And there is sweetness in the bitterness of knowing that you long for him still."

"It does not feel sweet," I admitted. "Do you...do you struggle with your choice sometimes?"

"Every day. Every night." His hand fell back to his lap. And in that moment, there was only naked grief and sorrow in his eyes. "It became the hardest choice I ever made. Sometimes I have to remind myself why I made that choice to begin with. Remind myself of the importance of protecting her." He swallowed hard, his eyes soft and shining as if tears threatened. Though his voice softened, it did not falter. "And I suppose I would tell her what I would tell you. When all of this is said and done, I hope you have a good life. I hope you find peace and joy. That you make a home with someone who loves and cherishes you. Someone who sees who you are and realizes that they are blessed to be able to experience life with you. You may have severed your mate bond, but that does not mean you severed your ability to find happiness, love, peace, and joy. Nor does it mean you don't deserve to be loved."

His words struck me like a physical blow. I couldn't breathe for a moment, staring at him across the table as something inside my chest twisted. The raw sincerity in his voice, the vulnerability in his eyes—it was too much. No one had spoken to me with such naked emotion since...I couldn't remember when.

My throat tightened. What could I possibly say in response? My own words failed me. "Ramiel," I started.

A muscle worked in his jaw as he gathered himself. "I apologize," he said quietly. "I didn't mean to—" He stopped, then shook his head. "I need to be alone for a moment."

He rose from his chair, a slight tremor in his hands as he straightened his surcoat. "We'll speak more soon. There's something I want to discuss with you tomorrow. Something important."

I managed a nod, still unable to form words around the knot in my throat.

He hesitated at the doorway, his tall frame silhouetted against the light from the hall. For a breath, I thought he might turn back, might say something more. Instead, he drew a deep breath and continued on, leaving me alone in the candlelight.

16

STABLE CONVERSATIONS

The abrupt ending to the night left me reeling, yet somehow my sleep was peaceful. A warmth similar to the one that spread over me at the campsite the night Zephyrus left came over me as I rested, and it stirred a longing for family and home deep within me. The tang of magic on my tongue and in my lungs was not so unpleasant despite the sweet, dark flavor of plums when I woke.

Had I really told Ramiel so much of my past? It had been years since I had spoken to anyone of my family. When I was part of the Resistance, my family was spoken about mostly in generalities. They were images and symbols for inspiration, not the people with strengths, flaws, quirks, and oddities.

And Ramiel seemed to understand that. There had been no expectation from him when we talked. It was just… talking. The way people were supposed to.

And I wanted to save him even more than before. I flexed my fingers and tested my aura. The restoration of my own power was slower now than I liked, but it wasn't a sign of anything dangerous. Just fatigue. And that could be managed. Today I'd likely be testing my own limits if I pushed too hard on removing those cursed knots, but if I paced myself, perhaps I could finish this within four days.

For now, I needed to dress and prepare for the day.

When I reached into the wardrobe, a new garment brushed my fingertips. I drew it out, then smiled. It was a soft pink travel dress with a wrap-around skirt and matching leggings, the sash and inner lining a beautiful rich turquoise. Certainly not for blending in, and today I didn't want to blend in.

I dressed swiftly, braided my hair, and then slipped down to the stables, eager to see Zephyrus. The familiar scent of hay and dragons filled my nostrils as I pushed open the heavy wooden door, only to find Ramiel already there in charcoal riding leathers with dark blue accents. He spoke softly to Thalorion, stroking the ancient dragon's jaw.

My steps faltered, and a bolt of heated energy shot through me. I still didn't know what to say in response to last night, though I desperately wanted to. A shyness crept over me, something I rarely experienced. Should I perhaps leave and come back later?

Ramiel turned at my approach. A smile spread over his face, gentle and warm. The way it reached his eyes made my heart stumble. "Good morning. The dress suits you. It's good to see how well the wardrobe is fulfilling its role."

"Thank you," I said, fidgeting with the sash's embroidered edge. "I—about last night—I wanted to tell you how much it meant to me. I'm usually better with words, but I just—I wanted you to know no one has ever spoken to me like that. And I know I broke into your tower, but you have been so kind and courteous. More than I deserved. You aren't a frost fiend bastard, and I know that we have not known one another long, but I will do whatever I can to save you. Not just in removing the curse. But...beyond that."

My words felt so fragile and weak, incapable of conveying the depths of my feelings. I swallowed hard, trying to steady my voice. "I also wanted you to know that I think you deserve happiness and peace as well. And if your mate knew what you did for her—I think she'd be angry but only because her mate was someone who put her well-being so far above his own that he was willing to deny himself rather than cause her pain. But I also know she would forgive you for that as well because I would do the same."

His brow drew up. Those soft lines in his forehead deepened. "Astraia—" he started.

"And what I am asking is that you please don't give up on you," I said, rushing the words out. "I know that you have to remain steadfast. And you are. But please…know that you aren't alone."

The edges of his mouth pulled up. "I know that. I'm glad that you are here though. I did want to talk with you more." He stroked Thalorion's neck. "I need to travel the Seam of the Chasm today to check for weaknesses and see if I can spot the leviathan. This was what I wanted to ask you about. Would you care to join me? You could ride with me on Thalorion."

The invitation made my insides flutter. The thought of sitting behind Ramiel, arms wrapped around his waist as we soared through the sky...

A loud chuff interrupted my thoughts. Zephyrus was watching us, his amber eyes burning with unmistakable disapproval. He sat up straight in his cell, head canted sharply to the side. Thalorion gave a long sleepy yawn, then clicked his jaws shut, and shook his head. Another huff from Zephyrus followed.

I couldn't help but smile. "Someone's jealous." I started to cross over to him, then halted, remembering the pulse-port. "I'm not saying I wouldn't love to ride with you, and, I know this is up to you, but…would it be possible for me to go with you and ride Zephyrus? It would probably be safer if we had two dragons with us as opposed to just one."

There it was. Perhaps one of the most important questions and one which could sour everything. I hadn't actually removed all of the cursed knots, and he might conclude I was trying to manipulate or trick him. Especially after that heartfelt confession. Had I known what he was going to ask, I'd have waited. But it was too late for that now.

He narrowed his eyes at me a little as if evaluating my request, then he set his arms akimbo. "Well...I suppose there is wisdom in that. In truth, I am curious to see how you do riding. Especially given your instructor. But..."

I braced myself for conditions, for demands of additional vows or proof of my trustworthiness. After all, I could easily break my word once the spell was removed. And he needed to protect his position, especially with the importance of weaver dragons for maintaining the Chasm.

He glanced between Thalorion and Zephyrus and then smiled. "Very well."

"Is that all?" My mouth fell open. "No other terms? Do you want me to bind or vow—"

"No." He stepped forward, raising his hand. Silver light danced from his fingertips as he traced a complex pattern in the air. The magic shimmered around me, forming a long series of runes. They slid through the air and then coiled over my heart. The energy surged through me, dissolving the binding and filling my limbs with a pleasant sensation. "Don't make me regret it," he said, but there was a soft note in his voice. The way he looked at me made everything inside me spin.

I tried to stop a grin from splitting across my face. "My particular path of vengeance would be to rearrange your furniture and mix up your casting runes."

"I'm aware." His smile pulled a little higher. "Truly, I'm impressed you didn't start mixing the sands."

"I—I couldn't," I admitted, surprised to hear myself speaking the words. "It felt disproportionate. And wrong. Besides, I left you more than enough evidence elsewhere of my displeasure."

"So you did."

I wanted to say something witty in response, but the cell doors clanked open and Zephyrus's head appeared from the stable. "Zephyrus!"

I could barely get my arms around his neck at the base, but I flung myself at him nonetheless. He coiled around me and nearly flattened me with his snout in my hair and his scales scraping over me. Tears rolled down my cheeks. It had only been a few days, but at the beginning, I'd been so afraid of losing him forever.

He chuffed and then snorted. Another dragon call from within the stable made him lift his head. Before I could comment, he dropped his head again to nuzzle me. He snorted and huffed, checking me over with gentle nudges of his snout, examining my wrists and focusing on the one where the thread had cut me.

"I'm fine," I assured him, stroking the sensitive spot beneath his jaw. "Just a few scratches. Nothing serious."

He rumbled deep in his chest, unconvinced, then twisted his head to examine me from different angles with exaggerated concern. I laughed as he pushed his snout against my shoulder, nearly knocking me over. Then he nudged my wrist again.

"Do you smell something, Zephyrus?" Ramiel strode closer as Thalorion's cell opened. He slid his hand beneath my wrist and held it out.

Zephyrus growled again, then licked my wrist.

"What're you looking for?" I asked him, frowning. My wrist felt fine. I was still a little weary from yesterday's knotwork, but that was common.

He licked my wrist again, leaving a sheen of saliva. Grimacing, I tried to rub it clean. I glanced at Ramiel. "What's he looking for?"

"Not sure." Ramiel frowned as well. He put his hand on the side of Zephyrus's jaw, then shook his head. "It's something to remember. Pay attention for further signs. You're certain you're not in pain?"

"No, not at all." I didn't mention the fatigue. "Seems to me you both just worry." I leaned to the side, pressing my head once more to Zephyrus's scales. He still smelled like thunderstorms and the wild mountain air despite being in this warm stable.

He made a satisfied sound and settled, though his tail still twitched. Leaning down, he bumped my wrist again.

"Hmmm." Ramiel still appeared concerned. "Well, if you find any additional symptoms, tell me. It isn't wise to ignore a dragon's observations."

"I promise—I'm fine." I looked between both of them, quirking my lips. "I don't think I could hide it if I wasn't."

He gave another nod, then offered a small shrug. "I suppose it's possible he just enjoys the scent of jasmine and vanilla. It was certainly very pleasant last night. Especially with the cashmere."

My eyes widened. My scent had returned? I hadn't intended it. Hadn't even noticed it had returned. It had been years. My cheeks had to be blazing red now. "It is a pleasant scent…are we going to get flying?"

He chuckled. "Yes. But first…" He removed a small silver pendant from inside his surcoat. It held a series of runes etched into the pendant itself as well as the beads that formed the body of the necklace. "This is a Sentinel pendant. It's hard to hear much beyond the thunder of dragon wings and the roar of the wind in flight. So…we use these to speak into one another's minds. May I?" He gestured to my neck.

"Does it let us speak with the dragons?" I turned and lifted my braid, exposing the nape of my neck.

"No, it's just for us to speak to each other," Ramiel said, his voice low and close to my ear as he slipped the pendant around my neck. "I hope you don't find that too odious."

His fingers brushed against my skin as he fastened the clasp, lingering. A shiver ran through me that had nothing to do with the cool metal against my collarbone. He drew my braid back from my shoulder, his knuckles grazing the sensitive skin at the nape of my neck.

I barely repressed a shudder, hyperaware of his presence. His breath tickled my skin. That wonderful cologne of his made me want to back up against him and burrow closer. Knowing he liked my scent made it almost impossible to remain still. "No, that's not odious at all."

He adjusted the clasp once more, then circled to face me. "There. It's very simple. To make it work, all you must do is envision speaking the words to me. If that doesn't work, focus on imagining the words traveling through the pendant and to the person with whom you wish to speak. Now I'll be able to hear all your complaints about our flight."

I raised an eyebrow, suddenly aware of how close we stood and how delightfully warm he was. "Bold of you to assume I'd complain. I'll be far too busy showing off my superior skills."

His lips quirked up. "Is that a challenge, little gnat?"

"Only if you're brave enough to accept it," I replied. "Remember I learned dragon riding from an actual dragon."

"And I can't wait to witness your prowess, my lady." He spread his arms in a slight bow at the waist.

The heat spiked through me again. A delightful cacophony of sensations spread at the same time, and suddenly I didn't know where to put my hands or where to look. Had he really just called me that? I pretended to play into it, mirroring the bow but averting my face. "And I cannot wait to witness yours, my lord."

Zephyrus huffed and then nudged me, nearly toppling me. I shot him a glare and pushed my braid back over my shoulder.

Ramiel stepped back toward Thalorion as the elderly dragon emerged from his cell, stretching his massive wings and then tucking them back. The ancient dragon's dark green scales gleamed with silver-green patches in the torchlight.

"Ready for a morning flight, Old Man?" Ramiel asked, patting Thalorion's foreleg.

Thalorion's voice rumbled in his chest as he lowered his head for Ramiel to climb up. Though more subdued than Zephyrus's enthusiastic greeting, there was unmistakable affection in the way the old dragon watched Ramiel settle into position.

"Sounds like it's time," I said, looking up at Zephyrus.

Zephyrus lowered his head, and I climbed onto his thick neck, settling into the familiar spot just behind his horns. The dress and leggings were quite comfortable, the slits on the wraparound skirt allowing me to move with ease and the leggings protecting my thighs and calves. As soon as I was in position, he tossed his head, pretending to try to throw me off.

"Oh, hey now," I laughed, gripping tighter with my knees. "I didn't forget, all right? I know how to hold fast." That had been one of the early things he taught me. Was he worried about me and trying to mask it? Did he really think that not flying for a few days would mean I forgot everything?

He chuffed and gave his head another shake. When I stayed in place, he rumbled his approval, straightened his wings, and moved back to let Thalorion pass.

Thalorion grunted in response, then stretched his neck up, reared onto his hind legs, and bumped the center of the ceiling.

With the heavy clicking and clacking of gears, a portion of the ceiling retracted, revealing a stunning morning sky. Soft lavender and peach clouds drifted across an expanse of perfect blue, and the morning light streamed down in golden rays. Fresh air rushed in, carrying scents of pine, distant mountains, and the crisp tang of high altitude.

"Let them get into position," Ramiel called, gesturing

toward a circular platform at the center of the open ceiling. "They know what to do."

Zephyrus strode to the back spot on the platform, his tail straight and resting in a groove on the floor. Thalorion followed, positioning himself a little ahead of us with precision. The platform beneath hummed with hidden energy, the subtle vibrations reaching me even through Zephyrus.

I stole a glance at Ramiel, and my whole being ached. Sitting astride Thalorion, his silver hair catching the morning light, he looked every inch a regal prince. His back was straight, shoulders squared, one hand resting lightly on Thalorion's neck while the other rested on his thigh. No saddle, no reins. Just trust and skill. The confidence in his posture spoke of countless flights and pure trust between rider and dragon.

Metal groaned against metal as the hidden mechanisms engaged. The square platform we stood on shifted slightly, locking into position with a heavy thunk.

Looking up, I frowned at the opening. I'd made it before with the purple dragon, and that had been roomy enough. But neither Zephyrus nor Thalorion were small dragons. The space did look wide enough for them, but... just barely. There was no room for error.

Zephyrus huffed beneath me, completely unconcerned. Thalorion similarly showed no signs of worry, his ancient eyes calm and steady.

Ramiel glanced back and smiled. "Hold fast, Astraia," he said, voice clear through the pendant and in my ears. "It's an intense ride."

Before I could respond, the platform beneath us engaged, and all four of us shot up into the air.

17

INTO THE SKY

My stomach dropped as we shot toward the opening. I instinctively flattened myself against Zephyrus's neck, gripping with my knees and digging my fingers in the ridges along his horns.

Ramiel and Thalorion remained perfectly poised, arrow-straight as we rocketed upward. Neither moved a muscle, completely at ease with the violent ascent. The walls blurred around us, uncomfortably close but never touching.

Then suddenly—we burst into open sky. The brilliant morning light washed over us, momentarily blinding after the dimness of the stable. I gasped at the exhilarating sensation of being launched into the heavens, loving the rush and the pressure. I let my eyes slide shut.

Zephyrus's wings unfurled with a loud thrum. They caught the currents, steadying us in the vast blue expanse. Glorious—completely glorious—freedom and connection melding into joy. The wind in my face and pressing against me with such force. I loved it!

"Look over the Chasm," Ramiel called out, his voice clear as glass within my mind.

Forcing my eyes open, I adjusted my grip and looked down. I gasped.

The Chasm stretched beneath us like a living entity—a river of deep purple mist that cut through the rocky valley. It billowed and frothed, tendrils of vapor reaching upward before dissipating into the air. Sunlight caught the edges of the mist, turning them silver and pearl. The section nearest the tower was the thickest and largest, like the base of a bottle. But it tapered into a narrower line as we continued flying north.

"It's beautiful." I caught the bitter and sharp scents of powerful magic. They stung the inside of my nose and lungs but filled me with exhilaration

The mist churned and pulsed with an otherworldly rhythm, steaming where it met the jagged rocks. From this height, I could trace its path as it wound through the mountains, disappearing into the distant horizon.

In all my travels, I had never seen anything like this.

We soared and swept high above, following the Chasm's path. What a wondrous place this was. Jagged mountain peaks rose like sentinels around us, their snow-capped summits gleaming in the morning light. Forests of pine and ancient oak blanketed the slopes in a rich tapestry of green that contrasted sharply against the mist of the Chasm. As the clouds gathered and crowded the eastern sky, the shadows below merged with the mist.

Ramiel guided Thalorion closer, the ancient dragon's wings barely seeming to move as he glided beside us. "Few ever witness it from this perspective," he replied, his voice clear in my mind despite the rushing wind. "There it is in all its glory. What do you think, Astraia?"

"Terrifying and magnificent." I couldn't tear my eyes away from the spectacle below. It was as hypnotic to watch as fire on a hearth or ocean waves lapping at the shore.

Zephyrus banked, giving me an even better view of the magnificent purple expanse. The filtered morning sunlight caught the mist, creating rainbows that danced across its surface. Utterly stunning.

The dragons continued to fly north. My heart raced,

my blood surging with delight. "So what exactly is the purpose of this flight?" I asked.

Ramiel pointed toward the Chasm. In the warm sunlight, the mist seemed more lavender than true purple here. "The Chasm itself runs for fifteen miles down the Seam. We're going to fly along the length of it and see if we can spot our wounded leviathan. I saw some signs that he might be hunting this morning. He still seems relatively stable considering how bad his condition was. I've been trying to get it close enough to the rifts to see what injured it. If we can heal him, he'll calm and stop trying to break through the barrier."

"You're sure about that?" I asked, frowning. How could he possibly know with such certainty?

He nodded, his gaze fixed straight ahead as he maintained a steady grip on Thalorion's horns. "The leviathan isn't meant to live in our world. It's a creature of liminal space. That's why it belongs in the Chasm. It would be like a freshwater fish swimming in the ocean. But its demise wouldn't be immediate. It would take days, and in those days, it would go on an ever more violent rampage. It starts trying to break through the Chasm when the pain becomes too much for it like a creature thrashing in the shallows."

Pity coursed through me. I could imagine how I might respond if I couldn't breathe. The nightmares often included that. Flailing, thrashing, struggling. Praying desperately that something would provide relief. "And you're really going to help him?" An almost painful softness stirred within me. I wanted to hug him.

"If I can." Ramiel adjusted his silver carver gloves. His shoulders dropped a little. "That will stop the incursions for now. If I can't, I'll go as far as I can with healing him and then use the last of my magic to seal the Chasm with my death throes. Maybe drag the omenfang in with me. The leviathan will die from that. Most of the dragons too if they disobey and try to intervene. But it will buy time. After I'm gone—"

"You won't be gone. We're going to figure something out," I said, sharper than I intended. "Remember what we agreed."

He laughed at this. "Yes, my lady." He raised his eyebrow as he met my gaze, hair flowing beautifully in the wind. "Now…we aren't likely to run into any difficulties with this stretch. Hopefully nothing difficult in our entire inspection, but why don't we take advantage of this stretch? Show me your moves, gnat." His voice was at once distant and distorted by the wind but spoken directly into my mind. And that sparkle in his eyes set me ablaze.

I cast a coy glance in his direction, savoring the burn of excitement deep within my chest and gut. Then I looked down at Zephyrus. "He wants to see what you can do, big guy," I said, scratching him behind the ear. "Start with a barrel roll and then just do what feels good, eh?"

Zephyrus huffed, then trilled three times. His warning for me to hold tight. I clenched my muscles and leaned down, tucked tight against his muscular neck.

My world flipped upside down as Zephyrus tucked his wings and plummeted. Wind screamed past my ears. My stomach lurched into my throat.

Knots take me, I'd almost forgotten how intense this could be!

We plunged toward the Chasm, purple mist rushing up to meet us. At the last second, Zephyrus snapped his wings open and barrel-rolled right above the vapor. I clung to him, fingers digging into scale ridges, thighs clamped tight.

He banked hard left. Then right. My body shifted against his neck with each turn, but I adapted.

A flash of silvered dark-green scales—Thalorion cutting across our path.

Zephyrus twisted, spiraling under the larger dragon's belly. I glimpsed Ramiel's silver hair streaming behind him.

Instincts guided me. I anchored myself to Zephyrus with a knot spell. Magic shimmered gold between us.

Up. Down. Sideways. The horizon spun like a child's top.

Glorious and horrifying all at once!

Zephyrus corkscrewed through the air, wings tucked tight. My blood thundered in my ears. The world blurred into streaks of blue and purple and green.

We shot upward, climbing so fast my vision darkened at the edges. Then—nothing beneath us as we stalled at the peak.

"Zeph—"

We dropped backward, freefalling in a move that squeezed the breath from my lungs. Oh, polph, I hated this one! But nothing beat the way my blood roared when it finished.

Thalorion appeared directly below us. Zephyrus threaded between his wings, missing by inches. I could have sworn that when we flipped upside down that my hair brushed over Ramiel's head.

The dragons wove around each other in an aerial dance, so close I could see the individual scales on Thalorion's hide. My heart hammered against my ribs. Sweat slicked my palms.

Another dive. Another roll. Another impossible twist that should have thrown me clear.

But my magic held, golden threads binding us together as we carved patterns across the sky.

Then I heard the most wonderful sound of all echoing in my head: Ramiel laughing. Not just some mild laugh or light chuckle. Full abandoned belly laughs. The most delightful sound I'd ever heard.

"By all the runes that fall and rise, you are a true dragon rider," he said.

I loosed my grip on Zephyrus's horn enough to tap my hand to my temple and sketch a bow. "I had a magnificent teacher."

Zephyrus chuffed in agreement.

Thalorion swept a look at us and rumbled a strange growl. Ramiel just chuckled and patted the side of the massive beast's head. "I suspect the dragons would all agree that they are the best teachers of all."

I found myself laughing, even though it wasn't especially funny. It just felt good to laugh and share this flight with someone else. As much as I loved soaring with just Zephyrus, there was something about this that was even more meaningful. I noted that Ramiel's hair still looked so elegant and had all fallen back into smooth waves. "You use that enchantment, don't you?"

"What enchantment?" His brow creased as he canted his head.

"The one to keep your hair elegant and flowing," I said, unable to keep the teasing tone from my voice.

His smile pulled up higher before he shook his head, speaking with mock seriousness. "I have my vanity, gnat. All fae do. What good is magic if you can't do a little something to make yourself feel better? Or perhaps you actually are blessed with hair that is never tangled or unseemly? I've heard that some royals are attended by the wee ones with their blessings and gifts and gorgeous hair is one of those gifts."

I giggled. "No. When I was born, some fairies gifted me with some gifts but nothing *that* substantial. The only reason I know you're using the enchantment is because I do something similar. That was all me though. Not a gift from our tiny cousins."

The way he smiled at me just made me come undone inside. The air whipped about us. His enchantment must have been a bit stronger than mine because his hair never cut across his face. Off in the distance, more dragons called to one another, low and throaty.

He shook his head, still smiling. When he looked back at me, my breaths quickened. No one ever excited me so much. "Well, gnat," he said, his voice rippling through my mind. "You wear your magic well."

"As do you."

We flew awhile longer, Zephyrus and Thalorion sometimes making additional maneuvers. Once we dove into a cloud bank, the cold rush cutting through me and then contrasting with the sharpness of the wind and the heat of the sun. Steam rose off the dragons in delicate patterns.

It was everything I could have ever wanted. My blood and heart sang with happiness, my cheeks burning and sweat and cloud condensation rolling down my neck. Knots take me. I didn't want this flight to end.

"Do you ever skim down along the Chasm or go inside?" I asked. "Before the curse stopped you, I mean."

"Oh yes, frequently but only for brief periods," Ramiel responded. He nudged Thalorion, and he drew alongside us. Hearing his voice in my mind while the dragon wings thundered around us was a strange sensation. "The Chasm is a beautiful place. But it's not intended for us. Especially not someone like me who is cursed."

"What was here before the Chasm? Or what made it tear open?" I realized I didn't know what precisely it was. "I always heard that it was like a portal into the abyss. But from up here, it looks like it's…it's like seeing the ocean on a foggy morning."

He chuckled at this. "Well, depends on who you ask. I explored the Chasm before the curse prevented me from entering. When I was boy and more of my family lived, there were even times when we danced upon the barrier and played with the deep swifts. Most Sentinels believe that there was once a portal here. Something that reached into the other worlds. Then something happened to rip it out, and this is what remains. An opening into accessible liminal space with all the creatures that it holds. It's dangerous in there. But that's why it leads to other points of liminal space."

"What happens if you go in? You mentioned that it

reacts to you?" I scratched Zephyrus's ear as he adjusted our height. Thunder grumbled in the distance. We now flew among the spires and tors, the massive natural structures dwarfing both dragons.

"Everything becomes hostile. The barrier weakens, but the air and space within…thickens. It becomes like the barrier's surface all the way through. Chasm wraiths seem drawn to my presence. And it escalates swiftly from there." He shook his head. "Once, my presence summoned ten night reavers. We barely escaped alive. The longer I am in contact with the mist, the faster it accelerates and the thicker it is. It feels like drowning and as if you are moving through clear molasses."

"And that isn't how it is for everyone?" I adjusted the pendant, tilting my head as I listened. My shoulder started throbbing more, and my wrist stung.

"No, Sentinels frequently enter the Chasm. It's one of the ways we protect it. Anyone from our realm can survive up to three days in the Chasm unless you get pulled into the aether. That's a whole other problem. They say if your spirit gets trapped in there, you stay until the end of time. So avoid chasm wraiths at all costs. If they bite down on you or grab you, your spirit will start to separate from your body. Their poison is contact based. It gets in the skin as soon as they touch you."

"Is that similar to what the omenfang is doing to you?" A pang of fear cut deeper.

He nodded, his expression grim. "The omenfang will drain my power and weaken me physically until I can be dragged away, whether just in spirit or spirit and body. But chasm wraiths work faster and have to be in physical contact with you. There aren't any near the surface right now. So…if you wanted to take a peek, you could have Zephyrus dip inside. He's especially skilled at that. I can't go with you though. So be cautious."

I started to nod. Exploration delighted me, and seeing the inside of something like the Chasm should have thrilled me. But almost as fast, a sharp pang of discomfort twisted inside me. No. Absolutely not. I could not enter.

"Is everything all right?" he asked.

"Y-yes. I just…I suddenly felt like I shouldn't go down there." I pressed my hand to my chest. The cold of the wind suddenly seemed far stronger, and the sun's warmth no longer reached me. Of course, it wasn't quite as bright either because storm clouds were building and covering more of the sun. My body ached. Especially my shoulder.

As I rubbed my palm across the scars, I looked around. The Chasm was far narrower here than elsewhere, more like a broad river that a strong swimmer could cross in three full breaths. Back at the Eye of the Needle, it had been more like a great lake. The mountains closed in more, the trees sparser and the rocks far rougher. There were small islands of stone, some large enough for three dragons to land on. These islands were a few feet above the deeper mist, but curling wisps of the purple mist still coiled around the stones. "Shouldn't go in," I repeated.

He hummed in contemplation, his brow knitting. "Well, it isn't the safest of places, so it is perhaps for the best that you don't." He snapped his fingers and pointed. "Look! There he is! The leviathan." He pointed down at a lighter portion of the mist in the Chasm. "Thank the Creator. Thalorion, we've got to follow if we can. Pray he doesn't dive down."

I leaned down, my thighs gripping tight and holding me in place. It took a moment for me to see through the mist. But soon, my focus improved. Through the purple haze, I caught a glimpse of dark scales, bobbing and diving as if swimming. Based on the angle and the style of the scales, I suspected I was looking at the leviathan's neck. He was massive, easily forty feet in length based on this angle. Possibly larger. His build reminded me of the brine iguanas in the south, except that his scales were thick as pinecone scales but much tighter and coarser.

"Where are we following him to?" I asked.

"Wherever he goes as long as he stays near the barrier," Ramiel responded, his gaze scanning the Chasm. "We need to spot the kind of wound he has and potential solutions. Looks like he's just finished a meal. He's swimming it off. He'll return to sleep for a time after this, but then he'll be roused and raging, trying to get relief."

"Why does he come up here when he's in pain?"

"The barrier has natural healing elements within it. Especially near the Eye of the Needle. If we're fortunate, he'll be trying to push the wound into the barrier itself. Focus on the places where the barrier is dimmer. It will be stronger and better for soothing the wound."

Zephyrus dipped to the side as did Thalorion, tracking along after the leviathan.

Now that I knew how to focus on the mist and see into the Chasm better, I picked out far more details. It really was like the ocean, though it did not look as if there was water down there. Another pang of alarm cut through me when I saw the thinness of the barrier at some points. "Are we too low?" I asked. "Could something come up and attack us?" Visions of shark attacks and crocodile ambushes flashed into my mind.

A smile flickered on Ramiel's face, but his focus remained on the surface of the Chasm. Thalorion had slowed his pace. "As long as nothing breaks the surface, they won't come out here. The surface is weakest near the tower. It's why we built it there. Here it would take a great deliberate force sustained for almost a minute to break through from their side. And it couldn't be just any crea-ture. This leviathan though, he's on his way to rest."

"What about on our side?" I asked. The leviathan continued to move along beneath the mist. He was massive. At least twice the size of Thalorion.

"It'd take a lot less, so be careful. If you do slip in, don't panic. It will feel like you can't breathe, but I promise you can. You'll need to keep your movements slow and steady and envision the action as you do it. It's quite disorienting down there, but focus on reaching the rocks and climbing out. You will sink if you stop moving. Just don't let your spirit get separated from your body. You know how to resist that, right?"

"Yeah…but if it's a big enough and dangerous enough creature, it's just delaying the inevitable."

"The delay is what matters. Sometimes it's all we have."

Thunder grumbled in the distance. My eyes snapped up to the darkening storm clouds. That did not look good. The scent in the air was changing as well, that crisp smell of fresh rain and cold stone. "Any interactions with storms we should know about?"

Ramiel cut his gaze at the clouds. "It can get pretty strong and worsen swiftly. Keep an eye out for the winds. A rock slide out here would be problematic. We should probably go." He hummed with frustration, his grip on Thalorion's horns tightening, weighing our options.

I understood that look. He didn't want to leave until he determined what was wrong with the leviathan. If we could figure it out and get it resolved, it might buy more time before the leviathan tried to escape again and Ramiel had to use so much of his magic. "Would you stay and search if it was just you and Thalorion?" I asked.

He tore his gaze from the mist and met mine. Concern radiated in his eyes. Then he nodded. "I've been trying to identify the source of the leviathan's injury for weeks. Knowing what caused this lingering wound would allow us to potentially resolve it, and he only ever gets his head and neck through before we drive him back and he resumes resting and healing."

"Then we stay. I know how to handle myself," I responded. "Trust me."

He weighed this. A muscle jumped in his jaw. Then another nod. "Then stay close. Watch for gaps in the mist. Enhance your sight if you need to. This could get dangerous."

18

BEASTS OF THE STORM

Zephyrus and Thalorion slid over the Chasm, taking care not to even brush against the mist as we followed the leviathan. The sunlight faded as the clouds darkened. I scanned the mist and the Chasm below, searching for any indicators of the massive creature's wound. He remained near the surface. Dark shapes stirred down below, occasionally creating pulses of dull light and void-like circles.

The wind picked up. My eyes ached despite the runes helping my vision.

We wove deeper into the valley, the mountain walls rising up around us into steep stone barriers. The spires and tors were thicker and larger here, some of the tors especially concerning with the way the erosion had left large chunks rounded and precariously balanced. The weather-polished stone contrasted sharply with the coarser chunks that had been recently broken off. With the wind howling louder and whipping at my hair, it was hard to tell whether the unease I felt was from my surroundings or my instincts warning me about something else.

Zephyrus growled. His head flicked to the right. I followed the line of his sight, seeing the leviathan turn beneath the mist, rolling onto his side.

There!

A spear embedded deep in the leviathan's shoulder, the flesh around it inflamed and infected. "What happened? Is that a bone fae insignia in the end cap?"

Ramiel's eyes widened. He leaned over Thalorion's side, his expression grim. "Yes. It was one of the last incursions a few months ago. Some bounty hunters from the bone fae and others." Ramiel urged Thalorion higher and out to the right. The rushing thunder of the winds intensified. His jaw clenched as he considered this. "Bone fae spears like that are enchanted. It'll keep burrowing deeper. We need to avoid disturbing anything else down there. Especially the leviathan. If we agitate them too much, the leviathan may attack the barrier sooner rather than later. Ithoks. Poor creature. No wonder he's been so aggressive. This will take very particular healing magic."

"Can we heal him from here? I know some neutralizing spells." I leaned down hard on the right, peering at the leviathan. He swam through the murky Chasm, sometimes vanishing within the mist and then reappearing. From this angle, the barrier looked like little more than clear gel, but the leviathan moved with the poised ease of a crocodile in tropical waters. "I don't know what your magic usage is at, so if you can't, could you show me the runes to make and I heal him?"

"It can't be done from this—" Another thunderclap interrupted Ramiel, closer now. He frowned, a muscle in his jaw jumping. "That wound is deep, but I know how to counter bone fae magic. It may not even require significant magical expenditure—more a proper mixing of reagents. If we can get it to the leviathan, it might be enough to allow him to heal himself. At least to start. Then we'll finish with runes if needed."

My shoulder throbbed again, a dull ache spreading across my old scars. I rubbed it absently, careful to keep my expression neutral. "Let's try it. Any solution that won't trigger your curse or advance its timeline is worth attempting." Getting the leviathan to calm down and avoid the barrier meant we'd have more time to heal Ramiel as well. I'd definitely take that.

The wind intensified, whipping my hair across my face despite my enchantment. The storm clouds had advanced with alarming speed, turning the sky an ominous charcoal gray. Lightning flashed, followed by a rumble that vibrated through my chest, louder and stronger than Zephyrus's growl.

We were in deep among the mountains now, and that meant we had much less room for maneuvering. Zephyrus slid around one of the spires and between another set. He scraped his claws across the rough granite and then thrust his wings down again as he got through.

Another boom of thunder shattered the sky.

Ramiel swore under his breath as Thalorion wove through another set. He vanished from sight though I could still hear him clearly thanks to the pendant. "We stayed too long. I'm sorry. I was too focused on tracking the leviathan." He glanced at the darkening sky. "We need to leave. Now." Thalorion uttered a long series of deep trilling calls.

Zephyrus growled in response and started flying up away from the Chasm, Thalorion leading the way. I scrunched down to shield myself better. The sharpness of the weather intensified, warning that rain was soon coming. It worsened by the second. My fists clenched tighter around Zephyrus's horns.

The wind howled around us, buffeting our dragons as they fought to gain altitude. Then the rain came, pelting hard and sharp. Each droplet stung. Zephyrus huffed and steamed, his wing thrusts steady. Thunder boomed directly overhead.

I tightened my grip, chafing at our pace. It felt as if we were hardly moving. Even Thalorion was struggling as the winds grew stronger. Lightning cracked across the sky in a jagged formation, nearly blinding me. I flinched and ducked my head. We were still amid numerous spires and tors which kept the dragons from going full speed as they had to weave through.

The air tingled, the hairs on my arms and head prickling. My focus snapped to a tall stone column that jutted up just a few feet away.

ZRAKT.

A blinding flash of light and a deafening crack shattered the sky. Thread rot! I barely had time to comprehend it. The bolt of lightning struck a copper-veined spire behind us.

My eyes widened. Stone shattered, chunks breaking free and crashing into a neighboring tor. The entire formation groaned, then collapsed directly toward us.

"Bank hard!" Ramiel shouted.

Zephyrus veered right as Thalorion swerved left, both dragons, desperately trying to escape the falling debris. I flung my right hand up. My magic zinged and spun over my fingertips in a ragged net. Narrowly, I swept it up and knocked one of the pieces away. Another chunk of the jagged rock still cut through and clipped Zephyrus's side. He roared in pain, faltering mid-air, wings stuttering.

"Zephyrus!" I clung to him as we dipped dangerously low. Vaguely I heard Ramiel shout something, his words booming in my mind but too distorted for me to follow.

Below us, the rocks struck the mist-covered surface of the Chasm. Instead of sinking through, they hung suspended, stretching the barrier like weights on a taut sheet, their points sinking into the gel-like substance.

Zephyrus struggled to regain altitude, his wing movements uneven. Blood seeped out from under the bruised and twisted scales from his wounded side.

I focused my magic, weaving golden threads into a healing knot. The poultice formed beneath my fingers, and I shot it down against his scales. His breaths were ragged, his shoulders rolling with the movement of his wings desperately seeking momentum.

"Come on, Zeph. You can do this," I urged.

Another gust knocked us sideways. My grip slipped, and I slid across Zephyrus's neck. No! I scrambled to get up, but my right hand plunged into a broad tendril of purple mist.

Cold—bone-deep, soul-numbing cold—shot up my arm. My vision blurred. Knots take me! What was that? I couldn't even breathe! Then my lungs loosed, but black dots danced in my vision.

Droplets of Zephyrus's blood fell into the mist like fat ruby teardrops. The tang of iron filled my nostrils. "You're all right, big guy, you're all right," I gasped, my right arm hanging limp and a band of fire along my wrist.

"Astraia!" Ramiel shouted, his voice now distant despite the pendant. "Astraia, get out of the mist. It's reacting to you!"

Howls rose from the depths—hungry, furious sounds that made my blood freeze.

The mist churned and bubbled below. the barrier warping and falling. My right arm hung limp, burning with cold fire from where I'd touched the purple barrier. I needed to focus. We needed height. "Up, Zephyrus! Higher!"

He pumped his wings, each beat labored. Blood oozed from his side, slowed by my healing poultice but not stopped. The storm's fury intensified, rain pelting us like tiny arrows.

Another shriek cut through the thunder, high-pitched and hungry.

Storm wyrms. Three emerged from the clouds, blue eyes glowing and serpentine bodies crackling with lightning-blue energy. They spiraled toward us, jaws open, rows of needle-sharp teeth bared. Two more storm wyrms appeared in the thunderhead. They hissed.

Thread rot!

The first wyrm dove at us. Zephyrus banked hard right again, nearly throwing me off. My wrist flared with pain so intense I screamed. It felt like something was sawing through bone and sinew, trying to sever my hand.

Ramiel and Thalorion swooped in from above. The old dragon's jaws caught one wyrm mid-air, snapped its neck, and flung it away.

Ramiel cut a series of silver runes that hung in the air and then wrapped around the other wyrm, sending it plummeting. It struck the surface of the Chasm, landing in the mist and on that strange slick gel-like substance. Its body twitched as it started to sink down with some of the fallen rocks, straining the barrier.

The third wyrm circled back, aiming for Zephyrus's injured side.

Zephyrus's breaths wheezed as he shot around one of the massive tors, talons scraping on the rounded stone. He thrust his wings down harder. The right one wasn't as strong.

I wove a golden knot with my left hand, fingers dancing and shaking despite the pain. "Hold fast, big guy," I gasped as I slapped the spell onto his side. The magic spread like warm honey, rolling along his scales.

Zephyrus made that chirring trill, warning me. I clenched my legs tight and wrapped my arm around his horns.

The world turned upside down. His wings stretched straight up and his body lengthened. We shot between two spires. The storm wyrm behind us followed, devouring the distance.

Ramiel pulled something from his belt—a curved horn etched with symbols. He put it to his lips and blew. A low, piercing call vibrated out into the air. A sharp scent like lightning and sulfur flared through the air, and a long beam of silver light formed in the sky like an eye irising open.

Zephyrus flew through another of the spires, trying to shake the storm wyrm that pursued us. Two more storm wyrms emerged from the clouds and swept toward Thalorion and Ramiel.

Below, the Chasm's surface bubbled violently. The mist coiled and thickened where... something... pushed against it from beneath the dead storm warm at the weakest point in the barrier.

My wrist throbbed. Horror poured through my body. I knew what that was instinctually. Not the leviathan.

No.

Oily claws pushed through the gel, trying to rupture the surface. Where it touched, color leached away, leaving nothing but opaque shapes.

A chasm wraith.

Zephyrus faltered again, drawing up just in time as another storm wyrm cut in front of us. The purple mist boiled around us, obscuring my vision.

"Get out of the mist, Astraia!" Ramiel shouted. His voice thundered in my ears, fear clear. "The barrier is weakening."

"Up, Zephyrus!" I urged him, leaning lower near his ear. "Come on, big guy. Come on. You can do this."

My right arm was still useless, that burning pain through my wrist and my scars throbbing as if I had just burned myself.

The color drained from the storm wyrm as the surface rippled and warped beneath it. The sharp scales of the dead dragon along with the pressure of the rocks cut deeper. A large bubble formed near it—growing—growing.

The rocks sliced through.

Claws swept up at once and grabbed the storm wyrm like it was a toy. All the color faded as the chasm wraith tore through the barrier of the Chasm. It sluiced and slicked off its massive form as it rose from the depths, a creature that seemed to be made of oil and with ever changing features that were impossible to focus on. It gulped the dead creature down in a single bite.

The surface of the Chasm bubbled again as more dark

forms pressed up. Zephyrus swept his wings down again in a desperate bid to gain more altitude. Ramiel and Thalorion battled more of the storm wyrms as that column of light in the sky flared and expanded wider and wider.

We had to get higher.

The chasm wraith twisted toward us. Though it had no eyes, I knew in my gut that it had focused on me.

Thread rot!

My breaths fled me. Everything spiraled down to that horrific creature as it snapped its hand out. Before I could even cry out, it seized me.

The whole world went ice cold as it lifted me away from Zephyrus. Some part of me was tearing. Color fled as my skin turned ashen. Black dots filled my gaze.

No! Let go. Let go!

I was tearing apart, my spirit desperately struggling to escape that soul-wrenching cold.

Ground. Breathe. I struggled to lift my head, pulling in memories. I was alive. I lived. My family's faces flickered through my mind. Each one darted out of my consciousness, thrusting me back into the void of nothingness.

The chasm wraith growled at me, claws clutching tighter as it brought me back to its rapidly distorting face. My heat and strength seeped away at every point of contact as its poisonous slime worked over me, but I held fast, rifling through my mind for a memory strong enough to ground me until I could get free.

One scene cut into my mind.

Those violet eyes gone soft and that deep voice low in my ears as I remembered him sitting across from me as we sipped mead in the calm: *"I would tell her what I would tell you. When all of this is said and done, I hope you have a good life. I hope you find peace and joy. That you make a home with someone who loves and cherishes you. Someone who sees who you are and realizes that they are blessed to be able to experience life with you. You may have severed your mate bond, but that does not mean you severed your ability to find happiness, love, peace, and joy."*

My spirit flailed and struggled in the chasm wraith's grasp. But I was here. I wasn't leaving. I had a future. I had a hope. And I—I wanted that life Ramiel spoke of. I...I wanted him.

If I got out of this, I was going to tell Ramiel I wanted to be with him. I loved him. I did. Knots take me, I loved him!

Ramiel and Thalorion shot around the chasm wraith. Ramiel carved out five runes in silver. His hands sliced through the air like blades, forming burning silver lines. Then the runes snapped out and embedded in the chasm wraith.

A deafening bellow shook the world around me. Zephyrus shot through the chasm wraith, his jaws snapping on the dark smoke. Color drained from him as he did, and the strangled roaring yelp he made cut me to my core.

But his attack worked with the runes. The chasm wraith evaporated. Black tendrils of greasy smoke vanished into the purple mist.

The world slowed as I sailed through the air and Zephyrus crashed in the opposite direction.

"Pulseport up to me!" Ramiel stretched out his arm overhead, staring down at me with terror in his eyes. His voice echoed in my mind.

It was perfectly clear. I'd land in the Chasm if I didn't act fast. But Zephyrus struck that stone island and rolled, his body limp. Pebbles ricocheted off. The force of his bulk and temporary weakness from the wraith would send him over the edge.

If I abandoned Zephyrus here, he'd be vulnerable. He was bleeding and stunned.

It'd be easier for me to get out of the Chasm than Zephyrus.

I had just enough magic left. My focus homed in on Zephyrus, and I wove a shaking lasso of knotted gold and swung it over. Only three strands and five loose knots. It barely shot over Zephyrus and stopped him from careening off the edge. Yes! It was enough! Some of the color had returned to his jaws and head.

SLICK!

Clinging greasy cold shot up my feet, my legs, my hips, my belly, my chest, my arms, my neck—my face!

I had plunged into the rift in the Chasm. The cold gel-like substance swept over me, freezing me and choking me at once as it engulfed my entire body.

19

CONNECTED

*S*hock radiated through me as I struggled in the strange gel of the Chasm.

"Astraia! Astraia, keep moving. Get to the side. I'm coming for you." Ramiel's voice echoed in my mind. "Keep moving. If you stop moving, you'll sink. But don't pulse-port. Get to the rocks and climb."

"I can't breathe!" Panic cut through me, fiercer than the cold as that gel filled my nose and mouth despite trying to keep it out. It tasted of algae and mud and rot, relentless and all encompassing.

"You can. It's an illusion. I swear it." The panic in Ramiel's mind voice did not comfort me. "Zephyrus!" Ramiel bellowed, his voice remaining in my mind though he was no longer talking to me. "Zephyrus, I command you: do not enter after her. You'll just trap both of you. We'll get her out. Giselle, Veyruneth, flank him! Get him strong."

The black dots spiraled over my vision. I remembered what he had said. I envisioned myself breathing and swimming. My limbs moved as if they had weights tied at every joint. My lungs ached. But I moved and I breathed, slowly —painfully slowly.

Above, I could hear Zephyrus's desperate roars dimly.

He was up! Two other dragons—the purple and the dark green-blue one shot across my field of vision. How had they gotten here so fast?

I pushed forward in the substance filling the Chasm, swimming through the purple mist and slick gel toward the nearest rock formation. My right arm was useless, that pain spreading from my wrist up to my burning shoulder. Each movement felt like dragging myself through molasses, and it immediately filled in after I moved farther, preventing me from gaining any momentum.

The cold seeped deeper, beyond flesh and bone.

Down below, red eyes opened. Multiple sets. Something brushed against my leg, greasy but solid.

"Hold on, Astraia. I'm coming for you. Just reach the rocks." Ramiel's voice echoed in my ears. "Get to the rocks, and I'll get you out!"

I twisted my head back, feeling that horrible cold slick substance filling my ears and mouth. Up above, I vaguely saw the dragons flying. Zephyrus's roar echoed louder, rageful and terrified.

Another greasy claw scraped against my leg. I yelped and surged forward, my fingers scrabbling against the rock. The red eyes below swam up closer. Three, four, five separate sets. I hooked my hand into a pocket in the granite and dragged myself closer.

The world exploded. Light and energy flared through. A hand seized me by the arm and dragged me up. Blessed warmth engulfed me as Ramiel pulled me into his arms. The greasy cold fled, all slicking off into the rift below. Claws swiped into that space, and a gurgling roar followed.

"I've got you. I've got you now," Ramiel said as Thalorion thrust his wings down.

We shot back up into the sky as the purple mist screamed. Runes hung in the air at regular intervals.

Four dragons swept down and snatched them up. The others wove back and forth. Silver light shone as they unraveled the runes, and the dragons worked in concert to weave the rift shut.

"Z-Zephyrus—" I stammered. I couldn't spot him yet, but my sight was limited to what I could see without turning my head. Where was he?

"He's fine. He's coming with us." Ramiel's hand pressed my head to his chest as he hugged me tight. His heart thundered against my ear. Even in my weakness, I could hear the straining of the curse as it tried to tighten around him and summon the omenfang. The wind didn't tug on my hair or chill me as I expected, so I guessed he had used some other charm or spell to shield us. I tried to tell him to let it go, to save his energy, but he shushed me as if he guessed. "Just breathe for me and hold fast, gnat. You're going to make it."

"I feel vile," I gasped weakly, my eyes watering.

His mouth quirked, his eyes bright with concern. "The curse makes it worse. Much worse." His thumb smoothed my hair back from my face, stroking my cheek. "My curse got on you somehow. It's still on me, but it's also on you. It shouldn't have gone like this. It didn't just change a little. It's like a full transference. Like it grew into you."

The threads. My wrist still burned, and I could see them trying to burrow in. Curses often changed. Was this just that? Maybe. My eyes slid shut. I didn't even know how Ramiel had gotten to me or how he did what he did. But if he hadn't, I would have died.

As Thalorion thundered up into the sky, Ramiel wrapped his cloak around me and settled me tight against his chest. "Just keep breathing," he whispered.

I managed a shaky nod.

He cut his hand across the air. A bolt of silver light struck the sky, and a long line formed, blinking ever wider. Thalorion circled it. "We're going to get out of here, gnat. I'm going to get you back home. You need rest. Rest and warmth and food. It's all right. Just stay awake, all right?"

My very spirit ached. I was raw. The throbbing in my

shoulder had intensified. I watched as the dragons began sealing up the Chasm in that complex aerial dance similar to the one they performed before. The purple mist closed in as the weak points in the Chasm vanished as if they had never been there. Except for one. The one where the chasm wraith had broken free and seized me. Maybe it was the curse or my magic or a combination that made it more resistant.

Ramiel hissed with frustration. That tension radiated through him. My hand settled over his heart. It wasn't beating as steadily as it should. He'd almost reached his limit. The knots were pulsing around his heart. I could feel them even from here. They were tightening and clenching, gripping him tighter.

I flexed my fingers against his chest, trying desperately to summon up some of my magic. I felt empty and chafed, but there—there was a little more in there. I summoned it as best I could.

"What are you doing?" he scowled as he looked down at me. His attention had to snap back to the runes.

"Breathing room." My tongue struggled with the words. I couldn't fully remove the knots right now, but I knew what was coming. I focused instead on loosening them. I was too weak to even cut one free. If I could just give him more space before they tightened after his magic expenditure, then he could breathe better. And if he could breathe better, he could fight the omenfang.

"Don't risk yourself, Astraia." His voice shook a little. "You've done enough. You've been through enough. Just trust me. I'll get you home safe. It's easier to fight it when we're in the tower. Just stay awake."

I just shook my head, breathing him in. Even with the afternotes of that horrid gel in my lungs and mouth, I could smell him and his woodsy and calming scents. My magic smelled more like burning cashmere now.

He lifted his gloved hand as Thalorion wheeled around.

He then carved more runes into the air. His breath hitched, a pained gasp choking him. He curled over me.

My fingers dug into his chest again. My magic faltered. It sputtered from my core, down my left arm, and into my fingertips. Loosen. Loosen! The threads writhed and stuttered beneath my grip. It lit up within his chest again. I could—I could almost see the central thread. The one thread I desperately needed to undo this curse once and for all.

His breaths shaking, he finished carving the last of the runes. The dragons darted in and seized them. That line of light had expanded. It opened into a silver-rimmed hole large enough for a full-grown dragon to fly through. The Eye of the Needle was on the other side, the tower jutting out of the forest and framed by storm clouds.

Thunderheads billowed behind us, but a darker spiral cloud formed. The red eyes of the spectral omenfang burned within. It had not yet taken its form. The stench of burning metal filled the air. Fear clutched me, locking me into place. It was coming.

"Faster, Thalorion!" Ramiel clutched me close, his body hunching over mine as if to shield me.

My hand clutched weakly at his tunic, fingers hooking in his pendant and the masking charm. Cold—so cold. But his heart was racing, thudding and constricting within the bonds of the curse. My own heart felt as if it was being crushed.

Lightning arced in the sky.

Zephyrus bellowed again. He shot up and passed through the omenfang. It vanished for a moment, the force of the wind whipping him back.

The other dragons took turns flying through the omenfang's oncoming storm cloud.

We shot through the portal into the air just above the tower. Thalorion's massive wings beat furiously against the storm winds. Ramiel's arms remained locked around me, his body shielding and warming me. I struggled to even keep my eyes open, the cold swallowing me.

A furious roar announced Zephyrus's arrival. He flew through the portal behind us, his scales gleaming with rain water and mist.

Through the portal, the dark column of smoke churned closer. One by one, the remaining dragons passed through. Each time they disrupted the omenfang, but it always reformed.

"The omenfang—" I tried to warn, but my voice emerged as little more than a rasp.

"I know." Ramiel's voice was strained. "The dragons are buying us time. It's not at full strength like it was the last time. We have to get inside."

My vision blurred as the other weaver dragons darted and weaved through the air, striking at the gathering darkness that pursued us.

As we neared the Eye of the Needle, Ramiel shifted me in his arms, pulling me tighter against his chest. His heartbeat hammered against my ear, struggling against those cursed threads I'd tried to loosen.

"Hold on," he whispered.

Without warning, he leapt from Thalorion's back, still clutching me to him. My stomach lurched as we plummeted through open air for a terrifying moment before the familiar disorienting sensation of pulseporting enveloped us.

We materialized in his library, the books rustling and the pages fluttering. The items on the desk jostled, the spindle with the thread falling off the edge and spinning on the floor in a stream of silver thread.

"Caein!" Ramiel called out, his voice strained as he laid me on a plush couch. A fire sprang up within the carved marble fireplace, but the heat did not reach me.

I tried to push myself upright but collapsed. The burning in my wrist intensified. I had to tell him.

"You'll be fine," Ramiel said, brushing my hair from my

face. His eyes held a desperate intensity that frightened me. "I'm not going to lose you now."

My eyelids were so heavy. I couldn't keep them up. My head slumped onto the soft arm of the couch. My spirit might not have been torn out, but I felt fragile. With the omenfang coming, either of us could die. And I had to—I had to tell Ramiel what I felt. That I loved him. The words burned in my throat, desperate to escape, but my lips wouldn't form them. Darkness edged my vision as consciousness slipped away.

"Ramiel, what happened?" Caein's voice floated into the room.

"A chasm wraith got her. It didn't fully rip her spirit out, but the curse—my curse—it's spreading to her. It wasn't a transformation. It treated her as if she was me." Ramiel's voice cracked. "We need to—"

The scent of burning metal filled the air, acrid and overwhelming. A dark cloud materialized in the center of the room, red eyes forming within its depths.

Ramiel stepped between the cloud and me, positioning his hands and slicing through the air. The runes burned bright. "Leave now, foul beast! I have no time for your games."

The omenfang's gaze hinged from Ramiel to me as the flames in the fireplace sputtered.

Those glowing red eyes burned into me, and my spirit screamed and tugged as if it might rip free. Those red eyes bore into mine even as my eyelids dragged shut again. It bared its dark teeth in a horrifying smile.

It was coming for me.

Ramiel swore, commanding it to fight him. He tried to cut in front of it.

I had to get up. Weave a net. Cut a knot. Something. Anything!

My body refused to respond, the chasm wraith's poison still pulling at my spirit and my consciousness. Nothing in my body responded. My vision blurred and hazed.

Vaguely I heard the battle continuing within the tower itself. Had a dragon broken in? Zephyrus's snarling bellows filled my ears. But the terror from the omenfang pressed in upon my consciousness.

Caein called out, shouting to Ramiel about something. Some ward or sigil to activate. It was garbled.

The omenfang loomed over me in my mind's eye. I forced my eyes open to make it vanish, the heaviness in my body present. Ramiel summoned the shadow creature to battle. He cut runes into the air. The light around his heart burned. The loosening had worked. For now. Not enough to free him entirely, but enough to strengthen him and allow him to fight.

And the omenfang—it wasn't paying attention to him now. It had found me.

The omenfang leaned back on its tail.

I struggled to push up, my hands shaking as I tried to summon my shield. My right arm no longer even felt as if it was there.

Black and violet static erupted over me. All the air vanished from my lungs. I—I couldn't breathe. Could barely move. My fingertips froze.

Then everything went still and silver light exploded.

As my vision cleared, Ramiel leaned over me, his arms wrapping tight around me as he brought me to his chest. "No, not like this. Please. Not like this. No. She doesn't deserve this. Astraia, please. Astraia, answer me! Don't die! Don't. Please! Hold fast, gnat. Hold fast!" His voice echoed in my thoughts as well as my ears, the pendant connecting us.

He put me back on the couch. I must have fallen off before. Had I? I—I couldn't remember. It was blurring.

Cold paint sloshed over me as he struggled to paint the runes on my chest.

"No, please. Please," he said, his voice shaking. Tears struck my cheek. Not mine. His?

I tried to lift my head, but all was blurred.

He pressed his forehead against mine. "I love you, Astraia. I love you so much. Please don't die. Please. I won't give up on you."

My heart swelled in response. Tears pricked my eyes. More than anything I wanted to say that I felt the same. Because I did. I felt as if I had always known him, and what I wanted now as much as I wanted to keep Zephyrus safe was to have a life with him. All the pieces snapped into place in this moment.

But the exhaustion kept me from speaking, and then…

REGRETS

I woke with sunlight streaming over my face and something fussing at the blankets. Caein loomed over me, the air shifting and shimmering in response to his presence. "You're awake. Oh, thank all that is good. We thought we'd lost you."

My eyelids fluttered. The brightness stung my eyes. My body protested, abnormally stiff and sluggish, my fingers and toes cold. Slowly I sat up and began to massage my fingers, then my feet. "I think you almost did. The omenfang, but also—"

"The chasm wraith." Caein sighed. His voice drew closer to my face. "Yes, I know. You need to rest. After a brush with chasm wraiths, your spirit will be especially raw and worn. Another encounter might let them sever you entirely and drag you into one of the liminal realms where you would be trapped until the end of time itself. The same holds true with the omenfang. You nearly died."

"I need to find Ramiel." I pressed myself out of the bed slowly, my head spinning with the movement. My insides clenched and my knees threatened to buckle as I remembered how he had protected and cradled me—how he had said he loved me. My breaths tightened. I had to tell him.

"I don't recommend it. Not right now. He is—"

"What's wrong?" My attention snapped up to the ceiling. Caein didn't usually sound this nervous. "Was someone hurt? Is Zephyrus all right?"

"Nothing is wrong," Caein started.

Darkness moved in the corner of the room. Another odd chill pulsed through me. That shadowy tentacle creature. It vanished almost as soon as I spotted it. I raised an eyebrow. Why did the energy in this room feel so off right now?

Caein sighed. "He knows you're awake."

"Is that a bad thing?" My stomach flip-flopped when I remembered what he'd said to me. Now I could say it back. As I stretched, I noticed how different everything felt physically as well as emotionally. The soft, magical hum was gone. I'd barely noticed it until it was gone.

"He's worried. You should know he doesn't do well when he's worried, but he wants to speak with you. He wanted me to send you down as soon as you woke."

"Well, I want to see him too." I opened the wardrobe. To my surprise, only my original clothing was present. My aura confirmed that the magic of the wardrobe was…gone. The garments were clean and fully mended though. "You're sure nothing is wrong?"

"Ramiel said you discovered the source of the leviathan's wound. He's confident that it can be countered, but what happened to you made him realize some things. It would be wise to give him more time than even he thinks he needs."

Yes, I'd realized some things as well. The thought of waiting any longer burned against every fiber of my being. "I need to talk to him as soon as possible." Stepping behind the silk dressing screen, I stripped off the shift and pulled on my old riding leathers. They smelled faintly of cedar and lavender with a touch of smoky soap.

"No, no, there's nothing that needs to be said right now that can't wait for another few hours or perhaps even a day. Please rest." Caein's voice hovered more insistently above me.

I strode to the door. It resisted my pull. "Caein," I said, my voice sharpening. "Ramiel and I need to talk."

The door shifted as if Caein pressed harder against it. "Just let him come to understand what has happened. What happened yesterday was significant for him."

I cut my gaze up at the ceiling. "You know about what he said then."

"I'm not certain what you're talking about." His voice was strained. "Why don't you come make bread with me? The conversation will be better after you have something to eat. I could use the help."

"I'll help you, but first, I have to talk to Ramiel." I wrenched the door open and hurried down the hall. With each step, I regained more of my strength, a giddiness making me even shakier. The ache in my shoulder intensified though. It was getting quite annoying. The sleep had been deep and restful though, and already I could feel the restoration of my magic returning faster than I had expected.

I raced to the staircase and down to the stable. There was so much I needed to tell him. That I loved him. And if I had succeeded in loosening the cursed knots around his heart—and it seemed that I had—that meant he had more time. With more time, that meant we would figure out how to get that central thread out and purge whatever happened with the omenfang from me. And with that added time, I wanted to spend it with him.

The stable doors stood ajar. Sunlight spilled across the stone floor, casting long shadows through the entrance. Bird songs filtered in from outside, their cheerful melodies bright but a little off.

I halted at the threshold, my hand grasping the door-jamb for support.

Zephyrus stood near the open double doors on the outer wall, his magnificent blue scales catching the sunlight. He wasn't moving, his head low, ears flattened against his skull. He wouldn't meet my gaze. All the other dragons were silent, mostly clustered together in one of the closer cells. Thalorion sat alone, his forelegs outstretched and his head high, his long whiskers brushing the flagstones. But even he seemed muted, his head slightly bowed.

Ramiel stood beside Zephyrus, shoulders squared, posture rigid. When he turned to face me, there wasn't a trace of warmth. His face was an alabaster mask, purple eyes flat and dull as cheap scuffed amethysts.

"You're awake," he said, the words clipped. None of the tenderness from before remained. This wasn't the same man who had pleaded with me not to die or wept over me.

My throat tightened, and my stomach twisted. Suddenly I wished I had listened to Caein. "Ramiel, I—"

"Your timing is exceptional." He gestured toward Zephyrus. "He wishes to leave. Per your vow, you will depart with him."

My steps slow, I looked from Ramiel's cold expression to Zephyrus's dejected posture. What had happened in the hours I'd been unconscious? "What about the omenfang? The curse?" I reached for his arm.

He drew away, his expression hardening even more. "Those are my concerns, not yours." His gaze flickered to my wrist. "The danger to you is too great. I was... mistaken... to involve you further. You did enough, and I am grateful for that. But now it's time for you to go."

I squared my own shoulders. His words cut across my heart like a blade. "What happened yesterday—"

"I told you to pulseport to me. I told you that the Chasm was reacting to you. Somehow the curse from the omenfang transferred into you, and it made the Chasm far worse for you. More dangerous for all of us. And more than that, you chose to save Zephyrus instead of letting me save you at that moment."

Lifting my chin, I braced myself. No one had spoken to

me this way for years, and suddenly I felt as small and weak as I had at the start of the Resistance. "I chose Zephyrus because he would have died if I had abandoned him."

Ramiel stared at me hard, unblinking. There was no softness or gentleness in his eyes. Only ice. "Perhaps. But your presence in the Chasm, like mine, worsened it and made it far more dangerous for everyone including Zephyrus." He held up his hand, silencing me before I could speak another word. "I do not fault you. You honored the bond between dragon and rider as one born to it. Your loyalty to him is profound as is his to you. Your life was at stake. You had to choose between obeying me and saving your dragon. You chose your dragon. So take him and go."

"Ramiel, please don't do this." My voice thickened. "We—"

"You gave me your word. You vowed that if Zephyrus wished to go, you would go with him. Do you intend to become a vow breaker?"

The ice in his voice chilled me to my soul. I swallowed hard. Tears burned my eyes, but I held them back. "I only say what I mean."

"Then go. I'm aware of your little crush on me. It seems there has been something of a misunderstanding between us. Let me make this explicitly clear: there is nothing between us. Not now. Not ever. We are on separate paths."

Those words struck me like a blow. I sought an answer, but my mind spun. "You—you said you loved me." My voice cracked. I hated how pathetic I sounded.

His expression changed for just a moment. A flash of pain perhaps. Or was it regret? "Did I?" He remained rigid. "The poison from a chasm wraith's grasp can be quite potent and cause exceptionally realistic hallucinations. I suspect that is what is at work."

"But...I—I love you."

Every muscle in his body tightened. His throat bobbed.

"Then that is most unfortunate for you. In time it will pass. You have my pity."

"I don't want your pity!" My hands balled into fists as I struggled to breathe. I wasn't going to cry in front of this man. "I know what I heard, and I know what I felt! I wasn't hallucinating."

He did not even flinch now, but his eyebrow arched. "Do not misunderstand. I do care for you. And that's why you should leave. Yesterday you asked me to trust your judgment. Matters did not go as intended, and while they may not be precisely as you remembered, I did find myself distracted and incapable of doing what needed to be done. You were also far more vulnerable to the harm of the Chasm than I anticipated, and that distracted me, which put everyone in more danger. You are loyal, Astraia. I commend you for that. But your stubbornness overturns your wisdom. Zephyrus's desire to leave is understandable."

My mouth went dry. Each word was a blow against my very being. What could I even say in response?

"I renounce your offer to help me. You have done more than enough, and you have my gratitude. The reagents are being finalized. We know why the leviathan attacks. It will be simple enough to fashion a cure."

"But…the Chasm—your curse—"

"It will be dealt with. Even beyond yesterday, I had a breakthrough while you were recovering," he said. The faint smile was forced, cold and sharp, not reaching his eyes. He moved farther away from me and gestured with a broad sweep of his arm toward the door. "You are no longer needed, Astraia. And Zephyrus does not wish to remain. See for yourself."

Zephyrus shook his head, growling low in his throat. He nudged me then and tilted his head down as he did when he wanted me to climb on.

I pressed my forehead to his jaw, struggling to calm my breaths. This wasn't happening. It couldn't be. I had finally felt something—I finally felt like I had a place and the possibility of a future.

"Ramiel—"

"Are you a vow breaker?" He stalked closer, glaring at me. "You made that vow. And if you are so fickle and faithless as to break it now when the dragon to whom you have made that pledge clearly wishes you to depart, then you are not the fae I thought you were."

My spine stiffened. A great hollow space opened within my chest, aching and throbbing worse than the cold of the Chasm. "So this is…goodbye. Forever?" I barely forced the words out, and they hung in the air filled with grief.

"If Zephyrus wishes to return, you may return with him," he said, his tone a little softer now. "But only when he wishes to return. Do not return for me."

Zephyrus nudged me again, more insistently. The vow itself tugged upon my spirit, an uncomfortable itch forming along my limbs as the magic reminded me of what I had promised.

The air shimmered above. "Words have meaning, Astraia. All words, no matter where they are spoken and even when they are not fully understood," Caein said softly.

"Caein." Ramiel's voice was even icier now. "Enough." His gaze was even harder. "I am sorry for your pain, Astraia, but it's time. I renounced my hospitality to you. Go,…gnat. I appreciated your company. Don't make this any more painful than it already is."

"Gnat" stung this time. As if I were nothing. A speck in the sea. A fleck on the wind. Had I hallucinated his whispers of love and pleas for my life? Was he—was he just trying to protect me?

Zephyrus nudged me again, growling low and soft. My throat tightened as the vow pulled at me, an invisible chain demanding I honor my word.

I climbed onto Zephyrus's back, my movements mechanical. His scales were warm beneath my touch, familiar in a way that should have been comforting. But nothing could ease the hollow ache spreading through my chest.

Low murmurs and grunts from the other dragons stirred the air. Zephyrus's ears remained flattened against his head. He started to turn. I pressed my hand flat against his head. He stopped, but his chuff warned me he didn't want to linger.

That was fine. I—I didn't want to either, but I had to say something.

"In the Chasm and when the wraith had me in its grasp, all I could think about was…" I closed my eyes. The words stuck in my throat. "I thought I was going to die. And—the thing I regretted was that I would die without telling you that I love you. Because I do. I—I wanted a life with you here, Ramiel."

His expression remained impassive, carved from stone. His arms were at his side, motionless except for the twitching in his right hand. "You will find a better life away from here. One day someone will love you and give you the life you deserve. Go in peace and forget your little crush, Astraia."

Zephyrus shifted beneath me, wings unfurling.

I set my jaw, willing the tears back. "Go in peace. Good-bye, Ramiel."

Zephyrus strode out of the stable. Low grumbles and murmurs from the other dragons followed us as we left. The soft clicking of his talons on the stone faded as he reached the packed earth. As we reached the knoll just outside the tower, Zephyrus turned his head and rumbled. His voice shook at the end.

The chorus of growls and chirrs rose.

I kept my spine straight and my shoulders squared. Part of me wanted to look back to see if Ramiel was watching.

But I didn't.

2 1

THISTLEDEEP

I couldn't focus on anything as Zephyrus flew away. Everything faded. There was nothing but pain and the tears came hard and fast. It might as well have been minutes or days when he landed. I jolted back into awareness, realizing it was nearing sunset and he had brought me to one of the fairy wells: Thistledeep. We'd been here often for translations and identifications.

From above, the fairy well appeared as nothing more than a dark circle amid tall grass. Even on the ground, it could be hard to see at first because of the enchantments surrounding it, but I knew better than to trust only my eyes. The ring of hawthorns and rowans surrounding it gleamed emerald and silver in the early afternoon light, their leaves rustling secrets in the breeze. Despite not being in season, red berries hung from the rowans.

My boots crunched on the packed earth as I slid off Zephyrus's neck and wiped my eyes. "Why here?" It was an odd choice. Especially given the fact he didn't like fairies. Yet he had brought me here on his own.

The well itself stood knee-high, its ancient stones fitted together without mortar, worn smooth by centuries of hands. Cool air rose from its depths, carrying the mineral scent of underground water and that distinctive tangy sweetness of wild fairy magic.

A dragonfly skimmed the surface of the dark water below, its wings catching the fading golden sunlight in iridescent flashes. The shadows of the trees dappled the clearing in shifting patterns, and somewhere nearby, a thrush called three times.

The fairies were our distant cousins, far, far removed. Some found them tedious. I found them amusing even though you always had to be cautious around them.

Zephyrus grunted and moved in front of me, his eyes narrowing. He then pushed his snout against my throat and huffed. Pulling back, he tried to use his claw to gesture at me roughly.

I held the pendant up, and he trilled.

Still frowning, I untwisted the clasp. It gave way easily. As I studied it, I noticed the runes and the writing. That phrase was on there again: *Natoumai ahme vahre.*

My stomach tightened.

I had to know what it said for certain. Zephyrus chuffed again, nudging me hard enough I nearly fell. "I've got it, big guy." For whatever reason, he wanted me to know what this meant. Fine by me. I wanted to know too. Then I could forget all about Ramiel…if that was even possible.

I'd used most of my rations so I had to gather items to make an offering and summon the fairies. Black raspberry bushes along the southern edges of the clearing held plentiful fruit, and I infused a handful with my magic. I'd come to learn what the fairies here liked well enough that I didn't even have to ask.

On the way there, I spotted spring onions growing at the river bank in the soft dark soil. A bit of good luck, and I'd accept any of that I could get.

I gathered the berries and spring onions and placed it on the mouth of the well. "Please. Accept this as payment and grant me a favor."

The water in the well sparkled, then hummed. A small circle of green light winked into the air above it, buzzing with excitement. "Astraia! Oh! Our little cousin is back! Clover! Cricket! Hurry!"

I found myself smiling a little more as Ivy darted around me. These fairies were precious but dangerous in an unintentional way. They had such short attention spans and intense emotions and random ideas. You never knew quite what you were going to get, and I'd learned the hard way to be cautious about accepting any of their aid unless there was no other choice. More than once their magic had backfired on me. And when I first came to visit them, they had "blessed" me with all manner of spells that had had numerous side effects, including my eyebrows changing colors with my mood for a whole six months.

But, all that said, there was no one like them when it came to translations and figuring out arcane meanings… provided you could get them to focus long enough.

Squealing with delight, Ivy flitted around me, circling the well and then shooting over to Zephyrus. He twitched his ears and cocked his head as sparkling dust landed on the tip of his nose. He wrinkled his snout, then shook his head.

A blue orb and a red orb darted out as well, Clover and Cricket. They spiraled around me and tugged at my hair and fussed over my clothing before turning to Zephyrus. He patiently endured as they fussed and bustled, not moving away or doing anything to slow their attention as if he knew the sooner they finished, the sooner we would get our answers.

"It's good to see you three," I said, grateful it was just the three of them and not all of their family. "I brought some magic-infused berries to pay for the translation. And I found some spring onions as well."

"Lovely, lovely." Cricket snatched up a berry. It was the size of a melon to her, and she bit into it as if it were an apple. Dark juice stained her lips.

"What are we translating today?" Ivy asked. Clover bounded up beside her, darting back and forth like a hummingbird.

"This." I held up the pendant. The metal caught the fading sunlight, the reflections iridescent on its smooth surface. "From the Sentinel tower near the Chasm."

"Oh—oh," Ivy and Clover gasped in unison, delight in their eyes.

Cricket nodded happily as she set aside the berry. "That's always a fun one. Northern rune fae roots with just a dash of the Aurora Isle and a bit of bone and silver mixed in for good measure. Just put it on the well, and we'll get to work."

As they translated the words, I turned back to Zephyrus. It still didn't add up. Dragons were exceptionally loyal. He clearly loved his family, and if there was danger, he would not want to abandon them. It didn't seem like he saw me as being in danger currently. Just a little battered. Certainly far better than I might have been.

I stopped, my hand on his chest.

The first thing Ramiel did when he found me suspended in the stable was search Zephyrus to ensure I hadn't added an incantation or spell to him.

I frowned, examining Zephyrus more carefully. Something wasn't adding up.

"Hold still," I murmured, running my hands along Zephyrus's scales. There—beneath the ridge of his left shoulder blade—I felt it. A slight pulse of magic, nearly imperceptible unless you were searching for it.

I traced my fingers over the area, then used just my fingers to direct my energy and undo the central knot. The thread unspun, revealing a series of runes that were already fading.

"Hmmm." I leaned in close, hand pressed to Zephyrus's side. These runes were familiar, but I didn't fully recognize them. They spelled out something specific. I recognized "take," "protect," and "stay." One of the runes was a marking for time.

Clover zipped over, her blue light illuminating the markings even more. "Oh! Hidden writing! I love puzzles!"

"Can you read this for me, please?" I asked, trying to steady my voice. Already I guessed what it said, but I wanted confirmation.

She hovered close to Zephyrus's scales, her tiny hands tracing the patterns. "It's an old runic spell that the Sentinels and Wardens use. Maybe a few of the north islanders in the west. Very specific. Very powerful." She canted her head, her curly ash blonde hair sliding to the side. "The Sentinel ordered the dragon to take you away. To protect you at all costs and not look back."

Ivy and Cricket joined us, their lights casting dancing shadows across Zephyrus's blue scales.

"One day's journey minimum," Cricket added, her red glow pulsing with excitement. "No specific place named. Just... away. Safe."

My stomach dropped as my head spun. Something was happening with the Chasm. At the Tower. And he was going to die.

"Well, there is some good news though!" Ivy spun in circles around my hand and then my neck. "The pendant is such a gift. So beautiful! I haven't seen one in ages, but *'Natoumai ahme vahre'* that's what Sentinels say to their beloveds!"

Cricket nodded vigorously. "It's difficult to translate directly because they shorten so many of the words and then combine them to make new ones. Very similar to the north rune fae in many respects. But essentially, that phrase means: The one whose soul was carved from the same star as mine, the one I will love through life, through death, and all that lies beyond."

"A mate-bond declaration and a vow of love," Clover whispered. "One of the most sacred bonds."

I staggered under the weight of those words. My gut

twisted. "Gnat. What if someone just said that, and they were a Sentinel…what would that mean?"

The three fairies looked between one another, their wings fluttering swiftly back and forth. Cricket just laughed, but it was more a nervous sound. "Well, if said alone, 'nat' means 'my beloved' more or less."

My heart twisted as my knees at last gave way. Collapsing on the ground, I dragged in a ragged sob. He had been telling me the whole time. He'd known from the beginning.

Zephyrus pressed his snout to the back of my head and grunted softly.

I couldn't breathe around the ache in my chest and the tightening of my throat. I hated him. I loved him. That rune-magicked bastard! It all made sense now. Thread rot, how could he send me away like that?!

"Astraia, love, what's wrong?" Ivy hummed beside my ear.

"He's going to face something terrible," I whispered, my voice shaking so hard I don't know how they understood me. My fingers dug into the dirt. "Something he doesn't expect to survive. He sent me away to protect me, and he isn't going to make it."

Zephyrus grunted again and looked back in the direction of the tower. Yes. I agreed.

"We have to go back." My whole body shook. "Right now! How much time do we have?" Dragging my hand through my hair, I drew in ragged breaths. "It can't be much. He only demanded Zephyrus fly a day. So—end of day today? Tonight? I've got to get back now! But we won't get back there before dawn even if Zephyrus goes at full speed!"

Cricket zipped around my head, leaving a trail of crimson sparkles. "Why not just pulseport back?"

I shook my head, struggling to regulate my breaths. "I can't pulseport with Zephyrus. He's too large, and I'm not strong enough to carry us both that distance. I couldn't even get myself that far without sapping my magic, and that might not be enough with just me."

The three fairies exchanged glances, then burst into tinkling laughter that sounded like wind chimes in a storm.

"Silly cousin!" Ivy grabbed my pinky finger with both her tiny hands. "You don't need to do it alone!"

Clover seized another finger. "Come! Hurry!" Cricket had already darted ahead, her soft red glow guiding the way.

They pulled me deeper into the forest, Zephyrus following behind and snapping through branches and crushing roots. The trees grew denser, their ancient trunks twisted with age. We stopped beneath a massive ash tree, its bark furrowed and gnarled. At its base lay a perfect circle of ivory mushrooms, glowing in the shadows.

"One of our circles," Cricket announced with a flourish. "Step inside!"

I hesitated. "What about Zephyrus? He won't fit."

Ivy flitted over to Zephyrus, sprinkling dust over his snout. "Of course he will!"

Before my eyes, Zephyrus shrank, his massive form compressing until he was no larger than a house cat. He let out an indignant squawk, wings flapping furiously.

I scooped him up and held him close. "I'm so sorry, big guy," I whispered against his scaled head. "It's just temporary."

"He'll return to normal ten seconds after arrival," Ivy assured me. "So get clear quickly! Otherwise, he'll crush you."

"Focus on your destination, dear," Clover said, zipping in front of my face and then back. "Pulseport as you normally would. The circle will amplify your power."

I stepped into the ring of mushrooms, clutching Zephyrus against my chest. He burrowed against my neck, his warmth familiar despite his diminished size.

"Ramiel," I whispered, closing my eyes. "I'm coming. I'll never forgive you if I'm too late."

I gathered my magic, feeling it rise within me—but something was different. The fairy circle pulled at my energy, demanding more than I'd expected. My strength drained as darkness enveloped us.

The world tore apart, then snapped back together. We landed hard on rocky ground. I stumbled forward, setting Zephyrus down just as the magic faded. We stood at the foot of the tower, facing the narrow bridge that stretched out over the Chasm's yawning darkness. Storm clouds billowed above us as lightning pierced the sky and thunder cracked.

One bolt of lightning illuminated the bridge and the Chasm. My heart sank. No!

22

MY CONFESSION

Lightning split the sky as I stared across the stone bridge into the chasm. My tongue burned with the taste and scent of magic and fire.

Ramiel stood at the center of the bridge's edge, his silver hair whipping in the wind as he faced the thrashing leviathan. The massive creature's scales gleamed wet with the purple mist that clung to his body. The bone fae spear jutted from his shoulder, the wound raw and festering. Part of the spear shaft had been severed, and fresh blood stained the stones and dyed the mist. Progress, but not enough.

Great rips threatened to tear further across the entirety of the Chasm, moving like waves of jelly beneath churning smoke.

Eight of the dragons worked in quads, their wings beating in perfect synchrony as they carried glowing rune strands between them. The magical threads shimmered silver, weaving an intricate pattern across the Chasm's surface, trying to stitch up the tears.

They were failing.

Badly.

Whatever pattern they sought to make frayed. The leviathan's constant movement weakened the barrier of the

Chasm with each twist and spiral. The dragons strained against the howling wind and the bubbling of the Chasm. Even from this distance, I could see three chasm wraiths trying to press through. Burning yellow eyes glowed within the Chasm at multiple intervals, pressing at the clear layer separating them from the rest of our realm.

Thalorion, Giselle, and Veyruneth tried to hold the leviathan in place with ropes of energy, but each time the leviathan twisted, one or two lost their grip, the rope either fraying in their mouths or slipping from their jaws.

Zephyrus launched skyward, his wings unfurling to their full span. The force nearly knocked me over. He joined Giselle and snatched up one of the fallen ropes, his dark-blue scales stark against her purple. Together they slammed the energy ropes taut, forcing the leviathan down against the bridge. Half its massive body hung in the Chasm, half sprawled across the stone. It was far larger than the forty feet I'd originally estimated. Its head alone was the size of a small dragon. He bellowed, lightning sparking from his jaws and making his eyes light up until they were yellow gold instead of deep orange.

The Chasm bubbled even more fiercely beneath them, purple mist rising in thick spiraling columns. Where the mist touched the bridge, it hissed and steamed. Through the fog, I saw another chasm wraith pushing against that invisible barrier, their elongated fingers clawing at the air.

Yellow-eyed creatures darted between the larger wraiths, their bodies little more than shadows as they tested the barrier for weaknesses. A few bat-like creatures escaped and swept along the ridge. Three of the dragons broke formation and dealt with them immediately. The runes faded in the air.

Ramiel dropped to one knee, his hands glowing with silver light as he traced runes in the air. His movements were sluggish. His shoulders sagged with exhaustion. The silver magic around his fingers flickered like a dying flame. He twisted his hands. The runes he carved into the air trembled, hanging there as the dragons returned to their formations and seized them. Then he cut new healing runes, his hands shaking as he formed them in front of the leviathan.

A column of dark smoke rose from the Chasm's edge. It twisted unnaturally, defying the wind's direction. The smell hit me next: burning metal. It was building slowly.

The omenfang was coming. We didn't have much time left.

I sprinted toward the bridge, rain striking my face.

Remnants of runes sparked and faded against the earth and the mist. The runes he now carved wavered and flared.

The leviathan thrashed against his bonds, his massive tail whipping across the stone bridge, sending fragments of rock into the churning abyss. Zephyrus and his trio worked to keep the leviathan down. Up above, the other dragons struggled to maintain their weaving pattern.

I skidded to a stop a few feet away and lifted my hands. Though I certainly didn't recognize all of these runes, I knew how to strengthen them. That was just as simple as tracing his pattern with my own energy.

Gold light flared from my hands. I channeled it up into the runes he had formed, sealing their bonds and strengthening him. The jarring from my encounter with the chasm wraith and the heavy use to pulseport here even with the fairy ring slowed my response, but I focused on my magic and forced it up into those runes and to support him.

Ramiel's shoulders tightened. He started to hinge his gaze back, but the leviathan roared again. "Ithoks—" He swore, the words distorted by the wind and bellows.

The runes turned silver and gold, marbling with both, pulsing with life. Our energy twisted together.

The leviathan bucked and flung his head back once more.

Ramiel curled his fingers and sliced his hand through the air. The glowing runes snapped forward, striking the wound and the broken spear. The spear wrenched up.

Blood spilled, splashing on the stone. A chunk of the wood snapped off, the swelling immediately reducing. Green smoke coiled up from it, fading in the wild winds.

Another pained bellow escaped the leviathan's jaws, and he dove back. He snapped at the nearest of the chasm wraiths that had gotten free. He dragged it with him on the way down, lightning bolts flaring around his jaws. He roared again, a terrifying tremulous quality to his voice as if he were trying to communicate something.

Ramiel cut new runes into the air. The dragons seized them and resumed weaving the Chasm shut. He spun to face me. "What are you doing here?" he bellowed. His hair fell back down to his shoulders, only slightly ruffled and tousled despite the wind. He strode toward me, a vein throbbing in his forehead and neck.

"You were saying it from the start, weren't you?" I braced my hands on my sash, meeting his gaze unflinching. So many emotions twisted within me, I could scarcely stand it.

"Saying what? To get out? Yes! You need to go elsewhere. Anywhere but here." He sliced his hand across the air and pointed to the tower. "Go inside. Wait for me there, and then we'll talk."

I lifted my chin. My voice shook. "Nat. You've called me 'nat' from the beginning. And I thought you were mocking me at first. Teasing me later on. But that was never it, was it? You were telling me who I was to you."

He halted, his jaw working. He braced his hands on his broad belt. When he spoke, his voice was low and rough. "Astraia, it doesn't matter. This is not how it should be. This isn't right."

"I helped you, didn't I?" I lifted my chin. "We work well together. If you had any doubts, and I don't think you actually do, you just saw proof for why we should be together right here. Our magic blends well. We strengthen one another. I am stronger with you, and you are stronger with me. We both make each other better."

That muscle along his jaw jumped, his gaze fixed on me hard. "I don't know what you think you know, but if you don't leave—"

"If I don't leave, what?" I narrowed my eyes at him, daring him. "What will you do? Show me, rune fae."

His expression hardened, his shoulders tensing even more. His eyes darkened. Something wild and desperate flashed across his face—he lunged forward, closing the distance between us in a single step. His hands caught my face, fingers threading into my hair as he yanked me against him. His mouth crashed down on mine, hard and hungry and desperate.

I gasped against his lips, shock freezing me for half a breath before heat flooded my body. My hands fisted in his tunic, pulling him closer as I kissed him back with everything I had. The taste of him—frosted silver, cinnamon, yeast, and cedar—flooded my senses.

"Astraia," he growled against my mouth, the word vibrating through me. His arms wrapped around my waist, lifting me off my feet as he deepened the kiss.

My fingers found the suppression charm hanging at his throat. I ripped it free, casting it aside.

Magic exploded between us—wild, ancient, and overwhelming. Somehow the mate bond roared to life, a brilliant golden thread weaving our souls together. I cried out as the sensation crashed through me. Ramiel's arms tightened, keeping me close as he pressed his forehead against mine, his breathing ragged.

"I tried," he whispered, voice breaking. "By all that is good and holy, I tried to keep you safe from this. I tried to protect you. I couldn't let anything happen to you. Yes, I knew from the start. You are my mate. You are the one I love more than any other who walks this world. But to be with me is to embrace death. I didn't want to do that to you. I've failed."

"You haven't failed." I clung to him, fingers curling into the fabric of his surcoat. "Whatever comes next, we'll find a way through. But I wouldn't trade all the safety and all the security in the world for this. What I want is you."

The bond between us pulsed and strengthened, years of longing and loneliness washing away in its golden light. I could feel him—his pain, his fear, his love—it beat as clearly as my heart. My shoulder pulsed, throbbing as if recognizing the violation I'd wrought against my own body all those years ago. I kept myself from grimacing, but somehow he noticed and cupped his hand along my cheek.

"You're in pain as well?"

"It's the mate bond…" I bit the inside of my lip, shaking my head. The sensation within me had taken on an unsettling sensation. "As we're bonding, it's like it's trying to reform. It's not coming together as quickly as it should, but…it is coming back."

He glanced around as the dragons continued their patrol. Another two yellow-eyed creatures clambered out, wings flapping clumsily. Giselle snapped them up in a single bite. Zephyrus landed over another rift and bellowed into it as if in warning. The other dragons followed similar patterns. Thalorion took up a position over the bulge in the surface where a chasm wraith tried to press through. He hissed and then roared, fire licking from his jaws. "The dragons are keeping a steady guard. The leviathan will likely return within the hour. I wasn't able to cure him or soothe the pain at all. Let me help you."

"But the omenfang—"

He pressed his finger against my lips, his brow knitting though there was such a heat in his eyes it made me melt. "Do you think I care what the omenfang will do to me in the future? My mate is in pain now. Should I not comfort her?"

Well…if he was going to put it like that. My stomach somersaulted.

He guided me to sit on a large stone. The spitting rain had stopped, the Chasm calming and the wind dying down. The dark storm clouds remained, but the setting sun turned them gold. Gently, he tugged at my sleeve, moving it down enough to reveal my shoulder.

I shivered, the air cool against my skin as well as his touch. His brow creased as he studied the scar. "You burned yourself deeply."

I bit back a wince. "I wanted to protect my mate."

That small nod of his said he understood. "You did this to yourself? You didn't have someone else do it?" He frowned more, his fingers tracing the lines of the scars gently. When I nodded, his brow tweaked further. He traced three runes onto the scar tissue, then leaned down and kissed them. "Nat."

Warmth flooded me, and my insides twisted to hear that name. "My heart." My fingertips grazed his collarbone where the charm once lay.

His eyes shuttered, a low groan escaping his lips. His throat bobbed. "Astraia…"

"Natoumai ahme vahre, Ramiel." I flattened my hand to his chest.

He pressed his hand over mine. "Natoumai ahme vahre, Astraia…I am yours."

"And I am yours."

"I don't know how long I have to offer you," he continued, leaning closer. The tip of his nose traced along the line of my cheek before he settled against me, arms tight about my waist. "I don't see how I survive this, but I want you to know that I have loved you since the day I saw you. You were—are everything I could have hoped for."

"As are you. And you come with dragons." I rubbed my forehead against his. My eyelashes brushed his skin as I tilted my head back and kissed him again. That little quaver of fear returned. I had suffered loss. I did not want to experience it again. "So have faith that we can make it. Don't give up on yourself."

"So long as you survive this, I will be at peace." He brought both my hands to his lips.

I winced again as the pain stabbed my shoulder once

more. Curse it all! Our mate bond still wasn't fully connecting. Like all mate bonds, it was transforming both of us but slower. So much slower than it should. The scarring on my shoulder from the scourging had not faded. It throbbed and pulsed as if I had just been stabbed.

His brow furrowed with concern once more. "I suspect that asking you to let me do this alone won't work. So I ask for another compromise. Don't go near the Chasm itself. Not any closer than you are now. The leviathan will likely breach again soon. And I will finish healing the wounds. I think that this last time will be sufficient. The spear is almost completely removed. But if we can get through that, the omenfang will be here. Even with you loosening the bonds, I will soon reach the tipping point."

"Then let me get as many knots free as I can. I can loosen them more and get you more time. More space to draw up your power and push it back. And the mate bond will strengthen us both! If we can just get you more time, that will be enough. I can even distract the omenfang if it comes for me again."

"No," he said firmly, holding my hands tighter. "Astraia, my curse was passing into you. Those threads were trying to become a part of you as they became a part of me." He clasped my hands between his. "That's why I sent you away. I realized that if you continued to help me, the curse was going to pass into you and I didn't know that I could separate it or save you."

"I—I don't care," I said. "Ramiel, you can't ask me to just let you die."

"I might not. You loosened the bonds and took the brunt of its attack the last time. That bought me time."

"Why can't we just destroy the omenfang then?" My voice shook. "There—there has to be a way. We've come this far. And—"

"The only way I know to destroy the omenfang is to remove all the points of the curse within me. Even if there was enough time, I could not risk it when your life would be on the line as well."

"So your plan is just to die?"

He kept his hand at my cheek, his expression softening. "No. You bought me time. I'll heal the leviathan. The dragons will help weave the rifts shut, and we will hope that the madness from the pain passes enough for the dragons to be able to tell the leviathan what we are doing and get him to help us again with driving back the others. And if I am able, then I will contend with the omenfang. If we get through that, we will celebrate. If I do not make it and my physical form falls into the Chasm, command the dragons to stay out of the Chasm. You must do that to save them."

The roar of the leviathan shattered the stillness. We were out of time.

THE THREAD

Ramiel whirled, one arm clasped around me as he faced the bridge. The leviathan thrashed against the largest of the rifts in the Chasm, desperate to get out and tearing it even more. A sour, bitter scent filled the air, mixing with the sharp tang of magic.

The barrier twisted and bulged against his movements, and the spear in his shoulder glowed with remnants of the healing energy. The poor creature flailed. His deep-orange eyes met mine. Madness surged in those eyes. If only I could tell him we were trying to help.

I locked into place, the creature's agony brutal and vivid. He flung his head back once more and bellowed. Lightning exploded around his jaws. The air near his head rippled as if he distorted it, and the Chasm's barrier rippled more and more.

Ramiel scanned the Chasm as the dragons circled above, his expression grim. "This is our last chance. Don't come any closer to the Chasm, Astraia."

I scoffed. "I won't come near the Chasm, but I won't abandon you either. We're in this together, Ramiel."

He opened his mouth to answer.

A thunderous crack split the air as the leviathan

slammed against the bridge. Stone crumbled beneath his weight.

Strange flying creatures shot up from the smaller tears. They scattered in all directions. The dragons swooped down and chased after them. The thunder of their wings intensified as the wind picked up.

I braced myself against the wind as Ramiel strode back to the edge of the bridge, his silver hair whipping around his shoulders. The Chasm roiled beneath, purple mist churning like an angry sea. Each movement of the massive creature sent waves of energy pulsing through the air.

The poor creature was suffering badly. My heart ached for him. The spear in its shoulder was nearly free, the healing magic working. I grimaced, shaking my head. Healing always hurt before it helped, but that didn't make it easy to endure. The pain in my own flesh reminded me of that. If he would just stop fighting it and let us help, he'd heal so much faster. But there was no way to communicate that.

Ramiel planted his feet on the bridge's edge as the structure trembled beneath him, far closer to the edge than I wanted him to be. His hands began to move, precise and deliberate, cutting glowing runes into the air.

I focused my energy, reaching out with my magic to strengthen each symbol as it formed. My aura stretched out as close as I could send it to find the weaknesses. Come on. Come on! The runes brightened, their edges sharpening as my power flowed into them.

I could see the strain in Ramiel's shoulders, the slight tremor in his fingers that others might miss. The power required to heal such a massive wound was taking its toll. Sweat beaded on his brow despite the chill wind.

The leviathan reared back, his massive jaws opening. Lightning crackled between his jagged teeth, arcing outward in a blinding flash. Ramiel barely pulled back, the brilliant streak of energy burning the stone near his foot.

A horrifying screech drew my attention skyward.

Another chasm wraith had broken free, its ghostly hand wrapping around Giselle. She twisted in its grasp, purple wings beating frantically as the color bled from her form.

"Ramiel! Above!" I pointed upward.

He glanced up, fingers still cutting runes into the air. Without breaking rhythm, he carved three new symbols over the Chasm, these glowing with a fierce silver-blue light. Zephyrus and a dark-grey dragon immediately dove toward the wraith.

Two other dragons swooped in, snatching the silver runes in their claws before soaring toward Giselle. Their coordinated attack tore at the wraith's misty form, freeing the purple dragon from its grip. The grey one swept beneath Giselle and helped her to fly to an outcropping as Zephyrus and Veyruneth bared their teeth and lured the wraith to the disintegrating runes where they would kill it.

The bridge shuddered violently beneath us. Thalorion landed beside Ramiel with a heavy thud. The whiskered dragon roared, a sound that seemed to shake the very air, and launched himself at the leviathan. Claws and teeth flashed as Thalorion drove the creature back from the bridge, creating space for Ramiel to work but without drawing blood.

Gritting my teeth, I channeled more power into Ramiel's runes. Almost there. The gold and silver spiraled together. Already though the scent of burning metal cut through the myriad of scents, present and growing. My skin crawled, my breaths tightening.

No! Not yet.

My magic surged as I strengthened the last of the runes Ramiel was carving. It hooked onto him momentarily, lighting him up. Maybe it was the mate bond that granted me insight even as it fought to seal into place. Maybe it was something from the Chasm. Maybe both.

But I saw it.

There.

My blood ran cold.

Ramiel was nearing the end of his strength, flagging badly though he kept up his grim expression. His heart thundered, its every pulse and throb highlighted by my golden light, the knots cutting in tighter and pulling closer.

And right in the center of his heart, peeking out just far enough was that central thread that bound the knots, layered around itself at least six times to form that crucial center knot.

He was right. It was hooked into the very essence of the curse and his heart, resistant to removal. If I pulled it free, I wouldn't have time to break it into pieces. I was already too weakened to do more than draw it out, let alone guide it. The whole thing would come loose, and it would coil around me as if I were the spindle on a spinning wheel. And I would die.

Funny.

Some curses really couldn't be escaped.

Mine had found me after all this time. After so much death and loss. It had found me.

I could run. Hide under a sycamore tree. Could probably call Zephyrus to me, and he'd come. Take me away from this place.

I really could.

In theory.

Ramiel would understand.

Pulling that thread free would unleash the fullness of his power, and it would condemn me. If I didn't, he would reach the end of his strength, collapse, and die at the omenfang's claws. The leviathan would not be healed. He would worsen and continue in this madness until he tore free and died a horrible death as he destroyed all he encountered. The dragons would continue fighting the creatures of the rift. But one chasm wraith could destroy any of them. Zephyrus would fall. I could practically see that, and tears stung my eyes. The rift would remain open with all the creatures of the liminal space free to pour through. And eventually everything would perish.

A small, sad smile tugged at my lips as I kept my magic steady. Oh, I could continue with the reasons. There were so many. But the fact that this would take Ramiel's life and almost certainly Zephyrus's was reason enough for me.

Creator of All, keep me strong, keep me steadfast. And please don't let it hurt too much.

Ramiel continued to cut the runes into the air. He sagged to the left, his breaths labored. Adjusting his stance, he stood again and called something out in a language I did not recognize.

Another agonized howl rose, spiraling in the growing darkness of night and storm.

Stepping forward, I removed my pale gold blade, tightened my focus, and snagged that central thread with everything I possessed.

It snapped around my wrist as if it had been waiting for me. Wincing, I gripped my arm, willing myself to hold steady. I had it! The power throbbed in my veins, building and singing as I willed that central knot to come undone.

Ramiel's posture tensed as soon as I connected. The muscles in his jaw and throat pulsed, his gaze hinging back though he barely managed to turn his head as he continued to support the runes and the dragons seized them.

"Astraia, no." I heard his voice in my mind through the pendant. That raw pleading nearly undid me. I heard the strain in his voice. Felt the pain of the curse.

"We can't escape some things, Ramiel," I said, both aloud and in my mind. "Sometimes we do our best, and we just have to let it be what it is. I love you."

With that, I closed my eyes and poured the last of my power into dissolving that core knot. The central thread surged free, and the world spun. It coiled around me, faster and faster. I couldn't even slow it. My arms were pinned to my sides, my legs squeezed together. It wrapped around my chest and my throat. Gasping, I thrust out with my aura and fought to keep the threads from completely choking me.

The ground struck me, knocking the wind from my lungs. Wheezing, I struggled to open my eyes again. My shoulder throbbed, my lungs ached. The cursed thread burned, seeping into my skin. But Ramiel—oh, Ramiel.

His chest expanded as he drew a full, deep breath. The silver-blue of his magic surged forth, radiating from him in powerful waves.

His eyes met mine, sorrow and horror etched into his face. "Hold fast, Astraia. Don't let it take you! You aren't done yet. I will save you." Raw anguish twisted his features before he forced it away, jaw setting with determination. He strengthened the runes in the air above the leviathan, their light intensifying until it hurt to look at them.

With a violent thrust, he sent the magic toward the leviathan. The creature froze mid-thrash, suddenly still. The runes eased into the puckered, ugly wound in his shoulder. The last bit of the spear dropped out, drawn free by the runes. The flesh knitted together, the swollen scales smoothing over.

Ramiel shouted something to the dragons—a command I couldn't hear through the roaring in my ears. Thalorion and Zephyrus responded immediately, adopting a tight formation above the Chasm. The rest of the dragons dropped down as well, reforming their quads and seizing the runes.

The horrible scent of burning metal intensified. That vile cold taste filled my mouth.

No.

Behind Ramiel, darkness gathered. The omenfang materialized, its kangaroo form grotesque and wrong, static crackling around its distorted limbs. Its gaze narrowed on me, pure rage and hate. It hissed, its entire aura pulsing violet and black.

Fear sliced through me, but I met its gaze, glaring back. Even if I was terrified, I wasn't going to let it see. The threads cut deeper, binding around me tighter and tighter.

What little resistance I could mount by pushing out with my aura and straining my arms rapidly weakened.

Ramiel spun around, his hand slashing through the air, trailing silver fire. "Do not touch her!" he bellowed. The blow connected with the omenfang's chest. It didn't evaporate this time. It screamed and staggered backward.

Yes!

It was corporeal now.

Murderous rage burned in Ramiel's eyes as he lunged for it. Runic blades shone in the air. "Release her now!" Those blades shot through the air and pierced the omenfang again and again.

A heavy thud shook the ground behind me. Zephyrus loomed over me, his heavy talons biting into the stone. His amber eyes blazed with terror. He howled and snarled, biting at the shadowy threads with the precision of a surgeon's scalpel but they reformed immediately. "No, no," I said, choking. "It's—it's going to be all right. I'm sorry, big guy. I love you too."

His jaws snapped with a sharp click. He nudged me frantically, whimpering.

My focus slipped. His talon clipped my side as he rolled me over and snipped again and again. It wasn't working.

He howled, then dropped his head level to me. Thrusting his snout against my body, he chirred and trilled and growled as he nudged at my ribs and my face. His steamy breath blasted against me, but there was no heat this time. Only damp.

The threads squeezed tighter. My vision dimmed at the edges. Each breath came shorter than the last. It felt like it was pulling me into the ground.

Ramiel skidded in front of me. He leaned over me, his hand pressing against my cheek. "Don't go, Astraia. Hold on. Just give me three more moments. Hold fast. I can save you. Just—just give me a few more breaths."

Zephyrus howled again. Then he spun and raced to the edge of the bridge. The rolling wail of a roar he made echoed in my ears. The other dragons flew closer, making a similar call.

I swallowed hard. Their voices deepened and distanced as a heavy hum filled my ears. Darkness closed in. I couldn't hold out much longer.

"Shh. You can do this. You saved me from my curse, now I'll save you from yours." Ramiel's voice was distant. "Keep breathing. You're holding on. That's right. Just a little longer." He etched the runes into my shoulder. But the scar refused to accept it as easily. It repelled his rune as much as it had fought the full connection of the mating bond. He gritted his teeth and pressed more energy against me, willing it against me. "I won't lose you," he said hoarsely. "I love you."

I gritted my teeth. It hurt in a different way. Like something was trying to connect.

The darkness closed in. One last breath sputtered from my lips, and the threads cinched tight. This wasn't just a dream. It was real.

I would never wake again.

THE NIGHTMARE

This was the nightmare. A nightmare that would never end. The threads vanished from around me. I lay on coarse dark stone in a great open space that was dark as a tomb.

Already the cold gnawed at my fingers and toes. Sound did not travel. Even my own breaths were so faint. As I sat up, the rocks beneath me scratched and itched my flesh.

If this was the liminal space spoken of before, then where were the other spirits? Shouldn't there be hundreds? Thousands?

Or…this was part of what made it such a horror. To be trapped not only in darkness, cold, and discomfort but alone. Completely and utterly alone.

On unsteady feet, I pushed myself up. It was so dark I could scarcely see my own hand in front of my face. As my eyes adjusted, I realized though there was simply nothing to see.

My chest tightened. This was it. I was trapped here. My magic was drained. Pulseporting wouldn't work. That part of myself felt as if it was dead. Ramiel had sworn he would not let me remain trapped. But did he even know where I was? Liminal space was massive. This curse had been connected to the Chasm, but did that really make a difference?

I pressed my hand to the pendant. "Ramiel?" I called out.

The darkness devoured my voice. It didn't even echo. There wasn't even a scent to guide me. No smell of stone or water. Not even the smell of me.

My fingers trembled. "Ramiel."

I moved farther away, wandering aimlessly. My shoulder stopped aching, though I massaged the scar tissue through my sleeve.

There was nothing in this place. Just darkness and rocks. Each time I moved to my right though, my shoulder started to ache.

Time no longer had meaning. I sobbed in a way I hadn't for years. "Please, Creator of All," I prayed. "Please don't let me stay here." I cried out, but my tears were cold, barely streaking down my cheeks. And the sucking ache within my chest could not be avoided.

From the first time I heard of the curse, this was the place I feared. The endless night and waking sleep, locked in a place of cold and dark. If what I'd heard was true, I would not starve to death here. Nor would I die for lack of water. I'd simply...exist.

Nothing but darkness, cold, and coarse stone.

I was going to go insane in here.

How long had it been already?

I tried counting each step but stopped after one thousand seventy-nine. There was something even more unnerving about realizing how little was changing. Was I even moving?

The only thing that changed was if I moved to the right, my shoulder hurt, the scar aching deep.

Why?

What was different in that direction?

I rubbed my shoulder again and then took three steps to the right. The pain in my shoulder worsened, radiating down my arm and across my chest. I tugged my sleeve down, then gasped. The scar was peeling away. Freshly healed skin met my gaze, the crimson mate bond struggling to form, the soft pink glow signaling that it was still healing. It was…it was still trying to complete the full mate bond with Ramiel.

Was this because of the runes Ramiel had placed against me or the mate bond or both? The burns had almost vanished, bits of the scar falling away. Something shone underneath, blindingly bright in the darkness. A golden red light—the mate mark. The mark I'd scourged was still returning, the mate bond still forming.

My magic had been drained by the omenfang and the fight. But the runes, binding spell, and mate mark were present. When I pressed my fingertips against them, the pain worsened. But in a different way. It was...were the bonds and the runes still trying to take hold?

I focused more, willing them to grow stronger. Come on. Would it make a difference? Who knew?

My energy sputtered, the magic resisting this place and refusing to regenerate like it usually did. Only a trickle flowed from my fingertips. I traced over the mark and then runes, pausing at the binding spell. What had Ramiel been binding to me? It obviously did not feel the same as the first one he put on me. It made me smile now, a bittersweetness passing through me.

I hadn't been able to find the weakness in the binding spell with Zephyrus. Binding spells made from love did not have weaknesses. That was a fact of rune fae magic. A law of sorts. A gift from the Creator. Did that in turn mean that it would more swiftly take hold?

My fingers drifted then to the pendant once more. I imagined my words traveling through the pendant to him. "Ramiel?"

A large shape loomed ahead, somehow darker than the shadows. Was that—was that the leviathan?

The darkness shifted. A low, haunting sound vibrated

through the void. Something like whale song. I froze, my skin prickling.

I stepped toward him, that eerie melody lulling me closer. Another step. Dull pain spread through my shoulder beneath the scars, making me wince.

The leviathan gave another low call and continued to swim, not getting closer or farther away. The hum of his voice filled my ears.

The mate bond pulsed stronger, hurting more.

I hesitated. Was this a warning or sign? I didn't know. What choice did I have in this void? Stay still and surrender to eternity?

"Knots take me," I muttered, pushing forward.

Each step intensified the discomfort and pain. My shoulder burned like molten metal. Still, I followed the leviathan's path.

The creature doubled back, swimming in long, sweeping arcs. It never approached me directly, instead tracing what seemed like an invisible boundary. Back and forth, back and forth, but never toward me.

Soon it seemed as if I was directly in front of it. I reached out, my fingers encountering resistance where nothing should be. A barrier. Invisible but solid as stone and slightly damp.

"I'm just outside the Chasm," I whispered, my voice swallowed by the emptiness.

The leviathan paused. He knew I was here.

Was that a good thing?

Well…worst that could happen is he ate me. That'd be a swift end rather than being trapped in this place until the end of time.

I pressed my palm flat against the barrier, channeling what little magic I could muster. Golden light spread from my fingertips. The barrier—it was like what formed the surface of the Chasm except thicker and sturdier. "Can you hear me?"

The leviathan's song changed, shifting to a lower pitch.

He began swimming deliberately to the left, his movements slow but purposeful. Slow enough that I could follow.

I followed along the barrier, matching his pace. "Are you the same one from before?" Were there others like him down here?

His song continued, low, then high, rumbling, then keening. It was almost soothing.

I winced as the mate bond pulsed again. "Healing hurts sometimes. I don't know that mine is going to do me any good down here. Are you—are you feeling better?"

The song continued. It remained the same, unaffected by my statements though he slowed his pace. Down here, he seemed to be at least sixty feet in length. Lightning arced from his jaws occasionally, lighting up the space and revealing there was truly nothing but rocks around me.

"Will you stay close? Ramiel said you're something of a guardian in this space." I hugged myself as we continued. The ache in my shoulder intensified. "I know you can't help me. You may not even understand what I'm saying. If I can't figure out a way out of here, you'll see me go insane." My shoulders dropped. "The only thing that comforts me is knowing if I hadn't done this, then Ramiel would be here. And I wouldn't know the first thing about saving him."

The leviathan continued. And I followed, speaking of nothing and everything. It unnerved me to hear how small my voice was in this place. And the leviathan's presence made me feel more aware of my isolation.

"Zephyrus, no. Don't go into the Chasm. Stay back!" Ramiel's voice was distant within my mind as if on the other side of a field.

I clasped the necklace close. "Ramiel?!"

"We'll get her back. Zephyrus, stop. Zephyrus, calm. Calm!"

I closed my eyes, focusing intently on the remnants of his voice. "Stay back, Zephyrus," I whispered, even though I knew he couldn't hear me. "Don't die because of me." I could practically hear his roars of rage and sorrow, and they gutted me. But when I really listened, I knew that was simply my imagination now.

The leviathan hummed again. He moved up and down slowly on the other side of the barrier as if searching for something. Vaguely I heard the faint squelching of pressure. Was it weaker here? Maybe I could summon my last remnants of magic and—he drove his blunt snout into the barrier.

Sharp pain pierced my shoulder, and light flashed before my eyes. Then it vanished.

My energy faded, and I dropped to my knees.

The leviathan's hum wove around me. He drove his head into the barrier again.

The leviathan's song grew distant. My eyelids grew heavy. I—I couldn't stay awake. I couldn't stand.

Before I could even register fear, I drifted into a dream. The familiar balcony materialized—the same one from my last dream with Ramiel. Stars glittered overhead like scattered diamonds against black velvet.

Ramiel stood at the railing, silver hair catching moonlight. He turned, his face lighting up as he spread his arms.

I rushed forward, collapsing against his chest, clutching his shirt. My fingers dug into the fabric as I buried my face against his chest.

"I'm afraid," I whispered, voice breaking. "I don't know how to get back."

His arms tightened around me. One hand cradled my head, fingers threading through my hair. The other pressed firmly against the small of my back, anchoring me to him.

"It's all right," he murmured against my temple. "Please don't give up. I'm coming for you."

"I'm tired, Ramiel. And I hurt so much." My voice cracked. "This place is draining everything. I know you're not here. You couldn't hear me before. This isn't any different."

He pulled back just enough to look into my eyes. "Trust me, Astraia. Just a little longer. You gave me back my life. I will give you back yours."

"Don't give me false hope," I whispered. A dream had never hurt this much, but how desperately I wanted all this to be true. False hope that would be so easy to take into myself.

Something cracked, a loud ricocheting sound like a cliff collapsing. The balcony shuddered beneath us. Cracks spiderwebbed across the stone. My stomach lurched.

No. No!

I tried to grab onto him, but my fingers passed through his surcoat and chest. I was fading. Fading and falling!

His arm snared around me, his other hand seizing me by the shoulder.

"Ahhh!" Pain shot through my shoulder, white-hot and vicious, twisting and curling. It was as if my arm was being wrenched from its socket and the joint burned from within.

"Hold fast, Astraia. Just trust me!" He yanked me forward. The darkness vanished.

We stood in the Covenant Chamber. Glass jars of gemstone sand hummed in harmonious chorus, casting prismatic light across the walls. Beautiful. Peaceful. Sacred.

Relief swept over me. The dream had changed. "Rami —" I doubled over, clutching my shoulder. Each breath came in ragged gasps.

He steadied me, his hand against my shoulder. "Trust me, Astraia," he said. "It will be all right. Breathe. And focus on me. Focus on our bond. Have we come this far only to lose one another now? Focus on me, nat. Just on me."

"It hurts so much," I said, my voice thick. "And I'm still so cold. That's all that's left, isn't it? Memories and cold and aching and pain and darkness."

"No." A muscle in his jaw jumped. He pulled me tight against him and pressed my ear to his chest. His heartbeat thumped steady and strong against my ear. The humming of the sand jars grew louder, resonating with something I could not place. "Focus on me, Astraia. Just focus on me."

Oh! Warmth radiated from his body, chasing away the bone-deep cold of the void. For the first time since entering this terrible place, I could smell him faintly—frosted silver and cedar, crisp and earthy. A hint of smoke and leather too. I inhaled deeply, letting his scent fill my lungs.

"Good." He held me closer. I curled in tighter, my hands fisting in his tunic, desperate for touch and heat. His fingers carded my hair. "Good. Focus on me, Astraia. Focus hard. You aren't alone."

"Ramiel—" I gasped again. That searing pain cut into my shoulder once more. Screaming, I buried my face in his chest again. My fingers tingled. My toes burned too. Heat crept through my limbs. The aching intensified. My body trembled.

The pain twisted deeper, shredding through me like a thousand white-hot needles. I couldn't breathe. Couldn't think.

"I can't—" My legs buckled.

Ramiel held me up, his grip fierce. "You can. You will. I know you can do this."

I shook my head, tears streaming. "It's too much."

"Look at me." His voice cut through the agony. His eyes locked with mine, fierce and determined. "I love you, Astraia. I loved you from the moment I knew you were real."

The pain crescendoed. I screamed, clinging to him.

"Feel me. Use all of your senses," he said, his voice rumbling in my ear. "Smell the air. Hear my voice. This is not an ordinary dream, and you know that. You're coming back to me now, Astraia. You're coming home."

Suddenly—scents flooded back. The gemstone sand jars' earthy bite. The sharp tang of magic. Ramiel's cedar and frosted silver, warm cashmere and burning wood.

Sounds sharpened. The vibrating hum. My ragged

breathing. Ramiel's steady heartbeat. The smooth silk of his shirt beneath my fingertips. Cool air and—my own tears, hot and wet, streaming down my cheeks.

"That's it," he whispered. "Come back to me."

"How—?"

"Trust me," he said. "Everything will be all right. I promise you."

The pain surged again. I cried out.

"Hold on," he urged. "Just a moment longer."

His hand cupped my face. His thumb brushed away my tears.

"I love you," he said again. "I will always find you."

Then his lips pressed against mine.

Light exploded behind my eyelids—blinding, golden, warm. The mate bond flared strong, bright and undeniable, burning and aching.

The world tilted.

Then stillness.

25

FAMILY

I blinked, disoriented. Wh—what? I wasn't standing. I lay on something soft.

A finished stone ceiling came into focus above me. A real one. Not a dream.

Ramiel leaned over me, his silver hair falling forward, his eyes wide with relief and exhaustion. His hand trembled as he brushed the hair from my face.

"Dare I ask what you're doing in my tower?" he whispered. Tears shone in his amethyst eyes. He stroked his hand down my cheek, cupping his fingers beneath my chin.

My heart raced faster. I was back. Back and alive, my hands shaking as I pressed my fingertips to his jaw, his cheek, his temple, his lips. "I'd rather not have this conversation while in such a position." My lips trembled.

His smile curled higher. Leaning down, he kissed my chin, then my cheek. His lips lingered. "Is it wise for someone in your position to make such demands?"

The deep rasp of his voice made me melt, the sparking within me now pleasurable. The mate bond hummed. "Oh, you have no idea the demands I'll make of you."

His mouth quirked up. He nuzzled me, the tip of his

nose grazing mine. "And I will happily spend the rest of my days granting them all."

A giggle escaped my lips, and I intended to tease him more. But as soon as I opened my mouth, he pounced and kissed me deeply.

It was hard to believe that somehow I had escaped both our curses. Somehow we were both here together.

His kiss stole my breath. His fingers tangled in my hair, cradling my head as if I might slip away again. I clung to his shoulders, anchoring myself to him, to this moment, to life itself.

When we finally broke apart, his eyes shimmered with unshed tears.

"For the most awful moments of my life, I thought I'd lost you," he whispered, his voice raw. "The moment you took my curse—I realized that the curse fulfilling in this way truly was the way that broke me most. I feared—I feared that this was the true fulfillment. That I would lose you forever just after finding you."

I twirled a strand of his hair around my finger, then curled my hand against his jaw. "Yet here I am."

"Here you are." He pressed his forehead to mine. "My brave, foolish mate who risked everything."

"I would do it again." I said softly.

His fingers trembled against my cheek. "I wasn't sure it would work. The binding spell barely took. It was Zephyrus who drew the leviathan back and passed on the message."

"Zephyrus?" My heart leaped. "Is he—"

"He's more than fine. Angry. Honestly, we should probably go and show all the dragons you are here. They nearly roused the leviathan to rage again, but somehow they told him what we needed. Rather impressive really."

I giggled a little at that, though my heart warmed. "So the leviathan was there to help me?"

"He tracked you and fractured the barrier enough that I could reach you and your magic could reach me. The curse dragged your spirit there. Your body was here, and I brought you up to the tower. Then—"

I swept my arms around him and kissed him fiercely. His eyes shuttered as he groaned against my mouth, and I melted beneath him. The mate bond hummed between us, no longer painful but gloriously alive. I tasted salt and cedar and desperate need on his lips. And the air smelled of him and…vanilla and jasmine. My heart clenched, and I flung both arms around his neck to draw him as close as I could.

A chorus of deafening roars shattered the moment. Apparently we had waited too long.

He pulled back and dragged his hand across the back of his neck, laughing. "Ahh…we may have waited a little too long in their estimation."

I recognized Zephyrus's indignant roar. The others did not sound too pleased either. "How long was I gone?"

"The curse snatched your spirit two days ago." He kept his arm around my waist as we walked, his body solid and warm beside mine. "I brought you up to the Covenant Chamber and tended to you there while the leviathan searched for you."

The air thrummed around me as Caein appeared. "I am so glad you have returned, Astraia. This tower was far less without you," he said smoothly.

"Thank you, Caein."

"Oh, and if I say welcome home, does that mean I am the first with that honor, or would a certain prince prefer to grant that honor himself?"

Ramiel chuckled and lifted his hand toward the ceiling. "If you would like the honor, it is yours."

"Ah." Caein's voice rose and fell as if he were moving up and down in a rough parody of a bow. "Then welcome home, dear Astraia."

"Thank you, Caein. I missed you as well." I smiled up in his general direction.

Another roar shook the walls.

"He definitely knows I'm awake." Blushing, I brushed my hair back over my shoulders and sheepishly made my way down the curving staircase. The stable doors were open, and the dragons all watched. Warm afternoon sunlight streamed across them, bathing them in golden light.

Zephyrus glowered at me from the doorway, his nostrils flaring. He cocked his head as he looked between us, his tail thumping on the flagstone path.

Shaking my head, I held up my hands. "I'm sorry about that, Zephyrus." My lips twitched in a smile.

He grunted. His gaze flicked between Ramiel and me.

Ramiel folded his arms. "Don't look at me like that, Zephyrus. Of course I spent time with her."

Zephyrus chuffed again, then cut his eyes at me. That and the small trill were the only warning I got. He pounced, his great claw knocking me over. As soon as I got to my feet, he thrust his jaw against my shoulder. Growling and chuffing, he nudged me again. I put my arms around his head as best I could. "It's all right, big guy. I'm fine."

He shook his head and huffed at me again. Indignation flashed in his face along with relief. He bumped me and then turned his head hard, offering his ear. Laughing, I scratched behind his ear and then down his jaw. His happy purr rumbled through me.

It took a great deal of reassuring and soothing Zephyrus to convince him to let up with his mock punishment. He curled around me, nuzzled my shoulder, and nudged incessantly at my wrist as if to ensure that the curse truly was gone. Even then, he insisted on remaining near me as the other dragons came to greet me and evaluate.

Life had changed yet again. The tower did in truth feel like home, though anywhere with Ramiel and Zephyrus would feel that way. And as beautiful as it had been before, it was even more so now.

The Chasm itself appeared to have healed so much, the

barrier no longer so murky and far stronger. The purple mist coiled and rolled above it, more peaceful and more like small clouds. Some even rolled on the bridge, varying in shades from pale lavender to rich purple.

There was one matter more that needed our attention. With the mate bond completed, we needed to commemorate our sacred bond. It only seemed right that we do it today. After all, who knew what tomorrow would bring? We had spent enough time apart.

I wore a flowing pink gown similar to the one I wore to dinner. Except this one was sleeveless. Some of the scar remained as not all of my wounds had fully healed, but the mate bond was now clearly visible. A simple mark that showed my connection to the other half of my heart and soul.

It was almost sunset by the time we were ready. Not a trace of a storm cloud on the horizon. The sun's brilliant gold blazed across the horizon, a masterpiece painted in strokes of fire. Crimson and gold streaked the sky, burning against the deep blue canvas that stretched above us. The Chasm caught the light in its purple mist, transforming it into a river of roiling amethyst.

"I never thought I'd see another sunset like this," I whispered as I stood in the doorway, waiting for the signal.

"I pray you are able to see many more," Caein responded.

I glanced back up at the ceiling. "Are you sure that you don't want us to find some way to bring you down to the bridge for the ceremony?"

"I can see from here. I promise I will grant you the full delight of my presence on many other occasions." The air shimmered, and a rough call sounded. "They're ready for you, little knotweaver. Go on."

Heart beating fast and palms sweating, I stepped out and made my way forward. Ten of the dragons lined up, five on each side in a path leading to the end of the bridge. Thalorion and Zephyrus sat positioned at the head in front of a pedestal table that had been carved from part of a grey stone pillar.

On top of that table sat three jars, one with the blue sand, one with the inscription, and one empty. Next to that were two large crystal formations, one of rose quartz that was larger than the ball my brothers played with as children and one turquoise that was about the size of my fist.

What stole my attention was Ramiel, my mate, my groom, my love, my heart. He waited for me by the pedestal, flanked by the dragons. His eyes widened when he saw me, and my heart quickened to see his response.

His amethyst eyes darkened as they locked with mine, and the hunger and need in them made my core tighten. I could drown in those eyes. The smile that split my face in response almost hurt. He stood tall and regal, shoulders squared beneath his formal attire, silver hair shimmering in the fading light. He wore a rich blue-violet surcoat, more luxurious than his usual and yet familiar. Runes had been stitched into the lapels, interconnecting and woven with iridescent thread. He held out his hand to me, only the faintest tremor in his fingers indicating his nerves.

My cheeks warmed at the intensity of his gaze, but I lifted my chin and accepted, sliding my hand to his. His touch sent sparks of delight and desire searing through me, and as he drew me closer, his wonderful scent filled my lungs.

"Astraia," he said, his voice low and rough. "When a Sentinel takes a spouse, they make vows to one another and combine the essence of their magic into a single vessel to honor the bond." He placed his hand over the jar that was half filled with blue sand. "This is mine, created from the first runes I carved into stone and refined with the remnants of the energy of the ones I marked in the air. You may, if you wish, create yours. I brought stones that reminded me of you." He picked up the rose quartz and the turquoise and placed them in my hands.

Smiling, I stacked the two stones over one another and

set them above the empty jar. My magic flared against the stones. Gold veins appeared in both like threads. Closing my eyes, I drew into my mind's eyes images of my family. My father. My mother. Sona. Loam. Elim. Not of their deaths but of the life we shared. Of baking peace loaves and weaving runic talismans. Of taking turns telling stories line by line. Of arguing passionately and intensely over the proper ordering of toys, books, plants, and food.

I would never forget them. And nothing would bring them back from the great expanse of eternity. If they could see me, I prayed they shared my happiness and were themselves at peace.

Then I saw Zephyrus. Remembering how he found me at the base of that hill under a sycamore tree, a scared girl grieving and broken. How he'd curled around me and kept me warm. How he'd taught me to hold fast as he flew and rolled. How he'd stood by me through the Resistance and led to my coming here. Our bond was profound, and I was grateful for it. Had he perhaps known of my connection to Ramiel? Or had he simply trusted?

My thoughts shifted then to Ramiel. My impossible, stubborn, powerful, gentle prince and the last of Sentinels. For now. The man who had become my heart.

I remembered his face when he'd first caught me in his trap, that arrogant smirk that had made me want to punch him when all the while he knew what we were to one another. The fierce determination in his eyes as he battled to protect the Chasm. The tenderness in his touch as he'd tended my wounds. The vulnerability when he'd told me about his curse and how he had accepted my help. The passion and affection when he spoke to me of "his mate" and what he would tell her. The selflessness as he had tried to put my future and wellness above his own.

Falling in love—finding a family—all of that had seemed out of my reach. When I scourged myself, I had not believed I could ever heal. Not truly. At best, I could protect him. But now—now even though part of the scar remained, the bond had formed.

No longer was I the broken, scared child who cowered beneath the tree, nor was I the vengeful, petty woman who'd broken into his tower. And he wasn't the cold, isolated Sentinel he'd pretended to be.

I sent a silent prayer of gratitude to the Creator of All. Life had taken so much from me—my family, my kingdom, my innocence. The path had been cruel and hard. But standing here with Ramiel, with Zephyrus and his dragon kin watching over us and Caein with his support and wisdom, I felt only gratitude and hope.

When I opened my eyes, I gasped. The stones had completely transformed, crumbling into fine, shimmering sand. Rose-gold and turquoise grains swirled together, glowing softly now and filling half the empty jar.

He took my hand in his and brought it to my heart. "Where your soul goes, mine follows. From this day to final silence and into all that lies beyond, I am yours. And even if your light falls dark, I will love you still. For if you fall, I will catch you. When you rise, I will guard you. You are mine through all that is and all that will yet be, and I am forever yours."

I gazed up into his eyes as I made my pledge to him, his heart beating against my palm. The words came to my mind easily, a blend of crimson and rune fae vows. "In fury and in joy, in passion and stillness. My blood bears the truth: I am yours and you are mine, and no force will tear our souls from the other. When your rage burns, I will be your calm. When your calm breaks, I will be your shield. I will fight for you, bleed for you, live for you, and you will never go alone."

Together we then poured each of our individual jars of sand into the empty jar with the inscription. They melded together, shifting in layers, creating purple and streaks of pink and blue with hints of violet and turquoise. Once it was filled, he took my hand and placed it with his over the mouth. He put his other hand over my heart. I mirrored this pose.

"Natoumai ahme vahre, Astraia," he whispered.

"Natoumai ahme vahre, Ramiel," I responded.

Our magic twined together, sparking between our palms and fingertips, gold and silver.

Our magic swirled between us, gold and silver light intertwining as the sand in the jar shimmered with our combined colors. Ramiel's eyes darkened to deep violet as he gazed down at me. His expression filled with such tenderness it made my very being ache.

He cupped my face with one hand, his thumb brushing my cheek. "My nat," he whispered, the words carrying on the evening breeze.

"My heart," I answered.

He leaned down and pressed his lips to mine, his touch soft, reverent. I greeted him with the same tenderness, leaning against him, my fingers finding their way to the nape of his neck, threading through his silver hair. A small moan escaped me.

His arm wrapped around my waist, pulling me flush against him at that, and his kiss deepened, becoming hungry, desperate—as though he'd been starving for this moment his entire life. I matched his passion, rising on my toes to press closer, my fingers tightening in his hair.

The dragons around us roared, the vibration of their calls thrumming through me as Ramiel's mouth claimed mine. Their wings beat the air as several dragons took flight, circling above us in celebration.

Ramiel finally broke our kiss, his breaths ragged. He caressed my cheek as he held me tight.

"I never thought I would have this," he whispered against my lips. "That I would have you. I'm never letting you go again, Astraia. You are the one my soul sought all these years, and you are the one who makes my life worth living. Even if you do mix my rune stones up when you're angry."

I tried to laugh, but it came out as a half sob and half giggle. "I'm glad. Because you're never getting rid of me."

"I noticed." He nuzzled me again, his voice even softer. "Thank you for coming back."

Another chorus of roars and bellows resounded. Most of the dragons had taken to the skies and flew in a circle. Zephyrus remained at the edge of the cliff, watching me expectantly. Crossing over, I leaned up on my toes and hugged him. He thrust his muzzle down and purred as Ramiel spoke to Thalorion. The ancient dragon inclined his head, eyes half shaded and whiskers trailing on the flagstone as he dutifully listened. Then he nudged Ramiel lightly.

Zephyrus trilled, drawing my attention back to him. He nuzzled once more and chirred in response. I pressed my cheek to his and kissed him gently. "You have been the best friend and family I could have asked for. Thank you for everything."

He huffed at me and blinked slowly, the picture of perfect contentment. Above, more dragon calls sounded. He turned his gaze upward.

Thalorion grunted. He jerked his chin up toward the skies. Zephyrus responded. They walked to the edge of the bridge, unfurled their wings, and leaped into the sky. Within seconds, they joined the dance above.

Ramiel smiled as he turned to me. "The only thing missing is music, my love."

"It's all—" I broke off as he started to cut runes in the air. Each silver line hummed and sang. The mist coiled higher, moving in time to the gentle beat as the sun sank behind the mountains.

"May I have this dance, my lady?" He bowed at the waist and extended his hand to me.

"It would be my honor, my lord." I curtsied. Then, in a breath, I was once more in his arms, melting and smiling.

So easily did we move across the flagstones, runes singing above, silver lines humming with a melody that matched our mood. His hand pressed against the small of my back, warm and steady and keeping me close.

Words couldn't express my joy as he spun me across the bridge, purple mist swirling at our feet. Night descended around us, stars piercing the velvet black sky one by one. The dragons circled overhead, their calls a primal chorus of chirrs, growls, and rumblings. Even from here, I could pick out Zephyrus's deep resonant growls. As I turned my face up to the sky, I watched in wonder, still letting Ramiel lead me. "I've never heard dragons sing before."

"They celebrate the sacred bonds," he said. His lips brushed mine. "And this is the most precious of any bond I have ever held."

"I never thought this was one I'd get to celebrate," I whispered.

"Nor did I." He nodded, his eyes reflecting starlight. We turned again, faster now, our bodies pressed tight. The music from the runes intensified, matching our quickening steps.

I laughed with delight, just shaking my head.

His smile broadened into a great slash of white, and he suddenly grasped my waist and lifted me in the air. He spun me as if I weighed nothing and then held me there as he gazed up at me. "Natoumai ahme vahre, Astraia."

I pressed my forehead to his, utterly content and grateful beyond words. "Natoumai ahme vahre, Ramiel."

THANK you so much for reading. Readers like you help keep this dream alive, and I am so deeply grateful to you. If you enjoyed, please leave an honest review on Amazon or whatever platform you like.

And if you would enjoy some bonus content related to this series including bonus scenes and some from Ramiel's perspective, come visit me at https://geni.us/toswayaprincebonus

ABOUT THE AUTHOR

Jessica M. Butler is an adventurer, author, and attorney who never outgrew her love for telling stories and playing in imaginary worlds. She is the author of the epic fantasy romance series *Tue-Rah Chronicles* including *Identity Revealed, Enemy Known,* and *Princess Reviled, Wilderness Untamed, Shifter King* along with independent novellas *Locked, Cursed,* and *Alone,* set in the same world. She has also written numerous fantasy tales such as *Mermaid Bride, Little Scapegoat, Through the Paintings Dimly, Why Yes, Bluebeard, I'd Love To,* and more. For the most part, she writes speculative fiction with a heavy focus on multicultural high fantasy and suspenseful adventures and passionate romances. She lives with her husband and law partner, James Fry, in rural Indiana where they are quite happy with their five cats: Thor, Loptr, Fenrir, Hela, and Herne.

For more books or updates:
www.jmbutlerauthor.com

Read More from Jessica M. Butler

(jmbutlerauthor.com)

facebook.com/jmbutler1728

x.com/jessicabfry

instagram.com/jessicambutlerauthor

ALSO BY JESSICA M. BUTLER

Standalones
Of Serpents and Ruins
Bound By Blood
Trapped by Claws
Through the Paintings Dimly
The Mermaid Bride

The Tue-Rah Chronicles

Identity Revealed
Enemy Known
Princess Reviled
Wilderness Untamed
Shifter King
Empire Undone

Tue-Rah Tales
Locked
Alone
Cursed